CHOCOLATE CHARLIE

CHOCOLATE CHARLIE

A NOVEL

BY

TOM FITZGERALD

Ashley books inc •
Box 768 · Port Washington, N. Y. 11050

Library of Congress Number: 72-91129

Address information to Ashley Books, Inc., Box 768, Port Washington, New York,11050.

Published by Ashley Books, Inc.
Manufactured in the United States of America

First Edition

to
Charlie

ACKNOWLEDGMENTS TO

Melissa Vaughn, who typed it—with broken nails
Gwen Costa, who edited it—with broken leads

and especially to
Joshua, Matt & Sean Fitzgerald, who inspired it—with an uncommon profusion of dirty diapers
and Laurie Fitzgerald, who believed in it—with an uncommon capacity to love

my thanks

CHOCOLATE CHARLIE

Chapter 1

She just stood there, her eyes narrowed with irritation. "Just look at you, David! Just look at all that mud!" Mama's precious baby was snuggled in the arm of her ocelot coat. As always. I had to kill her. I had to feel my fingers close around her warm neck. To feel them squeeze slowly, tighter and tighter. It had to be slow. There was no stopping me now, not this time. The hunger was overwhelming, beyond control.

But I wanted to stop! I really did. This was wrong. I motioned for the man to come, to stop me, to grab hold of me before I could strike, before it was too late. It was the only control I seemed to have left. My legs, not mine, were moving me closer to that face of blank hypocrisy. But the man wouldn't move. Why! Why did he just stand there? Couldn't he see the horrible thing I was about to do? Didn't my own father care, for Christ's sake?

The compulsion was boiling to a frenzy. I could feel sanity slipping away. I beckoned desperately for him to stop me. Oh, please! For God's sake, please! Goosebumps began to prickle through my flesh in wild electric bursts. My breathing grew heavy, then labored. Then violent. I could feel my eyes bulge with excitement, my heart pound. My hand stopped beckoning and suddenly tensed into a claw. It was too late! No longer was I driven against my will. Not now. I *wanted* to kill her. Wanted to dig my nails deep into the flesh of her throat, wanted to watch her choke, gasp, to watch her eyes bulge in cold terror. Pleasure swelled erotically in my bowels. Near orgasmic. I lunged . . . .

Awake. Breathing like a rabid animal. Gooseflesh standing up and down my arms. Clammy, cold sweat sticking to my body like glue. Shadows lurking in the corners of the room. Had to piss badly, nearly bursting.

I crawled out from under the damp sheets and fumbled my way into the bathroom. My stream wasn't that deep satisfying color which comes from hard physical labor, but instead that weak yellow which flows from eight hours of hard drinking. I avoided the mirror.

Head throbbing, I stumbled back into the bedroom. Even with drawn shades, the room wasn't dark enough to hide the snarls of clothes and clutter of debris strewn wildly over the floor. The air reeked of spent pot. My eyes gravitated to the dead weight lying on the other side of my queen-sized bed, her legs still spread apart. Right where I suppose I left her. I wondered who she was, and whether, when she awoke, she would feel like I was feeling, like an empty garbage pail.

I promised myself I'd go for a hard run and take a sauna at the Y just as soon as I got rid of her. Anything to restore enough self-esteem to get me through another week at the office. Christ! The office. No time to think about that.

Sick to my stomach, I ran back to the bathroom and stuck my head into the bowl. I hung there, waiting, peering down at the shit stains on the porcelain, but nothing came. The feeling was unbearable so I stuck a finger deep down my throat. It came.

Finished, I couldn't bring myself to go back into the bedroom, much less to bed. Naked, I walked out into the living room. I tripped over an empty bourbon bottle, then turned off the amplifier on the stereo, left on from the night before. A bagful of grass was open on the coffee table in front of the couch. Like the bedroom, the room reeked of it. Ashes were carelessly strewn everywhere and there were a few fresh burns on my rented couch. It was already so badly abused I knew I would end up having to pay for it.

Though the drapes were pulled, the room was bright with sunlight. I knew it was well past noon, but I didn't really want to look at the clock in the kitchen.

Instead I walked to the window and flipped on the air

conditioner, then parted the drapes to look out into the courtyard below. The playground was deserted.

I was about to turn away with coffee in mind when a movement caught my eye. The playground wasn't empty after all. One little boy, completely alone, was down under the pull-up bar. No taller than hip-high to me, he was trying, doggedly, to reach the bar. I parted the drapes further, then dropped to my knees to watch. The boy jumped and jumped but each time success eluded him by what seemed to me, from four floors up, no more than a fraction of an inch.

Then some other boys appeared. Older and taller than the little tyke under the bar, they gathered closely around him and began to mock and point jeeringly at him. The little boy stopped jumping and timidly backed off. The older boys immediately jumped onto the bar and began to perform their tricks of daring.

The little boy turned and walked slowly off. I followed him with my eyes into the empty shadows; then he was gone.

Chapter 2

It was one of those impulsive things a person does out of desperation. Purely an emotional thing. Perhaps to lighten a load of depression, to pump a little fresh air into nothingness, or, in my case, perhaps a little of both.

Some two weeks ago, when I first made the appointment, I certainly had every intention of seeing it through. That was the only way I could get the lift I needed at the time. There could be no hope where there was no commitment. But now the moment of truth had drawn near, with the same circumstances seeming a little less dramatic in retrospect. I found myself sitting at my desk nervously thumping two clammy feet smothered in imitation alligator against the floor and watching the wall clock speed dispassionately past two on toward three. I mean, what did the damn clock care! To make it on time I would have to leave soon. Too soon.

The whole idea was ridiculous. Downright absurd. You know, like all those promises you make to God when you think the hairy hand of Death's got you by the balls. You're all penance and promises. Then when the sun comes up next morning, as usual, you find yourself too embarrassed to look at yourself in the mirror and eternally grateful nobody overheard all those solemn oaths.

So I decided to let the afternoon of Friday, the 18th of June, slip quietly by. No one would ever know about my idiotic scheme or all those stupid good intentions. The secretary over at the Children's Agency on 3rd Street would simply cross my name off the appointment calendar, and some harried case worker would undoubtedly be grateful for an unexpected coffee break. For me, the whole deal wouldn't amount to anything more than writing one of those purgative letters one just has to write at the time but then never sends. I had simply needed something to hang onto. Mondays were always that way. I felt better already. And it was Friday!

In just a few hours I would abandon my desk to another layer of lemon wax and rush to my apartment to spray on another layer of cologne. Then I'd jump into my baby blue vet, put the top down, and rumble throatily over to catch Happy Hour at The Singles. That would mean a certain pick-up and with little effort another orgy at my place. I mean, for a score all you had to do was tell these scavenging secretaries and school teachers that you were a budding young associate with Wagstaff, Walbridge, Ottley and Martin; babble about your involvement in storefront movements during summer vacations from Cornell Law; drive them to your apartment in your vet with the cassette tape deck playing something "with it;" show them around your dimly lit pad so they could notice all the *Playboys* and *Penthouses* lying around; and finally blow a little grass to a few softly romantic records on the stereo. That was about it, guaranteed. Saturday night would be more of the same. Usually I would ask Friday night's pick-up out and most often take her to an expensive hang-out like the Purple Plum. They always performed better in the sack the second night if you allowed them to think you were getting interested after the first.

Two whole days of the real thing, right? I mean, it was not time to be thinking about Monday or the three o'clock appointment over on dingy 3rd Street. Right?

The intercom buzzed. A surge of excitement lifted me up like a rocket beginning to rise off the pad for the stars. I always felt that way when the phone rang, or the intercom buzzed, or when a first class envelope of high grade paper and clean type arrived in the mail. They always stirred up hopes for something new and exciting.

But then I saw that it was line 3 flashing. The rocket exploded and plummeted back to earth in pieces. The efficient, doctrinaire voice on the other end, the same type you would expect to hear over the PA of a POW camp, would be that of Sally Eckert, Stanley Walbridge's personal secretary. Stanley loved efficiency. Almost, I think, as much as he loved the status of having his own secretary and intercom line. I pushed the damn button, pausing a moment to feign ulcerous activity, then answered.

"David Dezengremel speaking." Strict aloofness and formality in communications between levels in the hierarchy of the firm—between salary and non-salary, degree and non-degree—were sacred commandments. Image, don't you know. Yeah. Dee here. What's up?

"Mr. Walbridge would like to see you immediately in his office. Please bring your notes on the Douglasson divorce case. Thank you." Click.

"Why certainly, Sally. Be glad to. Beautiful day, isn't it? What do you say you and I go outside for a while and take off our shoes and chase butterflies—"

I picked up the file folder which had been sitting conspicuously open on my desk in case anyone came in (which nobody ever did, because I was the juniorest of the junior, and the juniorest of the junior did all the walking) and left my one-window closet for the five-window gymnasium of Stanley Walbridge, Esq. A couple of important looking gentlemen were sitting in the reception room absorbed in late issues of the *Wall Street Journal* and *Forbes.* Miss Eckert informed me with the same brusque politeness she would have extended an indigent client, and without taking a finger off her typewriter keys, that I could go right in. I noticed she had so much make-up glued to her face that it looked as if she would need to bathe in turpentine to get it all off. If she ever took it all off, that is.

"Mr. Walbridge is waiting."

"Thank you." I couldn't help but smile at a mental flash of Miss Eckert chasing butterflies down the middle of Seneca Boulevard.

Stanley Walbridge was sitting behind his desk as I entered. Without glancing up, he continued to scribble his signature on some letters. I knew without looking that this was his latest epistle to various Republican dignitaries of the city and county, exhorting them in the bluntest terms possible to snub a luncheon next week in honor of Senator Osgood, "that goddamn bleedin'-heart liberal opportunist and the rest of his pussy-haired freaks." I had seen a copy of it on Miss Eckert's desk yesterday during the lunch hour (the only way I ever found out what was going on was to snoop around during the lunch hour). The best part, near the end, was something about every high school grad being conscripted into the Marine Corps for two years of character building. It occurred to me at that time that the only real difference between boys and men is that men have hair on their balls, for some reason.

Conspicuous on the credenza behind Stanley was a gold-framed photograph of himself and Governor Rockefeller with their arms clasped behind each other's back like long lost brothers newly reunited. They were smiling so hard their eyes seemed almost shut, and with their free hands they were holding up vees for victory.

"How's the Douglasson case coming along, David? Old Man Douglasson just called. Wants to leave for South America as soon as possible, but wants his old lady completely out of his hair first."

"The complaint is finished and being typed, sir, and I'm about to have—"

"What do you think about hiring a private dick on this, David? Personally, I think a little documented dirt could be of great help in keeping the alimony down, especially if Judge Comstock gets the case, which he probably will. He caught his own wife with an encyclopedia salesman, you know. You might say he's been a little down on wayward women since. Sam doesn't want her to get a dime. He doesn't care what it costs, just doesn't want any goddam sluts on his payroll, he says." Stanley chuckled with amusement; so David Dezengremel, junior associate, did too.

"Well, if that's what he wants, I guess—"

"Why not give Andy Mezzatesta a call. Christ, Andy loves this type of thing. Might even give him some more material for one of his movies. Ever see one of his stag films, David?"

"Uh, no sir. None of his. Saw a few at the fraternity, but–"

"Andy was at a little party we had over at Judge Ainsworth's last week. He brought along a couple of his favorites." Stanley chuckled; I smiled. "One was about this ugly woman and the biggest Great Dane. . . . "

I glanced over at the Walbridge family portrait resting on a corner of the desk. It was turned so it could be easily seen from my angle, but not at all from Stanley's. Along with his own, were the grim, tinted, brushed and polished smiles of his wife and daughter. Somehow you knew the daughter was safely packed away in some antiseptic girls' school, one where no serpents lurked in the garden.

Looking into the sober face of Muriel, Stanley's wife, I wondered if she was at all aware of Stanley's pet client, Miss Toothpaste Smile. And if she were, whether or not she gave a shit.

When Carolyn Sommers first came to Wagstaff, Walbridge, Ottley and Martin, for contract counseling, I think it was, she had no agent and was only doing an occasional toothpaste ad or two. Since meeting Stanley, however, her career had suddenly blossomed; almost overnight every billboard had become a Carolyn Sommers centerfold. And good old Stanley had blossomed as well, into the most avid sportsman of the firm, making three times as many "hunting" and "fishing" trips to the firm's Adirondack lodge as anyone else.

Perhaps Muriel knew but would only *care* when Stanley's affair became public knowledge and therefore a source of personal embarrassment. Like with my own parents.

Christ, what a farce that one was. A comedy in three acts. Polite noncommunicative cohabitation. Peaceful coexistence. and for what? Sex? Shit no! If the coexistence was peaceful, it was paradoxically pieceless. In all the years I lived in the same house I overheard the sounds of love from behind their bedroom door but once. I was up doing my homework as usual one night, struggling for that A in English, when I thought I heard a strange sound, sort of a squeaking. At first I thought it must have been the hour, mental fatigue, but I opened my door to listen anyway. The sound was even louder, more distinct. Heroic thoughts of vanquishing the prowler single-handedly began to parade into my mind. *YOUTH OVERPOWERS PROWLER.* But when I heard that crescendo of heavy breathing, the groans, I smiled and went back into my room. In 15 minutes I had finished what I knew was an A+ composition. My teacher even wanted me to polish it for publication as a short story. But I never did.

That was the only time. And the only time, too, I ever got an A+ in English.

No, not for anything so impractical as sex, or love. My parents were strict pragmatists. To them a tree was a source of wood. Ownership and exploitation were the things. Marriage was an opportunity, an investment. My father wanted to exploit the power my mother's money could buy, and my mother wanted to exploit the social position my father's good looks and political ambitions could give her. Mutual risks for mutual returns.

But as two people supposedly bonded in marriage, they were far apart. And, therefore, so was I. My mother's world was always being mentioned in some asshole social column in the same paragraph with the Boswells or the Pembertons; she and the house were always primed and polished as if expecting unexpected guests or a photographer from *Better Homes*. And she always had me dressed the same way. The greatest sin I could commit was to get dirty. Everything was for exhibition, for show. Especially me.

My father was almost a stranger, an acquaintance of the same surname who paid all my bills. His world was one of big business deals (which he would never talk about, so I stopped asking), frequent trips away from home (which I began to look forward to), and weekend golf at the country club with his "business associates." Golf. I hate it. Most men of business play it either as a crutch to reassure a paunchy male ego—hitting that tiny hard ball a mile with that big club—or because their boss does. My father never swung a club until the day he discoverd the senior partners at his law firm were all members of the same country club.

The only real interaction I had with my father was an infrequent game of catch on the back lawn, during which he would point out everything I was doing wrong (and the more he told me the more I did wrong), or an occasional fishing trip up into the Minnesota woods, where he'd get all bent out of shape over the fish not biting or some asshole's boat being too close to ours or the guide charging too goddamned much, then take it all out on me with persistent ridicule and nagging until I'd get so uptight I'd piss in my pants.

Performance was his thing. He expected everyone to perform to his personal standards of excellence, including his son, and if they failed, God help them. He would never say anything outright; he would let you feel his disapproval, let you feel it until your guts burned up in your own bile. It was easy to see why my father and Stanley Walbridge had been such good friends in their law school days.

My mother was forever suggesting to my father how nice it would be to take little David on more outdoorsy trips away from home, like our great fishing adventures, and whenever he would finally sigh his consent, she would immediately plan a grand backyard soiree for all the neighborhood ladies. A celebration at getting rid of us both, I thought. Anyway that's the way I took it. I'm not sure how my father took it, or if he took it any way at all. He was remarkably oblivious about anything that wasn't related directly to either business or politics. And for an intelligent man, I always thought that rather strange. Once in a while we got around to discussing—or rather him telling me about—things. But it was always fishhooks, Democrats, and the American Dream. Never once did we rap about things like feelings, emotions, or love—or why my mother always gave a party when we left town.

Divorce came up openly only once. It was right after my mother received a mysterious phone call one afternoon, which I listened in on (a kid who can't get dirty hasn't much else to do), telling her in graphic detail what a gifted lover my father was. The whispery voice was that of a young woman, and her information was obviously firsthand. The woman asked for $10,000 to keep her mouth shut.

My father was away at the time on business, as usual, and my mother fumed like a volcano about to blow until the night he got back. Whereupon she immediately called him into the den, and blew.

I listened in with a drinking glass pressed against the wall, and soon found myself enjoying it all. Like watching cocks fight to the death.

My mother spewed verbal garbage all over my father that night. Not because he had been unfaithful to some sacred trust, and had hurt her, but because he had jeopardized her standing with her friends, thereby threatening her with public humiliation. She finished with a demand for an immediate divorce. My father begged her to stay. Begged her in a voice limp with panic and desperation. He pleaded like a little boy whose weekly allowance was threatened. He said a divorce would tarnish his legal position with irreparable harm, but worse, it would ruin his chances for the governorship in the next election. He stressed the glories of the governorship, apparently reading a reaction on my mother's face, then promised her he would keep it zipped in his pants. He would make it worth her while; he would pay off the informer to keep any dirt out of the columns. He promised her everything but his soul, but I knew that he'd already auctioned that off. The bastard.

"I don't have to remind you, David, Sam Douglasson is one of this firm's more, shall we say, *important* clients. We have entrusted him to your hands in this divorce matter, quite frankly, because we think you're very capable for a young lawyer, and will be a valuable asset to this firm. Getting Sam off the alimony hook will make him a very happy, and very generous, man. Do what you have to, David."

I looked at Stanley Walbridge and saw a complete stranger and I knew then I was going to keep my three o'clock appointment. I had to. It was now or never.

"I'll get right on this, sir." Stanley nodded, but I could see his mind was already on other matters. The cheerleading session was over.

Miss Eckert didn't bother to look up as I brushed by. I wondered if she even knew what I looked like. The important looking men were still absorbed in the *Wall Street Journals*, joined now by the chicken-faced scowl of Mrs. Ouderkirk, a rich client. I could almost hear their computer brains hum with puts and calls and pork bellies. I noticed the tropical-type plant in the corner was dying.

I threw the Douglasson file down on my desk and glanced up at the clock. Christ, it was almost 3:00 already! I'd have to hurry.

I pressed in the third button on the intercom, the one marked SW.

"Yes?"

"Miss Eckert, I'm going out and will be gone for the rest of the afternoon. And I can't be reached at any other number—cause I'll be chasing butterflies." Click.

Chapter 3

The Children's Service Department of Social Services is located on the second floor of a dumpy, dirty brick building on West 3rd Street. There's a grubby grocery and a bar with ten thousand neon beer signs in the windows on the street level. The stairwell leading to Children's Service is sandwiched inconspicuously in between. One little sign, CHILDREN'S SERVICE, points in the general direction of up, but is tacked on to the wall inside the open doorway and could only be noticed by those who already know it's there. The bartender in the pub next door, the typical thick, red-faced, balding type, gave me directions. I fully expected him to point toward the back room.

It was 3:12 when I entered to the busy clatter of typewriters. It was an especially hot day and sweat was pouring off me as I approached a receptionist-secretary, who looked strikingly like my former Cub Scout den mother. She was wearing an everyday cotton house dress and a well-worn smear of lipstick.

"Uh, excuse me. My name is Dezengremel, David Dezengremel, and I'm a little late for a 3:00 appointment. I was tied up at—"

"Oh yes. Mr. Dez . . . uh, now how did you say that again? I'm just terrible with names."

"De–Zen–Gre–Mel. French. Some of my friends just call me Dee."

"Fine, Mr. Dez . . . Mr. Dee. And will your wife be joining us today?"

I could feel a flush flood my cheeks. That damned Celtic skin of mine.

"Uh, well, you see I'm not, uh . . . Well, I'm not exactly

married. Not at the moment, anyway."

"Oh, I see. Just engaged." Den Mother smiled. Then will your fiancee be joining us? It's customary to have both adoptive parents here for the initial interview."

I could feel the color deepen to a burn on my face. I'd probably have a nice tan by the time I got out of here. Christ, why the hell was I here anyway?

"Well, no, I'm afraid not. You see I'm not exactly engaged yet either."

I could see Den Mother's face tighten with that telltale Puritan astringency. I braced myself.

"Mr. Dezomogrel, I really think you should know, before going any further, that this agency cannot make placements with couples who are not legally married. I'm sure you can appreciate the rationale behind it. We have a public and a moral duty to provide our babies with the greatest levels of security possible."

"I appreciate that, Mrs. Uh . . . ?

"Mrs. Jordan. Ethel Jordan."

"I appreciate that, Mrs. Jordan. But I'm afraid I'm not shacking up either." I smiled—"at least not at the moment. In fact, right at the moment I'm *un*married, *un*attached, *un*involved—and completely *un*interested in *un*doing any of the un's."

Ethel gave me one of those *God, not another kook* looks.

"Well, you *are* here concerning an adoption?"

"Yes."

Her eyes surveyed me with a somewhat less than discreet sweep from my face down to just below my belt, and back up to my face, before she softened a little. Thank God my hair was of conventional length and my fingernails were clean.

"Just a moment, please. I'll tell Mrs. Oppermann you're here."

"Thank you."

She got up and disappeared into an office with a little sign thumbtacked to the door. *Mrs. Sylane Oppermann, Head Caseworker.* In a much larger room, directly adjacent, I could see a number of girls, through a doorway, pecking at their typewriters. A feeling of claustrophobia crept through me just watching them.

Ethel was gone long enough to fill Mrs. Oppermann in on the well-groomed kook waiting outside. I could feel my stomach tense up with defensiveness. She finally came out, smiling much too pleasantly.

"Mrs. Oppermann will see you now. Go right in."

I did, but only after stacking my pride up against a strong urge to retreat into the sleazy bar downstairs, and forget the whole stupid thing.

If Ethel was my den mother, Mrs. Oppermann was my Sunday school teacher. She peered up at me over a pair of amber heavy-rimmed glasses which seemed about to drop off the end of her nose. Her head was poised in just enough of a haughty manner to balm the air with a scent of righteousness. She was sitting behind an old painted wooden desk piled high with paperwork and sundry paraphernalia. A curious glass vase resting on one corner was cleverly fashioned from an old beer bottle, with the bottom cut off and somehow attached to the top. One pathetic greenish-brown vine was hanging limply down from it.

"Have a chair–Mr. Dezengremel is it?"

"Thank you. Yes. Dezengremel." I sat down.

"Unusual name."

"I guess it is. Ancestors came over with the French emigres after Waterloo."

"Interesting."

I could see it was.

She introduced herself as Sylane Oppermann–"two n's"–head caseworker at Children's Service, then she settled back in her chair, arms folded, and crossed her legs. She was wearing one of those silky summer-thin dresses gathered just under the bust (a somewhat modest bust, as busts go these days) something like baby-doll pajamas. And though I wasn't able to see her legs from where I was sitting, I assumed they were quite nice, and that Sylane knew it but that her husband did not. A satisfied woman has a certain look around her eyes. Her hair was in a ponytail, tied with ribbon.

She tilted her head back to look at me through her glasses. I thought I was about to get a reading from the Gospel. The urge to bolt was nearly overwhelming.

"I assume you're here concerning the possible adoption of a child, Mr. Dezengremel."

No, I'm here to solicit donations for the Salvation Army, but this is my first day in the field and I was so nervous I left my tambourine in the bar downstairs. "Yes, I am."

"You're not married; is that correct?"

"Correct."

"I see. And how old are you, Mr. Dezengremel?"

"Twenty-eight."

"Are you interested in anyone special at this time, Mr. Dezengremel?"

"Anyone special? You mean a kid to adopt?"

"No. I meant are you dating anyone special."

"No one special."

She turned a smile on. "Still playing the field?"

"I guess you could say that."

"How often do you date, Mr. Dezengremel?"

Whenever one of the boys in the band gets sick of blowing his horn. Christ! "Why don't you just come out and ask me, Mrs. Oppermann?"

She colored. It was nice to see someone else suffer for a change.

"What do you mean exactly, Mr. Dezengremel?"

"You're trying to ask me if I'm queer or not–right?"

Her eyes dropped down for a moment, then she looked up, her face set hard, and stared me square in the eye. "Well, are you?"

I grinned. "No."

She smiled back. "I didn't think so, but I had to be sure. We had a delegation from the Gay Liberation Front in here last month demanding we give up all our *gay* children to them. They were rather unpleasant and Ethel finally called the police to get them out. So I'm afraid we're a little edgy, and you being single and all, well, you understand."

"I do." Sylane uncrossed her legs and leaned forward to set her glasses on the desk.

"Mr. Dezengremel–"

"David." I smiled and began to loosen my tie. It was hot and stuffy, despite the window fan. "Mind if I get comfortable?"

"Oh, excuse me, certainly not. Gives me claustrophobia to even see you men wearing coats and ties on days like this." I slipped the tie through the knot far enough so I could pull the tie off over my head. I hadn't actually untied it since the day I first bought it. It would've been far less troublesome, of course, to buy those fake ties.

"Now, Mr. Dezengremel–David–just why are you here? You must realize, of course, that though we receive many inquiries into single adoptions, these usually come from single women–most often from those for whom marriage has become a lost hope. Frankly, as far as I know in the six years I've been here, you're the first single man we've ever had make a serious inquiry. You've taken us quite by surprise. Why?"

I smiled, feeling a little awkward.

"Well, because I don't like cats, I guess."

"Cats!"

"Well, not cats really. More what they represent. Love substitutes. You feed and pet a cat and in return it rubs up against your legs and purrs in your lap. And makes you feel loved. To me that's a waste. I'd much rather share my plate and my lap with a kid who really needs them."

Sylane flashed me a guilty grin.

"My husband said something very similar to that once, the day I brought home our third kitten. She swiveled in her chair a moment, her face pensive.

"Did you ever have a pet of your own when you were a boy, David?"

"No. Unless you could count a painted turtle I once found in the road. My mother said it would smell up her house too much so she made me get rid of it. Actually though, I sneaked him back into the attic and hid him but I guess it was too hot and dark because he died. I didn't have him very long."

"Any other pets?"

"None of my own, no. Mommy's Precious Baby was with us for

about twelve years, but it was certainly no pet of mine."

"Who?"

"My mother's castrated Siamese. Damn thing even used to sleep with her. More than my old man did."

Sylane dropped her eyes.

"I see. What do you think about marriage, David?"

Christ, we were back on that again. I got the feeling I was rapidly losing whatever upper hand I might have gained earlier.

"That it doesn't work anymore, I guess. Or at least not as well, or as often. My grandmother—one of those quietly wise women who never offered advice unless you asked—once told me marriage was like a seed: to flourish the seed must be able to sink its roots ever deeper into the fertile soil. But how far can a marriage sink its roots into concrete. I don't know anyone married who's happy."

"Are you happy, David?"

I noticed I was sitting on the edge of my chair. I sat back and tried to look relaxed.

"No, I guess I'm not. But I'm single and not paying any alimony yet, so I think I can still afford to have hope."

"For what, exactly?"

"I don't know. For something real and purposeful, I guess."

"You don't have any purpose now?"

"None."

"Where will you find it?"

"Here I hope."

"Do you ever intend to marry?"

I shrugged. "I don't know."

Sylane rested her chin in her hand, and stared at me through maternal eyes. "Are you lonely, David?"

My throat clotted. I swallowed. "Yes, I guess I am." I swallowed again, tried to push down my vulnerability. People weren't supposed to be so direct.

She stared at me a moment longer, harder, then settled forward on her elbows, picked up a pencil and gave me a detailed explanation of the adoption process, interviews that were necessary, the physical examination, the references, and finally the waiting list. I noticed the apologetic smile.

"I think I know how you're feeling right now, David. I had an adoptive couple in here once who had quite the same look in their eyes." She tossed down her pencil and settled back in her chair. She met my eyes with her own. Watching for every reaction I felt. "He was a telephone lineman and the most anxious adoptive father I've ever had walk in here. He and his wife actually wanted to take a baby home after their first interview." She smiled sympathetically; she was seeing right through me. "I told him their names would have to go to the bottom of a very long waiting list and that there was nothing for them to do but wait." She grinned—"So what's this fellow do but start calling me with his portable test phone every time he's up a pole just to ask how many names were still ahead of his. He had our ears ringing for nearly a whole year."

"A year? They had to wait a whole goddamn year?"

"Now he calls us up every five minutes to tell us all about his daughter's progress."

She went on to tell me about how the pill and the liberalized abortion laws, coupled with the increasing numbers of unwed mothers keeping their own babies had drastically reduced the number of babies available for adoption. Waiting periods of a matter of weeks had now become a matter of months and sometimes years.

I was being prepared for a big letdown. She was being kind.

"Of course, you understand, David, that this agency has an overriding obligation to place its children with married couples, whenever possible."

I nodded halfheartedly. Shit.

"And quite frankly, as a single, David, the possibility of your adopting a Caucasian child at this time is remote, at best."

She was watching me carefully, seemingly for a reaction.

"However—"

"I'll do it!"

"Do what?"

"Adopt a non-white."

"There are many things to think about, you know."

"Yeah. Do I have to wait a whole year?"

I found myself sitting on the edge of my chair, Sylane grinning at me, amused. I was suddenly alive inside, suddenly flooded with light. The thought of adopting a non-white child had never occurred to me, but now that a possibility existed, a *real* possibility, the very idea sent me soaring into the stratosphere. I was intoxicated.

"Well, David, I'm afraid there'll still be a lot of preliminaries. We both have to be sure. But to get you going, I'll place you in the hands of our caseworker, Miss Chesser. She'll conduct your interviews and get down to specifics. How's that?"

"Great." I glanced at my watch and saw it would probably be too late to see Miss Chesser this afternoon. "How about tomorrow?"

Sylane grinned.

"We're not open on Saturdays, David. There will be a number of people ahead of you. I rather doubt we can get you together with Judi much before two weeks."

"Two weeks!" Christ! Life is ten per cent living, ninety per cent waiting. Shit.

"Well, David, look at it this way. This'll give you two weeks to think the whole thing over. It's a pretty big step for a single young man, you know. There really are a lot of adjustments to be made, and not just your own. For instance, what would your family's reaction be, especially to a black or bi-racial child?"

"My father's dead. Cancer. Smoked three packs a day. But if he weren't already dead, this would certainly kill him."

"And your mother?"

"She still lives in St. Paul." I quickly changed the subject.

"When can I see Miss Chesser?"

"Mrs. Jordan will set up an appointment for you."

I picked up my coat and tie to leave. Sylane came around to my side of the desk. I hadn't been wrong about her legs.

"Oh, I almost forgot. Where do you work, David?"

"I'm with Wagstaff, Walbridge, Ottley and Martin. Just an associate, or *junior* associate as Mr. Walbridge prefers it."

"Lawyer, eh?"

"Yeah."

"This is a strange place for you to be. I thought all you lawyers wanted to be president."

"Yeah, once."

"What changed your mind?"

"A father who wanted to be nothing else."

We shook hands and I went out to make my appointment with Ethel for Friday, July 2nd, and was putting on my tie to leave when Sylane called me.

"David?" I turned. "Thanks for coming. You made my whole day." She was rearranging the ribbon on her ponytail and her eyes met mine in a way that was not church-like.

No, Dezengremel, I told myself as I returned her warm smile, don't screw things up. Then I put on my jacket and glanced over at a dumbfounded Ethel. I grinned, gave her a wink, and left.

The grin never left my face the whole time it took me to float on my cloud the several blocks to my apartment building (I never drove my vet to work anymore, after losing five wheel-covers the first month I was in town). In fact, if anything, the glow grew in intensity, like the sun, as I walked. I beamed into every face I passed, and at an intersection crowded with starched faces, I asked one if it weren't truly a wonderful day to be alive. Apparently it wasn't. What a pathetic thing it was, I thought, that it was really an abnormal condition to be happy. It occurred to me that our asylums were probably filled with the happiest people alive.

That night I was bursting to celebrate with someone, anyone, so I went out. Somehow, after a number of intermediate stops, I ended up in an upper northside pub drinking beer with a bunch of rowdies and singing a medley of lurid songs. But most memorable of all, in fact the last thing I can remember was when some clown went out and bought a birthday cake (apparently I had told them all I was celebrating my birthday) and came back and threw it full in my face. One gift deserved another so I followed up with a full mug of beer over the guy's head. Everything was a blur after that, especially how I ever managed to get home.

Part of the answer came the following afternoon, on my way to the drug store for some Alka Seltzer, when I found a note, scrawled on a gum wrapper, stuck in the horn of my car.

> some weels u got heer, bub. some pad too
> come back 'n see us at fredys agin.
> bring long the doptd boy u was
> talkin bout all nite
>
> Deke

I hadn't the foggiest notion who Deke could be. But I thanked God he was a friendly.

And I thanked God for Alka Seltzer, too.

Chapter 4

July 1

Dear Mother,

Looks like it's going to be a hot summer here after that horrendous winter. Never saw so much snow, even back in St. Paul. Hot there yet?

One of our secretaries got raped last weekend. Miss Eckert. Got into a phony cab. One guy nailed her in the back seat, right in broad daylight, while the other guy drove around. Then they switched places. She came back to work yesterday just as well-groomed as if nothing had happened. Her hair wasn't even mussed up. Mr. Walbridge put out a memo yesterday to the effect no one was to discuss "the unfortunate affair" with anyone outside the firm. Bad publicity, you know. Pretend I didn't tell you (and, of course, burn this letter in the fireplace).

Not much going on. Still working on that Douglasson divorce suit. This is Douglasson's 4th wife, and 4th suit. Wants to dump her but doesn't want to pay her any alimony. So now we've got a private investigator working round the clock recording all her extracurricular activities for airing in court. Won't be much trouble destroying her; apparently she's a nympho and shacking up with half the city (maybe even a few of the other half). Guess ol' Sam thought the world of her until he found out it wasn't he who was turning her on. Life is forever disillusionment.

If I get the old boy off financially intact, I'll score a lot of brownie points with Stan and the firm. Haven't opened the file in a week.

All for now.

As always,
David

PS

By the way, will soon be a father. Am adopting a little boy, a little black boy. Like the one on your back lawn, near the fountain, the one holding the lantern.

DDD

Chapter 5

I was a little early for my 4:00 appointment with Miss Chesser. In fact, I was well over a half hour early. But I hadn't been able to concentrate on anything *res legorum* at the office, so I finally quit pretending and took a leisurely stroll over to West 3rd Street, and found myself stopping off at the toy stores on the way to windowshop.

Miss Chesser wasn't in, so Ethel offered me one of those old unpadded fold-up steel chairs built for Spartans and masochists. Worn and battered, it looked as if it might have been a recent acquisition from The Salvation Army Thrift Shop. I sat down and picked up a five months old copy of *Parent's Magazine* and wondered what Miss Chesser would be like. I couldn't imagine how anyone who worked with children could still be a Miss.

The clock apparently espoused the "new" work ethic. Sometimes I had to glare up at the big hand three times in succession before it would be sufficiently intimidated into marching one step closer to four o'clock. But when four o'clock finally came—and went—I was still waiting, and still glaring. Christ, I hated waiting or for anyone to keep me waiting. And it didn't help any for Den Mother to keep smiling over at me ever so sweetly while I was boiling over inside, because that meant I had to smile ever so sweetly back, and that's the last thing I wanted to do. But it wasn't Ethel's fault. I mean, I couldn't really take it out on her. But then it was four-thirty and I was still sweating and waiting. I stopped smiling back at Ethel. I was just about to say the hell with the whole thing when, just after four-forty, I heard someone thumping up the wooden stairs. I rehearsed how indignant I would look.

The door opened. A girl limped in, sixteen at the most. Shit. This was getting absolutely ridiculous. What the hell kind of place were they running here anyway. I began to compose a letter to my Congressman in my head.

I noticed the girl was wearing a heavy metal brace on a severely deformed left leg that was considerably smaller than her right leg, as if it had withered up under intense heat or something. The left arm was the same way. She was a petite little thing, with fiery red hair, a face full of freckles, sparkling pale blue eyes the same color as my vet—and the chest of a sixth grader in her first training bra.

I assumed she was a ward of the court and still under the wing of the agency. I decided I would wait a little longer and settled back in my sweaty clothes. But five o'clock was the absolute limit. At five I was leaving. And that was that.

"Excuse me, sir, but are you Mr. Dezengremel?"

"Uh, yes—yes I am."

"I'm Judi Chesser and I'm terribly sorry for being so late." I jumped to my feet and melted into a blob of smiles. "I was at a birthday party for one of tots at the Foundling Home and I guess I got carried away and lost all track of time. You know how fast an hour can go by."

I mumbled something innocuous about how I hadn't noticed the time either and about how interested I had become in an article on tantrums in *Parents'* . But all the time I stood there, a picture of serenity, I was half-crazy trying not to squirm and wondering how in hell I was going to pull my sweaty undershorts out of my sweaty cleavage without being noticed by Judi in front and Ethel in the rear. Life . . . always a struggle.

Finally Judi asked me to follow her to her office where we could talk privately. As she led me through a room crammed with a refrigerator, a stove, somebody's desk, a few tables and what looked like last year's Christmas tree, I reached back and unglued my shorts. Ahhhh.

We passed through a children's playroom, then into a dusky hallway that reminded me of some dingy northside tenement (where I had intruded only long enough to serve a summons and run), then finally we entered a room about the size of the janitor's closet outside my office. There was room for Judi and myself, the desk between us, and perhaps an underweight three-year old.

I sat down on an old wooden chair that groaned and creaked everytime I shifted my weight. My body, tensed for the crash, refused to relax. There's no place to put your arms on that kind of chair, so I folded my hands awkwardly on my lap and prepared myself for the usual banalities. Judi switched on the window fan.

"Well, David—may I call you David?" I nodded. "Sylly tells me—we call her Sylly—short for Sylane, don't you know—Sylly assures me that despite your rather unusual request you aren't a fag or a weirdo or anything dumb like that." She grinned, amused. "God, you really put her down, didn't you? Sylly comes on a little snooty sometimes. Her husband's head honcho of the religion department at the University, and I guess the influence can be a little heavy. But once you penetrate that crust of hers, she's one of the greatest. I'm sure you've found that out already."

I could see the state of the weather was not on Miss Chesser's agenda. She looked up at me and apparently noticed the beads of sweat forming on my brow and upper lip.

"Gee, you really look hot. Why don't you take off some of your clothes and get comfortable? I never could understand why men felt they had to go around in suits and ties when it's ninety in the shade."

Though I was certain this little redhead would not have flinched in the least had I stripped down to my shorts, I opted for coat and tie only. Somehow I got the feeling she'd called my bluff before I'd even gotten around to making it.

She switched on another fan that was sitting on a table directly behind her. A few papers blew off her desk, and when she made no effort to retrieve them, I did. But she told me to let them all go to hell, that they were just a few more sheets of the toilet paper that rolled in endlessly from the State: mandates, amendments to mandates, amendments to the amendments . . . . So we left them on the floor.

"Mind if I ask you a few questions, David?"

"Of course not. That's why I'm here."

"Any siblings?"

"No. I was an only child. Apparently my father wanted more kids, but my mother didn't."

"Why not?"

"She didn't like them, I guess."

"Did she like you?"

I smiled, self-consciously. Even love-making was supposed to have its preliminaries, but this broad wasn't about to waste any time.

"Well, to her I always felt I was the means to something but never the end. I always felt she displayed more affection than she felt."

"How so?"

"She was always very phony, condescending towards me—like the way a kindergarten teacher is, especially when somebody's watching. Every little kiss on the cheek was like a bribe, a payoff for proper performance. Made my skin crawl every time she'd peck at me."

"But how about you? Do you like kids?"

"Yes, I do."

"How do you know?"

"Because I would've liked being one myself."

"You mean you never were?"

"No—I wasn't."

"How so?"

"There was never time. I was always too busy performing, making Mommy and Daddy proud. Piano, violin, staying clean, using the right fork. No time to be a kid."

"Would you like to go back, say under different circumstances, and start over?"

"I think I would. Yeah!"

"Why?"

"Because I feel cheated. Whenever I think back on my early childhood I can't remember a thing, not a damn thing. Everything's a vacuum until well after school age, just as if the whole thing never happened."

"Do you feel there's any of the little boy still in you now?"

"Yeah, I think there is. But it's buried."

"In what?"

"Plastic. Molded plastic."

"Molded? By whom?"

"Those who mold us all I guess; parents, teachers, employers. They pressure us to conform. You know, learn to use the pedals on your trike like little Albert down the street; don't get your clothes dirty so you'll look clean and cared for; get an A in English even if you hate it; never talk in school; success is money and position; God is an American Capitalist; successful businessmen play golf and bridge; "in" people ski and wear imported sweaters; everything a man of the cloth says is Gospel Truth; everyone should be fluent in a foreign language; America can never afford to lose a war; everyone should get married."

"Then you don't think marriage is for everybody."

I glanced over at Judi's shriveled up arm. "Definitely not. There's too much pressure in that direction, especially toward that until death do us part bullshh–"

"Feel free."

"Bullshit. I mean, people used to live to the ripe old age of thirty-five or forty, tops. Christ, now we drag on past seventy. Add longevity with its tedium and aggravation to everything that has complicated marriage–expectations, careers and communication substitutes, like TV–and you end up with flooded divorce courts and crowded psychiatric waiting rooms."

"Then where does sex fit in"–she grinned–"so to speak? I mean, isn't that one of the biggest pressures pushing kids toward marriage?"

I grinned back. "Talking about sex, since when do you have to be married to have sex? The Puritan Ethic slapped that one on us. Before the pill and the vasectomy, it was probably a socially valuable hangup. But it isn't anymore. Marriage needs commitment, but commitment doesn't necessarily need marriage."

The five o'clock rush had begun to jam up the streets outside. Horns blared with outrage, and I had to raise my voice for Judi to hear.

"I really think we look at sex from the wrong point of view anyway. We choose, for some reason, to see it only as a method of procreation. But actually, I think, we should look at it more as a means of population control."

"Interesting. How do you mean exactly?"

"What?" The din outside had reached rock band levels.

"I said, how do you . . . .HOW DO YOU MEAN THAT EXACTLY?"

"Well . . . .WELL–"

"LET'S GET OUT OF HERE, DAVID. THERE'S A BAR A FEW BLOCKS DOWN THAT'LL BE NICE AND QUIET. AND COOL. I'LL BUY YOU A DRINK."

"I ACCEPT."

Chapter 6

We fled the stuffy offices and walked the three blocks to the Brass Rail (I've never been in a town yet that didn't have either a Brass Rail or a Town House). I was astonished at Judi's agility as she walked along in that cumbersome brace, at what was more a slow run. On the way, we finally got around to discussing the weather and what a shitty place the city was to live in. We agreed we could do nothing about either, the standard resignations.

The place was jammed with after-fivers, their brief cases lined along the bar. The hostess seemed to know Judi quite well and showed us directly to a quiet shadowy table. I noticed there was no brass rail at the bar. There never was. We ordered a couple of gin and bitter lemons.

"You were saying?"

"Saying?"

"About sex. You know, as a population control gismo."

"Oh yeah. Right. Okay, let's look at it this way. What do you think would happen, say, if every woman in the world produced eggs that were already fertilized each time she ovulated?"

"She'd miss all the fun."

We laughed.

"Besides that."

"Well, I guess we'd all be pregnant from 12 to 40."

"Exactly. And you'd all produce about three dozen off-spring each, three dozen more baby factories, that is. Which, of course, would be suicide for your species, simply because our little planet could never support you all. You'd overpopulate it and pluck it barren in no time at all."

"You're a regular Arthur Godfrey."

"Talking too much, eh?"

"Oh no, I didn't mean that. This was a favorite topic on his programs. Go ahead. I didn't mean to interrupt."

"Well, the human species, as well as most others, may have developed sex not as the best possible way of reproducing itself, but as the best way of limiting its numbers. Sex introduces chance. Look at the plants. Even though each plant produces both male and female germs, it still goes through all the trouble and risk of having the wind or an insect get them together. Why bother? Why not put out the seeds and be done with all that silly dependence on forces beyond its control? Because, if it did, it would proliferate itself right out of existence. Sex, my lovely, is just a damn good way of holding down numbers to balanced levels."

"Neat." Her eyes never left my face. The waitress delivered our drinks. We both took long sips ending with deep sighs of relief. "Tell that one to the Pope."

"Yeah, I know. But what can you do?"

"What you're trying to do, for one thing."

Judi gulped down the rest of her drink and held up two fingers to the waitress. I chugged to keep up. When I put my empty glass down, she was staring me square in the eye again. I noticed how creamy white her skin looked beneath all those freckles.

"Tell me, David, what do you think about blacks? As a race, I mean. Do you think they're any less intelligent as a race than whites for instance?"

Jesus Christ! What the hell was this deceptive little bundle of innocence up to? First she gets you to relax and let your guard down, then BAM! I got the feeling there was a tape recorder playing in the heel of her left shoe.

I made a weak effort to laugh myself into a more dominant position. "Which answer do you want, PTA or locker room?" Ha ha.

"Smart aleck, eh. Well, which one are you gonna unload on your son the day he comes home from school and asks you himself?"

Ouch!

"Well, to tell you the truth, I've never really thought much about that before. But I certainly don't harbor any prejudices if that's what you're getting at."

Judi frowned at me with amused impatience.

"Good grief, Dezengremel. You sound like one of those fence-sitting politicians running for office. Is that the kind of answer you'd give your son, something to win his vote? I mean, the day he comes home all beaten up and tells you the white kids at school were saying that niggers are dumber'n whites or they wouldn't be the sorry lot they are now and have been for over two centuries?"

I searched for the right thing to say, wishing I didn't have to say anything at all. I wasn't prepared for this.

"No, I guess I wouldn't. I'd ask him who the bastards were and go and kick the shit out of their parents."

The drinks arrived and Judi immediately ordered round three before I could even get started on round two. It occurred to me that this deformed, redheaded lush of a prosecutor had designs for getting me loaded. Probably, I thought, to see what kind of drunk I was, Manic Depressive or Annual Convention, and too, to get me to divulge all those deep dark secrets we all hide from each other—like what we *really* feel.

"Well, that would probably do great things for your own wounded pride. But what about your son's? What about the doubts gnawing at his pride? Would it resolve those?"

"I guess it wouldn't, would it."

"David, do you really know what your own feelings about blacks are? I mean what they *really* are?"

"Certainly."

I realized I was jiggling both legs under the table. Shit. I had never been in the witness chair before, and certainly had never faced a female D.A., one who limped in front of the sympathetic jury.

"I don't think you do, David. I think you might be afraid to admit to yourself something you feel you must suppress because it's a no-no, a taboo."

"Admit what?" I stopped jiggling my legs and tried to look the picture of innocence.

"The average black is in fact less intelligent than the average wasp."

I shifted my eyes uneasily toward the bar and at the other tables. There were no blacks.

"Look, Miss Chesser–"

"Judi."

"Well, look, Judi, I'm not the enemy here. In fact, I'm probably as much of a bleeding heart as you are. My hair's not very long, and my sideburns are mid-ear at their daringest. But inside I'm as disgustingly liberal as they come. I never used to be, true. Simply, because I came from quite the opposite. But somehow, through it all, I managed to learn how to think for myself, to question anything and everything. I admit that my exposure has been somewhat limited, certainly much more limited than yours, but I am not a narrow-minded bigoted idiot. I'm just not." Judi nodded throughout my declaration as one does when they're really listening. Then she took a drink and smiled at me. She was beginning to appear much older than 16. Her boobs even looked bigger.

"That's fine, David. But just because you don't go around dumping your garbage on the jungle bunnies to make yourself feel superior doesn't mean you don't harbor racial prejudices. I can sense you're attempting to blot out that thought within yourself that wants you to admit Negroes are really intellectually inferior to Caucasians. You don't want to admit it because you don't think it should be true, or that it would be acceptable socially, so you're suppressing it, hedging around it. But, David, what if your son should detect your ambivalence? In his own father. What would that do to him?"

I had my head propped up in one hand and was diddling with the ice cubes in my glass with a finger. The coolness was soothing. "You're trying to stick pins in all my bubbles, aren't you?"

"I suppose I am, David. But it's easy to get caught up with the glitter and glamor of something exciting, especially when you're starved for it. We all do. But there are pitfalls, harsh realities. Sometimes they have to be pointed out. But better now than too late, eh?"

I nodded half heartedly.

"You think I'm starved for drama?"

"Aren't you?"

I nodded. Judi always made you answer your own question.

The next round arrived. We drained our glasses and set them on the waitress's tray, and Judi ordered still another round. I was drinking on an empty stomach and the gin was going right to my head, buoying me off my chair like a balloon, it seemed. I wondered if Judi had ever tried pot.

"We actually had this happen a while back to one of our own boys. He was attending one of the local mostly white junior highs. He came home from school all bloodied up one day and told his foster parents some white boys at school had been teasing him about niggers being dumber than whites. He had just flunked an English exam and one of the white boys snatched his paper to show around to the others. He and a couple of other blacks made a stand and managed to kick the shit out of a few of them including the one who stole his paper, but in the end they got pretty badly beaten up."

"Bastards."

"He was hurt far worse inside than out."

"What'd you tell him?" My hand brushed against her accidentally as I was reaching for my drink. Her flesh was soft.

"Well, I told him there was no disgrace in defeat, none in fear, and certainly none in having black skin, kinky hair or a squatty nose. Disgrace came only in running down others, and attacking their weak points, to make yourself feel superior. Which is what racial prejudice is all about, David. I told him the reason there were different races was because there were in fact *differences*. Differences in physical appearance, innate talents, skills, abilities, even in temperament and native intelligence. I said it might even be a fact that as a race distinct from others, the Negro might possess lesser intellectual abilities."

I thought I caught a glimpse out of the corner of my eye, of some people watching us—or worse, overhearing Judi's heresy. Paranoia began to burn my Celtic cheeks.

"Then I told him to count the number of blacks on a football team or in an all-star game, and compare it with the number of whites. I said each race has its advantages, but also its disadvantages, and that no race could be all things. I told him to take pride in those things about himself and his race which he found he could do better than his white friends, or enemies, but to accept and do his best with those things he could not. Judi swirled the ice cubes in her glass, then took a long drink.

"What'd he say then?"

"Nothing." She chuckled, obviously pleased. "That same year he joined the track team and broke every record in the 440, the 220 and the mile. He'll be a freshman in college this fall on an athletic scholarship. The kid who snatched his paper was arrested last year for pushing heroin."

I leaned forward on my elbows and lowered my voice. "Do you actually believe what you told him? About blacks not being as gifted as whites, I mean."

She frowned coquettishly—"Gifted?"

"Okay. As smart, then."

"You sound so amazed. Certainly I do. So what? I believe kikes are keener than guineas, too, Swedes are mostly blonds, Orientals are short, Anglo-Saxons tall. To me, the admission of a truth is not an act of condemnation. The way I look at it, it's the first step toward acceptance. I learned a long time ago you can't deal with truths by denying them."

I glanced again at that shriveled up arm.

The waitress arrived with our drinks; there were four instead of the two Judi had ordered. "I'm quite busy," the waitress said, "so I thought I'd stock you two up for a spell. Can't keep up with you."

My head was getting lighter and giddier by the minute; I was beyond the point of no return. I drained my glass and took up another. Judi was right with me; in fact, ahead.

"What's Sylly's view on this? She agree with you?"

"God no. We've had some battles over that one. She's as staunch a member of the *all men are created equal* sect as I am a nonmember and she'd rather burn at the stake then change her mind. But one thing for ol' Sylly, she respects my differences in opinion and allows me to voice them as I damn well please. None of this 'you'd better reflect publicly those views that will cause the least number of waves or else' crap. That's damned rare in a so-called public servant."

Judi's eyes were two little pools of melted inhibition. I'm sure mine were too. I wondered if she was a virgin. She drained one of her two drinks, then suddenly stared me square in the eye again. She was going to ask me to take her to bed.

"Have you ever washed out a diaper full of diarrhea in a toilet bowl, David?"

My stomach rolled up into a ball and died. "Uh, no. The pleasure's never been mine." Christ!

"Where do you eat? Do your own cooking, do you?"

"Don't eat breakfast except for the greasy donut and coffee I have at the office. Usually have lunch with some of the other solicitors. I sometimes eat dinner out, but more often settle for a TV dinner and potato chips in the peace and quiet of my apartment, watching some talk show."

"Outstanding eating habits, Dezengremel. Think that kind of diet would be healthy for your—son? And what're you planning to do with your son while you're at work?"

"Well, to tell you the truth, Judi," I mused with exaggerated seriousness, "I was sort of thinking about taking him along and letting him operate a Legal Help 5¢ stand along the street outside my office building."

Judi laughed. She had one of those easy laughs I could listen to all day, never forced, never polite, like a little girl laughing at the circus clowns.

"Well, I think I might have a better suggestion for you, though admittedly less lucrative. I have a friend, Hattie Walker, who's been one of the agency's foster mothers since before you and I were born. She's had some 182 kids of all races and mixtures in her home, 187 counting her own five. But since her husband died last year, she's sort of dropped out of things. I think she's just what you need. And I also think you're just what she needs."

"Think she'd be interested?"

"Sure."

"How do you know?"

"I already asked her. Said she'd babysit whatever hours you want. Even volunteered to stay on to fix your meals."

"Great."

Judi drained all but a last swallow from her drink. The din in the room had come a long way from the paranoic whispers heard when we'd first arrived.

"How's your body, Dezengremel?"

"My body?" I peered up at her—was this a proposistion?

"Yeah. Your body. How is it?"

I straightened my shoulders.

"A little on the skinny side, I guess. But nobody's laughed at it yet."

"Shouldn't be long, with your eating habits. Really shouldn't miss breakfast like that, David. Can't do well at anything 'til you get your blood sugar up. Most important meal of the day."

"So that's why I daydream all morning."

"You need a physical, David."

"Christ, do I look *that* bad?"

"You do. But that's not the reason."

"What then?"

"We require it. Don't want you to become a brand new father only to drop dead on us."

"Where do I get that? Give them yourself, by any chance?"

"Thought you'd say that. No, you'll have to see a doctor."

"Don't know any."

"I do."

"Who?"

"Roland Maynard Monaghan, MD."

"Christ."

"He's a GP. But he does a lot of obstetric and pediatric work, too. The agency uses him a lot. He's good—you'll like him. He's also a crusty old bachelor like yourself. Should get on famously with each other. He's in the phone book."

"Great."

Judi drained her glass.

"Know anybody who likes you, David?"

"Likes me?"

"Yeah. Likes you. Know anybody?"

"How well?"

"Well enough to write a glowing account of what an exemplary member of the Establishment you are. Gotta have some references."

"No."

"Well, maybe you can bribe somebody?"

"Well, how about the porter in the men's room at the Chateau de Laurier. I usually bullshit with him during the speech at Rotary Club. I guess he knows me better than anybody else."

"Can he write?"

"I doubt it but I'll write up the blurb and he can put his mark at the bottom."

"Fine. Oh, and I'll send you a form to fill out. Send it back as soon as you can. Do you attend church?"

"No."

"Well, start going. Every single Sunday. And be sure you get to know the minister. Shake his hand and suggest he publish his sermons or something."

"Why's that?"

"Another worker will want to interview your minister, as a reference. And for God's sake don't put atheist or agnostic down on your form. Put down Zoroasthianist if you have to. Sylly's pretty sticky on the religious bit."

"Want me to play the typical hypocrite, eh?"

"Right. Think you can handle it? Never know, you might even get something out of it." She fingered a St. Christopher medal hanging on a silver chain around her neck. "Some churches aren't what they used to be, you know. Why don't you check out Father Cummins, the Episcopal priest at St. James', over on Washington?

He's a practitioner of what you might call Divine Disobedience and he's been in jail three or four times already. I think you might like what he's got to say, and later on it might give your son an opportunity to meet some other tots, too. They have a nursery there. Lots of blacks and bi-racials."

"Guess I could make the sacrifice."

"Big of you."

I smiled leeringly at her.

"You're some broad, know that?"

"And you're very drunk."

"So are you."

Judi signaled the waitress over and ordered another doubled round.

It was nearly noon by the clock on the bed stand as I pried my eyes open to greet the sun glaring in my bedroom window. I searched my mouth with a tongue swollen like a bloated corpse for a little moisture, anything to cut the cotton-mouth, but there was not so much as a gluey drop of saliva. I peeled the covers back and almost passed out as I wobbled to my feet.

My head throbbed with one of those excruciating pains curable only with tincture of bloody mary.

I stumbled into the living room, on my way to the tabasco sauce, tomato juice, gin and lemon, when I spotted a white blur on the door. A note. The scrawl was crude, but familiar.

> took you sister home   u was in no
> condishon youself. see u agin
> Deke

I could remember a face. A laughing, sweating face. And a voice. Deep with that quality of quiet strength you associate with lumberjacks who refuse to cut down trees with birds' nests in them.

Good ol' Deke. Whoever the hell he was.

Sister?!

Chapter 7

1923 Summit Ave.
St. Paul Minn.

David dear

will arrive friday 9th for weekend stop american flight 431 stop tried to call stop

mother

Chapter 8

No theater, no manner of entertainment, can compare in fascination with a busy, bustling airport.

There apparently was to be a convention of Lions in town over the weekend. The main lobby was chaotic with straw hats, bright blue ribbons, slender round manila bags, and the exhilarated roars of newly liberated Lions. A couple of harried looking dudes at the doors where I entered, apparently the official welcoming committee, were shaking hands with one hand and packing droopy-eyed drunks into chartered buses with the other.

On the way to the American Airlines ticket counter, I passed by a group of Jesus freaks, all decked out in their sandals and white robes (old bedsheets on closer inspection), who had cornered two of the conventioneers and were pleading with them not to "stagger" from the straight path of Jesus over the weekend. One thing about these Jesus freaks that's lacking in any other group of fanatics—they've got a sense of humor. The two Lions, nipping from their manila bags, were listening in a dreamy state of amused awe. One seemed especially fascinated with the deep cleavage on one of the girls, whose bulging garment perhaps should have been a double sheet rather than a single. The man, red-faced and balding, probably figured the longer he stood and listened, or pretended he was, the longer he'd get to peer down that virgin cleavage. The girl, on the other hand, probably figured the longer the guy got to look, the longer he'd stick around to listen. Evangelism at its best.

The plane had been delayed in Chicago because of severe thunderstorms and would be about an hour late. So I drifted into a little bookstore, filled with overpriced souvenirs and a few paperbacks, and bought a newspaper. Then I strolled up to an elevated lounge above the main concourse, which contained a bar and a snackbar, conveniently grouped, it seemed, for those laid over by lengthy delays or stopovers. It was well filled, and my only choice was the center cushion of a couch, mashed between two unpleasantly plump senior-type citizens, both absorbed in the overhead TV. The organ music was choked up with intense melodrama. The man looked to be in his mid-seventies; the woman, a shriveled-up hundred and eighty if she were a day.

I people-watched, listening in on conversations within earshot, then opened my newspaper. I could no longer read the latest flashes on Indo-China, Russia, or the economy. So saturated, so bored, so skeptical of truth had I become. So I paged back directly to Peanuts and Andy Capp. Snoopy was telling Woodstock he had finally found the opening sentence for his novel: "What can you say about a Sopwith Camel who crashed?" Flo had decided to go on the wagon in order to present a proper example for Andy, but it all backfired when Andy greeted the idea, cigarette stub glued on lower lip as usual, with the greatest enthusiasm because it meant his pub money had just been doubled.

I was chuckling to myself when the elderly man to my right tapped me on the shoulder.

"Young man, would you be so kind as to turn the knob over to CBS for me. My program's coming on now and I just can't miss it. Made that man with the travel bureau *promise* me I'd be on the ground at four-thirty."

A sharp jab stung my left shoulder.

"If you do, young man, I'll never forgive you. *Spring of Forever's* right on this here channel. Haven't missed it once in twelve years.

Another tap on the right shoulder.

"Hurry up, son. The doc was just going to tell Kirstin yesterday if she was knocked up. Just flip it over to CBS like a good fella. Do it myself 'cept I can't reach it 'cause of my arthritis."

Another sharp stab to the left shoulder.

"Touch that knob, sonny, and I'll scream for the police."

Right shoulder again.

"Don't mind that old gum flapper, son. She can't even see her damn program, much less hear it. Just wants somebody to wait on 'er.

Fingernail right into the flesh of my left shoulder.

"That's the trouble with you younguns today. No respect. Too wrapped up in yourselves to care about an old woman who—"

I jumped out of my seat and flipped the channel over to the *Bugs Bunny and Road Runner Show* (beep beep), then fled into the dark shadows of the bar where I sat down at a vacant table and ordered a beer. I felt my coat pocket for the envelope I had brought with me.

I hadn't been there five minutes when a young man of my own age, perhaps a year or two older, braced himself against my table, leaned down and asked me if he and his "good parents," as he put it, could impose upon me by sitting at my table, seeing as none of the other tables had three chairs available. His breath was heavy with alcohol, his eyes bloodshot. His parents, standing behind him, especially the mother, looked terribly awkward and conspicuous.

"Certainly," I said. "I'll just find a spot at the bar." I started to get up.

"Oh, no, stay right there and let us buy you a drink. I insist." He insisted by pushing me back down with a heavy hand on my mutilated shoulder. Then with a flourish of chivalry he seated his mother and father, both of whom greeted me with those transparent smiles that are somehow supposed to hide embarrassment. The son waved over a waitress with hands flying like semaphores and ordered several drinks, including a case or two of beer for me.

The mother smiled politely over at me, then at her son. "Ricky, don't you really think we should be getting down to the gate to meet Annie?" She looked at her watch. "She'll be landing any minute now."

Rick looked straight over at me. "Aren't married, are you, chum?"

I shook my head and mumbled something unintelligible.

"Didn't think so. You don't have that married look. You know the look I mean?" I shook my head again. "Well, that's the look I have to face every morning in the goddamn mirror. Mirrors. World would be a better place without so goddamn many mirrors. Mirror, mirror, on the wall, who the hell's got it all?"

"Ricky, dear, don't you—"

"Mother, for Christ's sake. It was Annie's idea to go home to Mama, and Mama's idea to send Annie back to me. Lucky Ricky. She certainly didn't expect a bon voyage bash, so she's not gettin' any gala greeting either."

Mother crimsoned.

The drinks arrived. A double round for Rick and myself, singles for Mom and Dad. Rick downed his first highball in one gulp and started right in on the second. I was glad to have something to hold and sip at, something to do other than squirm. Dad, sitting next to me, seemed to be watching the planes through the tinted windows.

Rick looked over at me with a brow knitted in erudite thoughtfulness. "Know what's wrong with people today, chum?" I shook my head and braced myself. "They get married for all the wrong reasons, that's what. Men want something out of *Playboy* and feel cheated when they don't get it. Women want something out of *Love Story* or *Gone With the Wind* and resent it when they find themselves left out. When kids get married today they're just that, kids. Even when they're well into their twenties. They're still nothin' but kids, adolescents. Nobody knows what it's all about 'til it's too goddamned late. We live in a fantasy of commercial imagery until *Oh Promise Me*, then *Bang*!—reality. Christ!"

Mother reached over and rested her hand on her son's. "Ricky, dear, don't you think we should be going to get Annie now? I'm sure this nice young man has problems enough of his own without listening to all of ours, too." She smiled at me apologetically.

Rick drained his second highball, then continued to look over at me. I seemed to be the family focal point.

"Know what really tears us marrieds up, chum?" Again I shook my head. "Some ugly morning discovering your own marriage has become everything you loathed in your parents', that's what. All those promises you made to yourself, slowly, but surely sucked down the toilet bowl. Don't even know it's happening. Then it's too late."

Mother jumped to her feet. No more smiles, even for me.

"Well, *I'm* not going to put up with this childishness any longer. Somebody must meet Annie. Coming, George?"

George was coming. He turned back from the window, from the glittering birds, finished his drink and got slowly to his feet.

Mother scowled down at her slobbering son. I expected her to send him to his room without supper.

"Coming, Ricky?" Her voice was restrained just enough to prevent the people at the adjacent tables from overhearing.

"Couldn't possibly walk that far, Mother. Maybe you can find a porter who'll lug me in his baggage cart. Otherwise we'll be waiting right here."

We? Christ! Two beers and I was already a member of the team.

"You'll be sorry!" Mother huffed off to find Little Orphan Annie, George following. Rick sighed, seeming to buoy up in his chair, and immediately called the waitress over, less dramatically this time, and ordered us another double round. After the drinks arrived, he continued to babble on freely about himself as if I were his psychiatrist, biographer and closest friend. It all came gushing out. At one point his voice choked up with a lump, his eyes watered, and he had to drain a highball in order to regain control of himself. I could only think of a rabbit caught in the hunter's iron trap, desperately gnawing at his own leg to free himself.

No sooner, it seemed, had they left than Mother and George were back. But between them now stood an almond-eyed brunette, her face streaked with mascara. She was wearing hot pants coyly hidden beneath a slitted coat, which, I thought, would be especially teasing on a gusty day. George held a suitcase in each hand. He was looking out the window again.

Annie dabbed at her eyes with a handkerchief and sniffled a little. Rick looked up at her through swollen bloodshot eyes, then groped clumsily to his feet. He smiled like a man about to jump out of a plane, then held out his arms. Annie threw herself into them. They stood there, unsteady, but clinched.

Mother's triumphant eyes were searching the room, apparently for looks of approval. George was still staring off toward the soaring miracles of flight.

Chapter 9

Shortly after five, I walked out to Gate 11 to wait for Mother's plane. On the way, I remembered the envelope in my pocket and checked it once again. I was relieved to find it was still there.

Outside, a thunderstorm began to unleash its fury. Eerie fingers of lightning flashed against the blackened sky as thunder clapped and rumbled off into the distance. Sheets of wind-driven rain began to sweep over the acres of concrete and macadam. Suddenly I found myself wondering what it would be like to plummet to earth in a plane struck by lightning. Ugh! The screams. The weightless, helpless falling. The smell of ruptured, twisted machinery. The fear, the horror of violent death, of finality. A brutal nightmare with no awakening.

A voice bored with sweetness and servility announced the arrival of American flight 431. Mother was one of the first off the jet and into the reception area. First class always unloaded first. I checked my pocket again when I spotted her.

She was dressed to be picked out in the crowd, in a bright summery, flower print suit. Her hat was one of those wide-brimmed things, with the nest of flowers on one side, which looked like it could easily double as an umbrella. She looked young for her years. She saw me and rushed over. After a hug and one of those public pecks on the cheek, she stepped back to examine me. As usual. She frowned and pronounced me diseased with malnutrition.

"Oh, David, just look at how scrawny you've become. Still not eating any breakfast, I'll bet." She talked on as she always did, incessantly. "Goodness. Marilyn sends her best. Saw her yesterday at the club. Still isn't married, you know. And not for lack of opportunities either. Clarence Horvath has been wooing her. But everybody says she's still waiting for you. Chris's going to run for governor, you know."

Christopher Larson, my father's former law partner and heir apparent to his political ambitions, had about as much chance of becoming governor of Minnesota as Eldridge Cleaver did. And Marilyn, his only daughter, had the worst case of chronic sewer breath and matrimony mania you could possibly imagine. I had taken her out twice, once during a Christmas vacation from college, because my mother and her mother wanted me to, and once, just after her period, because she wanted me to. We've been star-crossed lovers ever since, or so I've been told.

"How was your trip, Mother? Bad storm, eh?"

"Frightful. Goodness me, it was so terribly bumpy up there that at one point I thought surely we were going to shake apart. You know how I hate to fly, David. I wouldn't have done it at all had it not been so important."

"Important?"

We followed the signs toward Baggage Claim. Thunder was still rumbling off in the distance.

"Well, David, your letter kind of took us by surprise." Us was herself and whoever read the social column. "Quite frankly, David, it upset me so much I haven't been able to sleep nights."

Good ol' Mother Dezengremel. Right to the point.

"Upset you?"

"Well, it was so unlike you, David. I thought, well, I was afraid you might have been using those disgusting drugs. You don't smoke marijuana, do you?" She examined me closely again. "I was afraid you might have been on something when you wrote. You know how mothers worry over every little thing."

Shit. Every *little* thing. Never the big things.

"Of course, I knew you would never do such a thing, with your career and all, but I felt I should come anyway, in case there was something really the matter. Tell me, David, how are you and Stan getting along? I'm so anxious to hear. You know what your dear father thought of Stan, that he was always telling you how a young lawyer could get no better start in law or politics than under the wing of Stanley Walbridge. His being a personal friend of the Rockefellers and all."

I sighed. "We're bosom buddies, Mother. He thinks I have all the potential in the world. Says that's why he earmarked me for the Douglasson case."

Mother's eyes sparkled with pure delight.

"Oh, that's wonderful, David. Your father would have been so proud."

We went through the automatic doors and out into the main concourse. I noticed the Jesus freaks had cornered three more Lions. Unlike the other two, however, these were antagonistic and were heatedly chastising the freaks for being a bunch of filthy, lazy, freeloading slobs. Four airport cops were keeping a close watch, and seemed itchy for some action. I doubted they would get it.

"Now, David, about that letter. Had you been drinking or something when you wrote it? You wouldn't do anything to jeopardize your career would you? Not now. You've worked too hard to get this far."

"Jeopardize my career?"

"Oh, I know your intentions are well-meaning, David. You young people are so much more social-minded than my generation was. Then again, we had a depression to survive and wars to fight. What do you think Stan will think about this, David? I mean, he has to consider the image of his firm and all; people aren't accustomed to this sort of thing. You haven't said anything to him yet, have you, David?"

I tightened. "What sort of thing, Mother?"

"You know, about taking in this little mulatto."

Mulatto! "No. I haven't told anybody yet."

She looked greatly relieved, as if the demonic storms had failed in their attempt to foil her sacred mission.

"You know, David, I was talking with Marge the other day, and she said these poor unfortunates often suffer terribly from identity crises when they're taken out of their own environment and put into ours. Goodness, just think what it would be like to be a little white face all alone in their world."

Good old Marge.

"Marge is president of our Christian Charities Society now. And with her at the helm, I think we'll break every fund raising record in the book. She's such a spunky little thing." *Little* Marge goes two fifty if she goes a pound. But *spunky* I can't deny–her first husband died at thirty-six, in bed, of what the doctor called "physical exhaustion."

We arrived at Baggage Claim where there was already a throng. The luggage from 431 had not yet arrived.

"I really think that's the best way we can all help those more unfortunate than ourselves, David. I mean, there are so many helpful charities today, all doing such a marvelous job."

"Helping us beat those higher tax brackets."

"There, you see. Everybody benefits, and nobody suffers any identity problems."

The baggage train arrived. I went and got Mother's bag and set it down on the floor beside her. My mouth tight, I slid the envelope out of my pocket and handed it to her.

"Why, what's this, David?"

She opened it and slipped out the airplane ticket.

"It leaves in forty-five minutes, so you won't have to wait long."

She looked up at me, stunned. "David!"

"Let's let distance lie where distance is, Mother. I can't explain what I don't think you could ever understand." I don't know why, but I kissed her on the cheek. Her skin felt cold. "Good-bye, Mother."

I turned quickly and left her standing there. An electric eye jerked open the door, and I stepped out into the washed air. The concrete smelled of wet heat.

Chapter 10

The first clue to the fact that Roland Maynard Monaghan was not exactly a conventional doctor came when I tried to make an appointment to see him. Every other doctor in the city, I knew, took Thursday off. Midweek R&R, I guess. But not Monaghan.

I called on the Monday after meeting Judi. I was eager to get the paperwork out of the way as soon as possible. On the phone Monaghan's nurse—*nurse* rather than *receptionist*, because the phone rang eleven times before she finally answered it—sounded like a gravelly-voiced Portuguese fishwife.

"Yeah?"

"This is David Dezengremel speaking, and I—"

"David *who*?"

"De-zen-gre-mel. D-E-Z-E-N-G-R-E-M-E-L. French, don't you know."

"Right. Medicaid or Medicare?"

"Excuse me?"

"Who pays your bills, bub?"

"I do."

"*You* do?"

"Yeah."

"One of those, eh?"

"Yeah, 'fraid so."

"Okay. Now what's your hang-up?"

"I need a physical."

"That all?"

"Yeah, for now."

"Okay. The doctor's booked this week. How 'bout next week?"

"That the earliest?"

"That's it, sunshine."

"Okay, Monday then."

"The doctor's not in on Mondays."

"He isn't?"

"Nope."

"I thought Thursday was the big day for the MD's around here."

"Not for Monaghan."

"Tuesday?"

"Right. I'll put you down for Tuesday at five. The doctor does his physicals after regular hours."

"Fine. Thank you. See you then. Bye."

"Peace, bub."

The waiting room was empty when I arrived, shortly after five. The fishwife greeted me with a smile. Usually the face never lives up to the voice (especially with disc jockeys). But this one did. Dark, leathery, lined with "been there."

"You the French taxpayer?"

"That's me."

"Fine. The doctor will be with you in a few moments. He's sewing up some kid's arm right now. Knife wound. Have a seat. I'm leaving so you'll have the joint to yourself. Have a ball."

She left. I sat down on a stiff wooden chair which was nearly as comfortable as the one at Children's Service.

The walls of the waiting room were cluttered with colorful paintings, apparently originals, of different species of wild birds. These, with the tree-like plants in every corner, and hanging vines, gave me the feeling of walking through the aviary of the San Diego Zoo. I scanned the walls and recognized only a robin and a song sparrow. Then something definitely out of place arrested my eye. It was a bird all right, but not the feathered sort. I got up and walked over for a better look. There was a title: ROSY-BREASTED PUSHOVER, by Anonymous.

A door opened and a teary-eyed boy of about ten came out holding a heavily bandaged right arm against his chest. His mother followed. The boy's clothes looked as if they'd yet to witness the inside of a washing machine, and the mother looked as if she had yet to witness the inside of a tub. The boy was carrying a huge red lollipop in his left hand. The mother looked blankly at me, and my clothes, then left.

A man appeared from the same door. He was wearing a pair of bright plaid bermuda shorts, a solid colored tee shirt, and sandals very similar to the ones I'd seen on the Jesus freaks at the airport. He was wiping his hands on a towel. When he turned fully toward me, I could see an inscription on the shirt. *St. Bernard's Seminary.*

"You Dezengremel?"

"Yes I am."

He held out his hand. His vice-like grip nearly put me on my knees. Uncle.

"I'm Doc Monaghan. Friends call me Rollie. Not-so-friendlies call me Maynard. Come on in."

If the waiting room was an aviary, the examining room was a conservatory. The wall paintings were a colorful riot of what I assumed to be wild flowers. I assumed, because after recognizing a dandelion and a buttercup I had exhausted my personal knowledge of botany. But, as in the waiting room, here too there was one startling exception to the smooth flow of things. It caught my eye immediately. It remotely appeared to be some sort of trophy, but only because of the little brass plate attached to the wooden backing. The backing itself looked like a well-weathered board, something perhaps off an old weather-beaten barn. Above the plate was one brownish, fibrous, irregular blob of a likeness totally foreign to any athletic activity I was familiar with. And I was familiar with most.

"Physical?"

"Right." A shiver ran up my spine as I spied one of those gargantuan needles used to inject adrenaline into arrested hearts. Christ!

"Strip to your shorts."

I started to take off my clothes. What is there about taking your clothes off in a doctor's office that is so different from the locker room? Perhaps it wouldn't be so bad if the doctor took his off too.

"Who did all your paintings?"

"I did. Well, most of them. One of my *birds* in the waiting room was contributed by Elma, my nurse."

I chuckled. "Yeah, I think I know the one you mean. The Rosy-Breasted Pushover. Quite a bird."

Rollie grinned as he pressed the cold metal of the stethoscope against my bare chest. "She was trying to tell me something, I think. Breathe deeply. So I left a copy of *Mr. Universe* and an empty Coke bottle on her desk."

I snorted and nearly blew out Rollie's eardrums.

"You did all the others yourself though, eh?"

"Yeah. It's sort of a hobby with me. I photograph the birds and wildflowers in their natural habitats in the spring and summer months, then spend the winter doing paintings from the photos."

Next he wrapped the blood pressure thingamajig around my arms and pumped it up until I thought my arm would fall off.

"Looks like you're quite an artist. Man, I couldn't do anything like that if my life depended upon it."

"Ever try to?"

"Not really, I guess."

"Then how do you know? Say, ahhh." He jammed an oversized popsicle stick down my throat. I shrugged my shoulders to answer his question.

Finished, he threw the stick into a hopper. "How long have you been able to talk?"

"Gee, I don't know. Since I was still shittin' my pants, I guess."

"Can you express yourself with words?"

"Yeah, sure, I guess so."

"Can you write?"

"Yeah. Sure."

"Do you express yourself with those funny little squiggles?"

"I try to."

"Then what makes you think you couldn't express yourself equally as well with colors and forms? Cross your knees."

I shrugged, feeling a little stupid, and crossed my knees.

Rollie started to rap my knee caps with a little mallet that looked suspiciously like a five 'n dime store nutcracker.

"You know, Dezengremel, just about everybody who comes in here says the same damned thing. *Gee, I could never do that.* But, like you, none of them have ever tried it either. And I suppose you're going right out now and buy your son about ten thousand new coloring books?"

Now how the hell did he know about that! I knew I hadn't mentioned anything to the fishwife about the reason for my physical. Quite frankly, for fear she'd hang up on another nut.

My surprise must have shown.

"Judi told me. She called the other day. Apparently she's taken quite an interest in you. She wanted to know if you'd made an appointment yet."

"Thorough, isn't she?"

"You bet. The best caseworker they've got over there. You're damn lucky to have her on your side. Stand up, please, and drop your trousers."

Christ, why the hell did they always have to do this?

Rollie grabbed me above the right testicle. My Celtic skin began to flush like he had painted it with one of his red watercolors.

"Cough, please."

I coughed and felt my nut jump up against his hand. He grabbed the right one; I coughed again. I could see the firemen bursting through the door on a false alarm. Christ!

"How did she get like that, Doc?"

"Born that way. Okay, bend over and spread your cheeks."

Christ!

I was eternally grateful the fishwife had gone for the day.

"Some twenty-nine years ago Judi was left on somebody's doorstep. The note said something about her father not wanting any deformed babies around. Probably offended his masculinity. But nobody else seemed to want her either. She spent eighteen years at the Children's Foundling Home, the only one she's ever really known."

"Christ!"

"You see, Dezengremel, most people adopt mainly to fulfill their own needs, and if the child doesn't quite measure up to their standards, well, tough shit for the kid. Let somebody else worry about that one. Okay, you can get dressed now."

I pulled on my clothes with a feeling of relief, like crawling back into the old blanket.

"Now take this asshole war in Vietnam. When that's over–if it's ever over–all those orphans left in one piece, the ones with cute little dimples and pretty fat faces, will soon be snatched right up by loving, lily-white parents. But those maimed and scarred and unsightly will just end up like Judi. Banished somewhere to some obscure outpost so their ugliness can't unsettle any Christian consciences. Know what I'd like to see, Dezengremel?"

His voice grew tense. "What?"

"I'd like to see everyone of those bastards in the war department be required to adopt at least one maimed child from Vietnam. It'll never happen though. They'll publish their memoirs instead, to defend themselves and I'm gonna use Lyndon's for my dart board!"

Even when ruffled, Rollie had the eyes of a basset hound, an Irish basset hound–drooping, softly sad, almost pleading with gentleness, but blue instead of brown. He had the kind of face you might wish to look up into at the moment of death. At least you would know one person cared, really cared, and perhaps would even remember for a while. I glanced again at the lettering on his tee shirt.

"Did you study to be a priest, Doc?"

"Do I sound like it? I get a little sermony sometimes, I guess. Can't help it. Can't sound off to *them*, so I sound off to my patients."

I pointed to the *St. Bernard's* on his shirt. "No, I mean your shirt. The seminary bit."

He looked down and smiled.

"Yeah. I did. Three years of minor, or what was minor back then. This isn't my shirt, though. My kid brother's. Became a deacon last year, and'll be ordained a priest this fall. He went to med school and dropped out for the priesthood; I went to seminary and dropped out to become a doctor. Crazy, eh?"

"Different."

"He couldn't tell people they were going to die; I couldn't tell people they were going to hell. So we switched places."

I noticed the shiny purplish circles around Rollie's eyes. If I ever looked that beat, I knew damn well I'd simply call in sick and sleep it off. And I knew damn well, too, that I'd never run myself into the ground over my job, not now. I had once, at school, during the final exam weeks. Filled with uppers, I'd go a week without sleep, anything to get those goddamn A's to please the parents. But never again. Rollie was probably in his late thirties, but he looked fifty.

"Well, David, you still haven't told me about those coloring books. Are you or aren't you?"

"Am I what?"

"Going to buy the stores out?"

"Well, probably. Thought I'd get him a little desk and chair, too, if he's old enough."

Rollie shook his head. "Going to put the screws right to him, eh? Do unto mine as was done unto me."

"How's that?"

"One of my pet peeves. Perhaps one of the reasons you never ventured into new areas of expression, like art, is because you were probably discouraged from it when you were a kid. Take a real good look at this goddamn coloring book bullshit. You're handed a coloring book and crayons and praised to high heaven only if you tow the mark and conform your expressions to those preordained by the lines in the book. But nothing is your own! Nothing comes from within yourself. You simply learn what those sacrosanct *education experts* want you to, which is what they themselves learned—how to become a dull, docile, timid member of a semi-conscious society."

David: "Not everybody can paint."

Rolly: "Why the hell not? Friend, the best thing you can do for your kid is buy him the fattest pad of paper you can find and a few pencils and let him have all the freedom he wants. That's where it's at! And when he draws a circle with two other smaller circles for eyes—one inside, the other out—then adds a penis about a foot and a half long and says it's Daddy, then, buster, that's just exactly what it is! Daddy. *His* Daddy. The way *he* sees him."

"Amen."

Rollie laughed at himself, and I suggested that perhaps he should return to St. Bernard's. Then he got a bottle of whiskey out of the refrigerator, where the other perishable drugs were kept, and we sat around and chewed the fat for well over an hour. Finally, when I was about to leave, I remembered that bizarre collage hanging up on the wall.

"I meant to ask you. What the hell is that?" I pointed at the fibrous blob.

Rollie chuckled. "It's a trophy I won back in '68. When I was State Cowchip Throwing Champion."

"Cowchip!"

"Yeah. I broke the state record that year, which won me the right to compete in the nationals in Kansas. But I got drunk in Lawrence the night before the finals and broke my arm. I fell off a Brahma bull at two o'clock in the morning, on a dare. That's the chip I used for my record throw."

On the way home, I wondered to myself, why, if I hadn't been sick, did I feel so much better. Perhaps, I thought, it was because I had just met a man who hadn't been dead since puberty. Cowchip Throwing Champion. Christ!

I found myself laughing out loud in the elevator.

Chapter 11

When it comes to housekeeping, I'm a slob. I mean, how turned on can you get over a kitchen that's really an operating room or a living room that's really a museum. Life's too short to waste half of it impressing the neighbors with how clean and neat and antiseptic you are. Which, I think, is why most people are clean and neat and antiseptic.

Judi had called me at work late in the afternoon to inform me she would be around sometime Saturday morning for a home visit, and that she would have another caseworker with her. The other caseworker, she said, happened to be the agency's self-appointed expert snoop, who was especially gifted at telling the person from the way he lived, and whose opinions carried considerable weight at the agency. Christ! Thanks for all the warning.

I stopped off at a supermarket on my way home and dumped every kind of cleaning product into the cart that I could lay my hands on—soaps, detergents, bowl cleaners, brushes, window cleaners, antiseptics, polishes, towels, a couple of pails, and a sponge mop. Then, for personal fortification, I added a couple of six-paks and a box of potato chips.

It would have been overwhelming to tell myself I had to scour the whole pigpen in one goddamned night, so I talked myself into thinking about only one room at a time, as if it were the only room in the apartment. Life is tolerable with the aid of illusions. I spun an empty bourbon bottle; it pointed toward the kitchen. The kitchen, therefore, was the only room in the apartment, at least for two hours and thirteen minutes. I scoured the top of the stove, then opened the oven door Christ! Now where the hell did all *that* shit come from? Not from me, because I myself hardly ever used the damn thing. I mean, how much grease is there is a TV dinner? After convincing myself it must've come from the slobs who had the apartment before I did, I attacked it as one would another person's toilet bowl. But the crap was so thick, so baked on, I finally had to dive in and scrape it off with an old knife. Christ!

I wasn't even going to bother with the refrigerator, because, as everybody knows, refrigerators never get dirty. They can't. I mean, can you imagine Alaska ever looking like Birmingham? But then I recalled a movie in which Walter Matthau, playing a private detective, opened up Gregory Peck's refrigerator to find out what kind of guy he was. So I opened mine. Have you ever noticed that orange juice mingled with wine and strawberry jam in the bottom of your refrigerator forms a flypaper-like glue that never fully dries but keeps snaring up everything that touches it, including your fingers?

The bathroom could have qualified for a federal disaster grant. So stubborn were the shit stains in the toilet bowl, for instance, that they refused to loosen their grip until I plunged right in with my grease-scraping knife and flaked them off. I damn near barfed. Afterwards I held my hands under scalding hot water for ten minutes and threw the knife in the trash. The bathtub ring finally surrendered after a series of repeated assaults consumed one whole can of Ajax cleanser; I had forgotten porcelain could look that white. The mirror on the medicine cabinet over the sink was so clouded over with toothpaste spatterings that, peering into it, I could only see a ghostly apparition mimicking my movements. I scrubbed it with my toothbrush until it revealed every flaw in my face. I liked it better dirty.

My bedroom reeked of fermentation and neglect. And I soon learned, after scrubbing the floor for the fifth time, that the wine, whiskey and pot of a year's worth of debauchery is impossible to expunge in only one penitent night. So, early Saturday morning, after but four and a half hours sleep, I ran out and bought a dozen air fresheners and tied them under the bed to the springs. My debauched arena was suddenly a virgin Adirondack forest! While I was out I stopped at a little Catholic shop and bought a discreetly sized crucifix and nailed it to the bedroom wall facing the bed. That meant the Playmate Calendar on the opposite wall would have to go; I kissed Miss July farewell and threw her and the other eleven apostlettes in the trash can, in company with my shit-scraping knife.

The spare bedroom, which would become my son's, was crammed full of junk–skis, a tennis racket, a basketball, two trunks, scuba gear, suitcases, thirty-five empty bourbon bottles, a couple of rusty barbells, seven years of back issues of *Playboy,* psychedelic wall posters, and an old disassembled English bicycle.

When it has to be, the human mind can be truly resourceful. The apartment was small and a bachelor's wardrobe already engaged what little closet space there was. So, the bourbon bottles, thoroughly smashed up, went in the trash can; the larger trunk, wrapped in psychedelic posters became a cocktail table, and the smaller one, also colorfully wrapped, became a chest at the foot of my bed; the suitcases, loaded with the *Playboys*, went under my bed, as did the scuba tank and the bicycle parts; the tennis racket, the barbells and the skis all went beneath the couch and chairs in the living room. The basketball remained in the bedroom, my son's first toy. Enough dust had accumulated on the floor to start a potato farm, which, at the time, seemed like a better idea than cleaning it up.

The living room looked a little bland after being sterilized, so I quickly ran down to a five and dime store (what a misnomer that is) and bought some leafy plants to spice the place up. The salesgirl said they were next to impossible to kill, and when I noticed the vines looked like the one on Sylly's desk, I believed her.

Finally exhausted and soaked in sweat, I sat down for a moment to catch my breath and gulp down the last can of beer from the two six-paks. It was hard to believe I was still in the same apartment. Then I quickly took a hot shower, being very careful not to mess up my nice clean bathroom, and got dressed.

Panic! I had forgotten something. I pulled the scuba tank back out from under my bed and detached the regulator; then hurriedly I pulled the hoses off the mouth piece and holding the end up so as not to spill any, I rushed the hoses into the bathroom and shook the contents out into the toilet bowl. I flushed the toilet and watched three ounces of the best Mexican pot one could buy swirl down the drain. Christ! That hurt.

A knock on the door. I threw the scuba gear back under the bed, took a deep breath, let it out slowly, then answered the door. It was Judi. She was alone.

"You ready, Dezengremel?"

Judi was dressed casually in slacks and a long-sleeved blouse and looked like a little doll, almost too good to be real.

"Ready as I'll ever be, I guess."

"Well, then let's go."

"Go? Go where?"

"Shopping, of course."

"*Shopping*! But–"

"Yeah, I know. You worked your ass off all night long and now you want me to come in and admire your newly washed soul, right?"

She limped in and glanced quickly around.

"Very nice."

"Well, aren't you going to see the rest? My stove? The bedrooms? Not even the toilet bowl? Christ, Judi, I spent a whole hour on that goddamn toilet bowl alone. A whole goddamn hour!"

Judi just smiled up at me and limped back out the door.

"Well, Dezengremel, now you know what it feels like to be a woman. Rewarding, isn't it? Come on, let's go."

"But where's the snoop?"

"Home in bed with the flu. Come on, let's get going before the stores get crowded. I don't like to step on people with my iron leg."

"But where we going?"

"Got any credit cards?"

"Credit cards? Yeah, sure, lots. Bank Americard, Master Charge, American Express, Texaco–"

"Fine. Now tell me, Dad, what do you think you're going to need around here to feed, shelter, clothe and entertain a three-year-old boy?"

"A three-year-old?"

"Yeah, a three-year-old. He's waiting for you over at the Foundling Home, if you want him." I was stunned. Judi took a snapshot out of her handbag and handed it to me. "Name's Charlie. Anyway, that's what the sisters call him."

I looked down at a wide-eyed little black face and felt my heart begin to pound. The reality of it all was suddenly overwhelming. Was this all really happening? I mean, was this little kinky-headed guy really to become my son? Judi sort of led me down to my car and asked if she could drive since she knew the locations of all the better shops. I gave her the keys.

I was still glued to Charlie's picture as she pulled out into the street. She tapped me on the shoulder.

"By the way, who the hell's Deke?"

It soon occurred to me I should have lied about my income on that application form Judi had sent me. No sooner were we in the first store than she was spending my money faster than I could sign the credit slips. Comfort came only in the knowledge I was damn well certain of getting my money's worth. Judi was a wary shopper and drove a hard bargain. She snatched up nothing on impulse, as I would have, but mumbled over every little detail. And if she thought something was a piece of shit, she would call over a salesclerk and say so–loud enough for every other shopper in the store to take notice.

The first stop was a furniture store. In the span of little over an hour, I acquired a junior bed, a chest of drawers, a little table with a matching chair, a rocking chair (for me for reading bedtime stories in, she said), a highchair (Charlie was still too short for a regular chair, she said; besides kids are forced to grow up too fast, she added), a small bookcase (we would stop by the bookstore later, she said), and, of course, a little training toilet (shit! I said). I winced at the total as I signed the credit slip; a very delighted salesclerk said they would be only too happy to deliver everything Monday evening.

Next on Judi's agenda was a clothing store. Which was really more of a children's boutique, I thought. Judi told me there was a fag hairdresser in back doing a landslide business fitting eight-year-old girls with hairpieces, falls and wigs, and that she wouldn't have brought me here had they not had the best selection of high-quality clothes in town. The place was bustling with silver-haired grandmothers; and to me everything seemed priced accordingly—the grandma markup. Christ!

"Let's see, now. Charlie is just over three. February, March . . . his birthday is February 11th, by the way. Or as near as they could tell. February, March, April—"

"Whatdya mean as near as they could tell?"

"Well, they couldn't tell exactly because Charlie was a foundling. The doctor sort of guessed at it from Charlie's level of development et cetera at the time."

"You mean he was just *found* somewhere?" I shouted. "I mean, abandoned, like Sylly's goddamn cat?"

"Yeah. In a garbage can, over on the Northside. Some old bum woke up in an alley one morning and heard faint screams coming from one of the garbage cans. He found little Charlie, half dead, and rushed him to a priest. After three months in a hospital he was placed at the Children's Foundling Home and he's been there ever since."

"Jesus Christ! What the hell kind of animal does it take to do something like that? I mean, how could anybody just stuff a helpless little kid in a garbage can like so much rotten baloney. Christ Almighty!"

"I know what you mean, David. It's hard to understand. Most don't want to. She put her good hand on my shoulder. A helluva lot of people in this ugly world, David, are hapless victims of pretty cruel circumstances, people born into a living hell. Mothers who shouldn't be mothers, fathers who shouldn't be fathers, and children who shouldn't be born. Put the three together and I'm afraid you've got many an unwanted baby in a garbage can. But whose fault is it? I mean, really?" I hugged her impulsively because she was so damn good.

Just then a salesgirl came up and asked if she could help us. Judi said no, we were just looking. The salesgirl stepped back, but kept an eye on us.

"I guess Charlie's pretty lucky to be alive then, eh?"

"He is now."

"When can I meet him? I mean, can't we stop over at the Home this afternoon, just for a minute or two?"

"All in due time, dad. I haven't even told Sylly yet."

"Christ! Then it's not for sure? I mean, she could still say no and I wouldn't get him?"

"That's always possible, I guess. Though she usually takes my recommendation. But, then again, she hasn't interviewed Father Cummins yet, so, well, you can always bring all this stuff back. Just don't get it dirty. Now, as I was saying, Charlie's about three years and one, two, three, four, five months, so he'll need fours."

"What's he like?"

"Well, as you may have noticed in the picture, he's got two arms, two legs, a rather dark complexion, kinky black hair that's hell to comb—wears it in an afro, don't you know—a mouth that's always got something in it, usually chewing gum, a—"

"Forget it. Christ, I should've known better. Let's get on with it."

Shirts, pants (I insisted on a couple pairs of bell bottoms), underwear (including training pants, because, she said, the nuns were having trouble potty training the little rascal; apparently he was using it as a weapon. Whenever the nuns gave him hell, he'd go sit in a corner and shit his pants. Christ! Shoes and sneakers (size 9½—Christ had to be black, she said; who else would've had feet big enough to walk across water), socks, pajamas, bedding (you'll need lots, she said, and she didn't have to tell me why), a pair of swimming trunks (but there's no uncontaminated water within a hundred miles of here, I said; for the "Y" swimming program, she said), and a couple of summer windbreakers (we'll do the fall shopping later, she said, after you've earned some more money). And, oh yes, she said, you'll need rubber pants and a dozen or so diapers; he still wears them to bed. I closed my eyes and mortgaged my soul to Marine Midland.

"Tell me, do you sophisticated young lawyers ride bikes or is that all beneath you guys?"

"Well, I have one, if that's what you're asking me."

"Good. Then we can put a seat on the back for Charlie. And what do you think about getting him a tricycle, too?"

"Sure. As long as it has a seat on the back for me."

Next we drove to the toy store, a place called SANTA'S WORKSHOP. Was nothing sacred?

Unlike the clothing store, however, this one had more men milling around in it than women, and I must confess I immediately felt more comfortable (my mother used to take me with her when she went shopping for panties and bras. Christ). Many of the toys were getting a good workout, the more mechanically intricate or clever the toy appeared to be, the more fascinated the fathers were. Toys, like baby foods, are designed to appeal to the parental palate.

Judi headed straight for the bike department, but I was suddenly twenty years younger, surrounded by mountains of toys, immersed in an eight-year-old's heaven. They were all mine.

Judi returned to take me in tow. Apparently I looked what I was feeling.

"I blew it, didn't I, Dad? You've gotta have 'em all, right?"

"Right."

"Well, if you do, why don't you just keep all the toys yourself and give your son the boxes to play with? Most of this stuff is just cheap plastic gimmickry, but pretty. And it's all stamped EDUCATIONAL to soothe the parental conscience.

I smiled sheepishly, "Some of it's nice."

"Listen, Dad, a child's best toy always was and always will be his own imagination. I mean, what kid, if left to his own devices, can't turn an empty box into whatever he damn well pleases? She steered me out of the store. Parents are brainwashed into thinking their children need toys in order to play. But what they're really doing in giving them every so-called *educational* gadget advertised on *Captain Kangaroo* is stifling their kids' imaginations. It's a damn shame."

"You know, you and Monaghan ought to go to Washington with your soapboxes and address a few Congressional Committees. You don't know what you're missing. You're a couple of real crusaders."

"Aren't you?"

One thing that fascinated me about this little redheaded kangaroo with the funny-looking arm was the way she confronted you with the goddamn truth. She was always a mirror, unobscured with toothpaste spatterings, in which you could really see yourself. Most people confront you with whatever least complicates the situation or puts themselves in the best light in your eyes. They tell you what they think you want to hear, and don't tell you what they think you don't want to hear. The illusions grow and the truth dies and you die with it. But not with Judi. She told it like it was.

We stuffed the trunk with a fender seat for my bike (made in Japan, of course; but would be easy to put on my bike, she said, if I could ever get the damn thing put back together), several sets of blocks, a tricycle (they didn't have a rear seat for me), a little teddy bear, several Tonka trucks, a dozen big fat pads of blank paper, crayons, water paints, brushes, finger paints, modeling clay (so he wouldn't play in his own shit, she said), a big red fire engine, twenty-three books (many of my old favorites, including the Mr. Small series), sundry other vehicles—and, of course, several empty boxes.

The goddamned salesman was a maddening picture of good cheer as I signed the goddamn credit slip. SANTA'S WORKSHOP. Christ!

Chapter 12

On the way back to the apartment Judi suddenly pulled up in front of one of those bargain furniture stores, always going out of business, having a fire sale or an anniversary celebration.

"What now? I'm broke."

"I almost forgot the most important item of all. Won't cost you a cent."

"And just what could that be?"

"One of those big empty appliance boxes. Kids just love 'em. Cut in a few holes for doors and windows and before you know it it's their second home. The nuns at the Home once had a kid move right in one, clothes and all; ate and slept there for over a week."

"Somehow I get the feeling it'll be Charlie in my bed and me in the box." She laughed.

Everything was being "given away" at fantastic discounts. Old prices were crossed out, with one thin line only, and new, lower prices screamed boldly for attention. You wondered why the second price always took up twice as much space on the tag as the first price.

The salesman in the appliance department was talking with a young couple, so we waited. The couple's four kids, apparently all under seven, were running and jumping around, opening up and slamming doors, turning dials, and crawling in and out of ovens and dryers. The salesman, well-groomed and unctuous, wore a look of strained patience on his face. You knew the ingratiating smile came only from the imminent prospect of a fat commission. We were well within earshot and could hear him extolling all the incomparable features of a particular refrigerator and how easy he could make it their own on the store's easy budget plan. The couple listened attentively but finally looked at each other to confirm what they already knew. It was just too expensive; they hadn't realized prices had gone up so much. The salesman vainly pleaded the easy budget plan again, but the man explained they never bought anything on credit and smiled a thank you anyway. Just then one of the kids slammed an oven door shut directly behind the salesman. The smile was gone.

"Goddamn you, get away from that stove! Jesus Christ Almighty. Spend forty-five minutes of my valuable time with people who don't know what the hell they want while their goddamn little brats bust every appliance I've got."

He turned to storm off, but then noticed the two of us standing next to the freezers. His face flashed into another oily smile as he approached.

"May I help you folks?"

Before I could kick him square in the balls or tell him to go fuck himself, Judi was on my arm snuggling possessively against me.

"Oh, you certainly can," she cooed. "You see, this is Horace, my fiancee, and we're going to be married next month. My daddy said we would need a few things to furnish the kitchen in the new house he just built for us up on the Heights. You know, stoves and refrigerators and things like that. He told us to hurry on down here and pick out just whatever we wanted. So, here we are, aren't we, Horry dear?"

Horry dear! Christ. "Yep, here we are. And don't you think we should pick up a few items for the servants' kitchen, Puss, I mean, as long as we're here?"

The salesman's smile became a solar glow.

"Oh, Horry, what would I ever do without you? You're so organized."

The salesman looked over at me, beaming. "Well, congratulations. I can tell you're going to be very happy together. And I'm sure we can help you furnish it right.

Judi squeezed tighter against my arm. "Oh, Horry dear, isn't this fun. I'm so glad Daddy likes you so much. He's probably got you down in his will already!"

"He did take the news about the baby rather well, didn't he, Puss?"

Judi nearly exploded in laughter but managed to hold it back. She picked out appliances faster than the salesman could write them all down. She asked to see only the most expensive items, all in harvest gold (Daddy's favorite color, don't you know), and took whatever the salesman showed her. Two ranges (an electric one, of course, but one in gas, too, in case of a blackout), an enormous refrigerator with ice-maker and the works, two twenty cubic feet capacity stand-up freezers (one for steaks and the other for lobsters), a washer and dryer (for the maids, don't you know), a hood for the charcoal pit, and a complete set of harvest gold pots and pans. With that done, she then went back and ordered another whole set of everything, in plain white, for the servant's quarters. At the end, the salesman, with his eyes dilated, upper lip beaded with sweat, cheeks flushed, appeared on the threshold of an orgasm.

He totaled the order three times, apparently to make sure it was all really happening, then added the sales tax and looked back up at us, breathless.

"And to whom should I charge this?"

"To Daddy, of course."

"Uh, well, excuse me, Miss, but, uh, well, who's Daddy?"

Judi scowled at such a dumb question.

"Stanley Bertrand Walbridge, E-S-Q, that's who."

Cardiac arrest.

The salesman smiled apologetically and started to write down the name.

"Wait a minute!" The salesman froze. "Horry darling, do you really like this harvest gold or would you really prefer some other color?"

"Whatever would make you happiest, Puss."

The salesman sprang to his feet and pounced on a near-by range. "How about loden green. We've got everything in loden, too—even the hood. Lovely color. Very popular. Very chic."

"Oh my, no. Much too drab. Daddy wouldn't like that at all. I was thinking more of a magenta. Do you have anything in magenta?"

"Ma-genta, ma'am?"

"Yes, sort of purplish, don't you know."

"Uh, no ma'am. Uh, I've never heard of–"

"Oh, that's such a pity. Daddy would be so thrilled with magenta. Drives a magenta Ferrari, don't you know."

"Oh, but I'm sure your daddy would take to this harvest gold, ma'am. Such a vital color. Very masculine."

"But the poor man has more gold in his life now than he knows what to do with. It'd be such a bore."

The salesman looked cautiously over at me. There was desperation in his eyes. "Well, ma'am, may I respectfully suggest that this kitchen is for you and your husband here and not for–"

"Well! I *never* in all my life. Wait till Daddy hears about *this*. Such gally people. Come, Horry, let's you and I find a store where the capitalists are of a little more breeding."

Judi grabbed my arm and we started out, noses up, chins out. The salesman followed with a flourish of pleas, apologies and special discounts for newly-weds.

Judi turned at the door. "Forty-five minutes of our valuable time, wasted. All because of this, this ill-bred imbecile. Daddy'll be just furious."

We squealed out into traffic and left the salesman standing at the curb, watching us streak away, his fat commissions with us.

Judi stopped at another store and we picked up a refrigerator carton, Charlie's second home. I couldn't wait to give him his first.

Chapter 13

Have you ever confronted a drunken basset hound at your front door—Irish basset, that is? Neither had I until that Sunday I answered a melodious knock at my door, the first two bars to *Oh, What a Beautiful Morning*. It was mid-afternoon.

I opened the door to find droopy-eyed Roland Maynard Monaghan, MD, standing unsteadily in the corridor, a case of Canadian ale at his feet, one arm loaded with all shapes, sizes and scents of fresh-baked bread, the other nesting a large manila grocery bag. He was wearing another wild plaid pair of shorts and was barefoot. Before I could stop laughing, he had an ale in my hand and was slicing off two thick slices from a long cylindrical loaf of bread.

It dawned on me, finally, why Monaghan was the only doctor in the city who took Mondays off instead of Thursdays.

"Where ya been, dad? Tried to call you all morning, to take your order, but I guess you weren't in."

"My order?"

"Yeah. For your favorite kind of bread. I bake it every Sunday morning, over a few brews. Don't eat a helluva lot of it myself, so I peddle it around to friends. Myself, I just like to smell it while it's rising and baking. Turns me on. Sorta like sniffin' glue, I guess. You weren't in so I baked you a couple loaves of French. Thought that would be appropriate for anyone named Dezengremel."

I took a bite from the well-buttered piece he had thrown me. It was still warm and the aroma was fresh and deep and good. What is there about fresh-baked bread that evokes such deep feelings of contentment and hominess? I wasn't surprised to learn our bird watcher was also a bread baker.

"This is really good, Rollie. Christ, I haven't had homemade bread in ten thousand years, at least."

"Would've baked you anything you wanted; would've called earlier for your order but didn't expect you to be out so early on a Sunday morning. I mean, without a fire in the building or something."

"Couldn't sleep."

Rollie paused and looked straight through me with one of those *ah, come on* sort of grins.

"Well, it's noisy around here in the morning. Truck route goes right by the building."

"How was it?" Rollie snapped open two more bottles of Molson's Blue. I was only half way through my first bottle, so I chugged to keep up.

"How was what?"

"Church."

I choked on a mouthful of ale.

"Now, how the hell did you know about that? Goddamnit all, has that dizzy redhead been blabbing again?"

"Judi? Oh no, not at all. I just added an unanswered phone on early Sunday morning to an adoption application, and divided it by a groovy rebel who obviously hasn't seen the inside of a church since adolescent disillusionment set in, and came up with David Dezengremel kneeling in the front pew of St. Andrew's mumbling a few *Our Dads*."

I laughed and guzzled down half my second ale. Euphoria was rapidly taking hold; I hadn't had much to eat, only a bag of chips and half a brick of stinky cheese, but I had learned the hard way, during a weekend in Montreal, that Canadian beers and ales were far more potent than their American counterparts.

"But how did you know I went over to St. Andrew's?"

"Figures a young intelligent wolf like you wouldn't fit in too well with the Catholic flock; thought Fr. Cummins would be more your speed. And you his. Good man that Jeff. I put up his bail last time he was in the clink. What'd he harangue about today?"

"Well, unlike you, he doesn't preach. In fact he's the first Rev I've ever met who doesn't just stand at the pulpit to play God and tell us how degenerate and selfish we are. He made us draw our own conclusions. He had the ushers pass around pencils and paper and asked everyone in the congregation—the place was packed, by the way—to list ten reasons why they should be admitted to heaven, if there was such a place."

Rollie smiled. "Well, how many?"

"What?"

"How many reasons did you list?"

"Fuck you."

Rollie laughed, then drained his bottle, drawing out the last stubborn trace of suds, and snapped open two more bottles. I had to chug again to keep up. With the ale, he served a couple of slices of pumpernickel, which, he said, happened to be his own favorite, not because of its taste particularly, but because he liked the name. Which was also the reason pumpkin was his favorite kind of pie.

"Well, dad, I've been doing some professional thinking lately, not often, just lately, and I've decided you can't really be an effective double parent in this deal of yours unless you can somehow become a mother as well as a father. The latter I have no doubts about, but you can't very well lay any claims on motherhood until you have yourself a baby, right? So how about coming up to the hospital with me sometime to have one?"

I gagged on another mouthful of ale and nearly blew my lungs out coughing. On top of three Canadian ales the unexpected is one thing; but coming out of a slobbering blue-eyed basset hound with hammer toes and bright plaid shorts, it's quite another.

"Sorry, doctor; I've tried but I just can't seem to get myself pregnant. Perhaps an operation would help."

"I don't think we'd have to be that drastic. How about a simple vicarious involvement instead. I'll give you a call on my next delivery and you can come up and watch the whole show."

"Me? Watch? You gotta be outa your goddamn mind."

"Why not?"

"Christ, Rollie, I'd pass out. All that blood and gore, people screaming, knives and needles . . . Christ."

"Ever seen it before?"

"NO!"

"Well then, how do you know how you'd react?"

Oh, Christ, not that pitch again. I gave him a dirty look.

"I just know, that's all. I came across an accident once and some boob made me help him get a body out of the wreck. Took 'em ten minutes to revive me; thought I was dead too."

"Birth is hardly death."

"Maybe to you it isn't. All that screaming and blood . . .Jesus."

"Typical. You probably think life's greatest experience is a hole-in-one, don't you?"

"Christ, Rollie, I thought you came over here to drink beer and eat pumpernickel."

I drained my bottle and found myself ahead of Rollie. Rollie finished his own and got up to open two more; he delivered mine with a slice of banana bread. The symbolism was obvious.

"Chicken, aren't ya, dad. You'd rather ply along in the pacific waters of your bathtub than venture out into–"

"Oh, for Christ's sake, Rollie, I'll do it. I'll DO it, you bastard! Now get off my goddamn back."

"Thought you would." He chuckled. "I'll give you a call. Got one due most any day now."

"How the hell you going to get me in? I mean, I may chase ambulances, but I don't drive 'em."

"Speak French, dad?"

"Yeah, my grandmother taught me. Used to stay with her a month every summer. We'd speak nothin' but French."

"Good. Then leave the rest to me. No sweat."

What in Christ's name had I gotten myself into? One impulsive move, one innocent phone call. Now I was about to become a mother. Christ!

"Well, dad, with that settled I suppose it's about high time we got down to business here."

"Business?"

"Yeah. We doctors sometimes have to mix a little business with our pleasure. It's the only way we can get everything done that has to be done. And, believe me, this *has* to be done."

Rollie reached down into the manila grocery bag he had brought, the one I assumed to be full of bread for other stops, and pulled out a large naked doll with long, curly locks of corn silk hair; big blue eyes that blinked with innocence, the tip of an erasure pencil, about an inch and a half long, scotch-taped between its legs. Facing me, it cried out twice for "Mama."

"Christ, Rollie, what in God's name is that?"

"Well, I'm afraid it's a bit of a hermaphrodite, but the only doll Elma could come up with for me was this women's lib type. So, being from an old Navy family, I just jury-rigged the necessary apparatus between its legs and presto! we're in business. Sort of a reverse Christine Jorgenson, you might say. Pretty resourceful, huh?"

"Oh, very clever. But what the hell's it for? You going to tell me about the birds and the bees and the coconut trees or somethin'?"

"Well, dad, Judi tells me Charlie's still in diapers nights. You ever change a diaper?"

"Christ, no."

"Then it's about time you learned, don't you think? I mean, the little guy's gonna be here pretty soon, right?"

"Right. But how the hell we gonna do that now? Christ, I'm half stoned."

"Well, if you can do it stoned, you can do it anytime. Like in the middle of the night when your kid's got diarrhea."

"Christ."

"Okay, I've got a couple of diapers here, and some powder, and some safety pins, and a pair of rubber pants—and a kid who won't yowl when you jab 'im. Or it. You got prefolds or what?"

"Prefolds? What the hell are they?"

"You know, diapers that're already folded."

"Christ, how the hell would I know. Just a minute." I went into the spare bedroom and got the diapers Judi and I had bought.

Rollie tore open the package and took out a diaper, unfolding it.

"Nope. You blew it. Now you'll have to fold 'em as well as put 'em on. See these stitch lines here?"

"Yeah."

"Well, that's where you fold it." Rollie folded the diaper and smoothed it out. "Nothin' to it, really; just another pain in the ass when you've got everything else to do, too."

"Christ, when will this kid be potty trained, anyway?"

"Oh, this could go on for years. Some kids use it as a weapon, you see, sort of a trump card. You may be bigger and stronger, but he can still shit all over you, so to speak."

"You're kidding. Christ!"

"Happens a lot where mothers try to push their kids too hard, too early, too often. Dad may want to brag about his son's catching a fly ball at two, but Mom wants him to shit in the pot at nine months so she can mention it, quite casually, of course, to the girls at bunco."

"Bunco?"

"It's a game. Something to do with your hands while discussing episiotomies, the length of your husband's organ, and how smart your kid is."

"But what happened to Charlie? I mean, he didn't have a mother or father to rebel against."

"Not *a* mother. Christ, he's got a whole shitload of 'em. Seventeen to be exact. You see, no matter what else a nun may be, she's also her mother's daughter. And what was done to her, she has a tendency to do to little wards like Charlie. Sort of a vicious circle."

Rollie arranged the doll and all the necessary paraphernalia on the breakfast bar so the doll was lying in front of him; the powder, diapers, pins and rubber pants in front of me. He rolled up his sleeves and took a deep breath.

"Now watch closely, dad."

"Right."

He held out his hand. "Powder."

I slapped the can of powder into it. "Powder."

There was a cloud of white dust.

"Double diaper."

"Double?"

"Yeah. Always double up for a night of it."

Christ. "Double diaper."

"Pins."

"Pins."

"Rubber pants."

"Rubber pants."

"There. See, nothin' to it. Take a look, then try yourself."

I examined the finished product while the proud doctor rewarded himself with another ale.

"But what should I do about the anemia, Doc?"

"Oh, just include some iron-rich foods in—what anemia?"

I rolled down the diaper for Rollie to see. Both safety pins were firmly attached to the doll's rubbery waist. Rollie frowned, scratched his head, then removed the diapers.

"Powder."

"Powder."

"Diapers."

"Diapers . . ."

It was just after midnight when a burly cab driver showed up at the door to drag Rollie home. No one had called a cab, but I could see from their mutual familiarity that this was all part of the Sunday act.

At work, next day, I caught Miss Eckert several times staring at my two bandaged thumbs.

Chapter 14

Jesus of Nazareth, head crowned in thorns, face drawn and bloody, fell heavily to his knees. He struggled to regain his feet. The earth and his lips were parched, were one. Suddenly he threw his cross to the ground, his brow furrowed with disgust, and bolted for the cliff. Nathaniel and a horse ran alongside. At the precipice, all three leaped far out into the void and plummeted toward the angry green sea below. I was a little off to the left, watching, as the three splashed heavily into the water. Then in a spectacular display of fury, the entire outcropping of rock began to fall in on top of them. Just then the church bells began to ring.

My eyes popped open. The bells were still ringing. Judgment Day! Bewilderment. Confusion. Christ, it was the goddamn phone ringing. A blur of luminesence from the nightstand told me it was 2:12 A.M. I fumbled for the receiver and knocked it crashing to the floor. I pulled it up into the bed by the cord and finally managed to stuff it under my ear.

It was Rollie.

"Hey, dad, it's about my eardrum. Next time kindly blow your beer farts in some other direction, will ya."

I growled something about jamming the goddamn receiver up his ass then sewing it shut. He chirped back something about what a great obstetrician I would have made. Which brought him right to the point.

"Okay, dad, this is it. I've got a big mama on her way in right now. Contractions heavy and regular. Shouldn't be too long a labor, either. This is her third."

"Oh, for Christ's sake. Look, just tell her to wait till morning, will ya?"

"You're a real drag, dad."

"Go to hell."

"Meet you at County General in about ten minutes."

"Ten minutes!"

"Yeah, ten minutes. Frank'll be pounding on your door in about twenty-three seconds. And if you don't answer within five, he's going to huff and puff and blow the damn thing down and *drag* your lazy ass up here."

"Who the hell's Frank, for Christ's sake?"

"The cabbie you met last Sunday night, the one who scraped me off the floor and carted me home. I called him before I called you and asked him to pick you up."

"You're a dirty rotten lousy sneaky low down sonofabitchin–"

"Sure you're fluent in French?"

"–bastard. French? That all Frank can speak?"

"He's Armenian. You fluent or not?"

"Fluent enough to tell you to go fuck yourself."

"Fine. Okay, from the very minute you arrive at the Emergency Room at the hospital–Frank'll drive you right to the door–I want you to speak nothing but French. Understand?"

"Yes, but–"

"Ten minutes. Better get dressed."

"But–"

"Come on! Hurry."

"Goddamn it, Rollie, I gotta work–"

"See you, dad, er, mom."

"Look, I–"

Click.

Christ.

Frank delivered me to the emergency entrance, after running seven red lights and four amber, then accompanied me right up to the girl behind the typewriter. Frank took his job very seriously. I tried to pay him but he refused, saying he'd already put it on the Doc's tab. Then he left. Or did he? I had a feeling he and his muscles were outside waiting for my attempt to escape from this incredible madness.

In front of me, a rough looking character with a pocked, deeply tawny face was bleeding to death from a gaping wound in his left arm. The girl behind the typewriter, bored with the whole deal, was asking the guy about his insurance, next of kin, and, I suspected, the family mortician. The guy's face blanched whiter and whiter as he sat there, and I began to rehearse in my mind how I was going to catch him without getting blood all over my suit. But then, just as his eyeballs rolled up into his head, an orderly and a cop stepped forward and caught him. As they dragged him off, the girl sighed, then glanced up at me. I felt I should apologize for my intrusion.

"Yes?"

"Oh, uh, je m'appele David Dezengremel et je cherche Doctor Monaghan. Pouvez-vous m'aider s'il vous plait?"

The girl's face flashed into a radiant smile. "Oh yes, you're the French obstetrician Doctor Monaghan was telling us about." There was something more than admiration in those eyes; they were all but handing me the key to her apartment. "He's waiting for you up in maternity. Go right on up."

French obstetrician! I could feel the quicksand sucking me deeper into Monaghan's quagmire.

The girl must have construed my dumb look for a lack of comprehension. She stood up.

"Just go down the hall." She pointed. "And take the elevator." She pointed up. "To the fourth floor." She held up four fingers. "Then turn right." She turned right. "And ask one of the nurses for Doctor Monaghan."

I bowed and smiled with unctuous appreciation. "Merci beaucoup. Vous avez ete une etaile dans la nuit." Should I have kissed the broad's hand?

As I stood waiting for the elevator, I glanced back toward her. She was still smiling at me. Christ, why hadn't I thought of this tactic before? It was perfect. But as the doors closed gently behind me, I knew it was too late. I was committed. I was about to become a mother.

Christ!

Chapter 15

Monaghan, all decked out in his blue-green surgical cap and gown, was pacing the corridor directly in front of the elevator. It was the first time I had seen him in long pants.

He greeted me as if I were a long lost buddy from the continent.

"Ah, Doctor Dezengremel. Welcome." He wrapped his arms around me and planted a big, fat kiss on each cheek. Christ. "So good to see you again. And I'm so glad you could be with us this evening."

The nurses at the floor desk were taking it all in, especially one sour-pussed old bat who just had to be the head nurse on the night shift. Monaghan took me by the arm and led me over to all the ladies, who seemed to be waiting for me.

"Ladies, this is that handsome hunk of European I was telling you about, Doctor David Dezengremel." I bowed with suave deference.

Monaghan introduced the nurses and flattered each by remembering the first name that went with the last on the tag; the younger girls all responded with blushes and self-conscious smiles. Heather Walters, *Miss* Heather Walters, however, neither blushed nor smiled. She just stared right through me—at the truth, I thought. I babbled a few meaningless phrases in melodious French and struggled to look as casually medical as possible.

"Well, Doctor, let's go and get you dressed for the occasion." He nodded to the girls and specifically to Miss Walters. "Excuse us, ladies."

I beamed and bowed, and considered pinching Heather on the end of one of her prodigious boobs. I mean, what could be more

European than that?

As we turned away, Monaghan began asking me, in something less than a whisper, about my flight and how everything was going in Paris. When we were well out of earshot, however, he asked me why I thought head nurses in maternity wards were always bile-tempered, overweight old maids.

Rollie led me into a room between the labor and delivery rooms where I scrubbed up and put on a surgical outfit. While there, Rollie told me there were no other doctors in at the moment, that his was the only labor in process, but that if anyone should show up, I was just to keep speaking French, *nothing but French*. I called him a deceitful, conniving old bastard and told him before the night was out I would be disbarred and he delicensed. To which he shrugged, "So what?"

Come to think of it, I thought, so what? Once, it would have been the end of the world; but now, well, it would only be the end of *a* world.

We were just about to go into the labor room to check Mrs. Henderson, whose labor, Rollie admitted, was not progressing as rapidly as he had anticipated, when we both froze to a clamor of screams and oaths coming from down the hall. It sounded like an all-out barroom brawl.

We looked at one another, apprehensive at first, then rushed out into the corridor. There, in front of the nursery window, sprawled on the floor, were three hairy-armed orderlies wrestling with a long-haired hippie-type man and a very pregnant hippie-type girl. The girl apparently had just kicked one of the orderlies in the balls; he was doubled over in agony, clutching himself. Behind them all, old Sour Puss, stern and invincible as a hefty Napoleon, was directing her troops. The other nurses were supplying most of the screams.

Monaghan ran up the corridor and called off Heather's gorillas with a few barks that woke up every baby in the nursery. Two of the orderlies got right up, but the other remained on the floor, still clutching his nuts, groaning miserably. Some of the nurses rushed into the nursery to quiet the wailing babies.

Rollie turned toward the scowling puss of Miss Walters, his eyes a fascinating paradox—sad with basset-like softness, yet furious with outrage. Though fuming, you still knew he was the kind of guy who could never thin out a row of lettuce, never decide who stays, who goes.

"What the hell's going on here, Heather? Christ almighty! This happens to be a maternity ward, you know, and I happen to have a woman in labor just down the hall."

Miss Walters snapped right back, but without any basset-like softness—a veteran lettuce-thinner. "Don't you foul-mouth me, buster. Give it to them. It's *their* fault." She pointed one stubby, accusing finger at the hippies. I noticed their wrists were handcuffed together. The girl was now on her back, eyes closed, limp, panting like an overheated dog. Her husband, or whatever (it was impossible to tell anymore), was timing her with his wristwatch. "They just barged right in here as if they owned the place, with those ridiculous handcuffs on, and *demanded* to have their baby together. Miss Waite asked them who their doctor was and that one"—pointing at the man— "asked who was here, and Linda made the very serious error of saying Doctor Monaghan and Doctor Dezengremel were and that one"—pointing at the girl—"said you were their doctor. At that point I took over and asked them very politely to get out, at once. They refused, just sat right down there on the floor like a couple of gypsies, so I called the orderlies."

"Did it occur to you, Miss Walters, that this girl is about to have a baby and might, just might, need our help? This *is* a hospital, you know."

Heather soured. Her face reminded me of the time I got an Alka Seltzer tablet lodged in my throat during fraternity hazing.

"Of course it did! But this hospital has rules, Doctor, and these Yippies or beatniks, or whatever they are know it. They know they have to register, they know they have to arrange for a doctor, just like anybody else, and they know we don't allow husbands, if he even is her husband, in the delivery room. Her voice was shrill. And you know it too, Doctor. And *I'm sure* you also know that if we didn't enforce our rules, these unbathed kooks would swarm in here like flies and take right over. And where would we be then, Doctor?"

The man looked up at Rollie, his face apprehensive, concerned. "Contractions every three minutes, Doc. Gettin' pretty heavy, too. But she's still in control."

Monaghan turned toward the orderlies; the third, now on his feet, still looked a little peaked. "Okay, tigers, get 'er onto a table. Fast. But don't break her concentration. Move her between contractions." The orderlies scurried into action. "Miss Waite, you're her nurse. Get 'er prepped."

The man looked back up at Rollie; I detected a little embarrassment. "Uh, excuse me, Doc, but she's already prepped. We did it ourselves. You know, in case I had to deliver myself."

"Enema too?"

"Yeah."

Rollie smiled, paternally. "Fine." Then looking over at me, "David, go get a gown and mask for Dad here."

Heather's eyes narrowed into slits. "This will be reported, Doctor. I will not have *my* ward turned into a circus for entertaining these unwashed hedonists."

"Miss Walters . . . go fuck yourself."

She gasped, then stormed off.

I left to get "Dad" his gown. When I returned the orderlies had the girl on a table and were wheeling her toward one of the labor rooms. She was panting very hard and massaging her swollen stomach with her finger tips. They stopped long enough for me to get Dad partially into his gown.

"Name's Tim," he said. "Thanks."

"Il n'y a pas de quoi, mon ami. Je m'appelle David." Tim scrutinized me as one scrutinizes any foreigner, then nodded politely.

Monaghan gave me a sly wink. For remembering who I was. Then he turned to Tim. "Lamaze?"

"Right on, man."

"Fine. You take charge then. We'll assist whenever necessary.

It's your party."

"Outa sight."

"You got the key to those things?"

"No. I swallowed it."

"Well then, I guess we'll just have to get the stomach pump out after the party. Can't very well leave you two like that for the rest of your lives."

Tim's eyes swelled into shooter marbles.

The orderlies wheeled the table into a single labor room where Miss Waite quickly took off the girl's clothes and draped her with a gown and a sheet. Rollie ducked into the next room to check on Mrs. Henderson and her nurse, but was back in a minute. The guy was positively electrified with excitement.

He waited for the girl to pant through a contraction, then spoke softly to her. "Hi. What's your name, little mother?"

"Amy."

"Your first?"

She nodded.

"Fine. Amy, will you pardon me while I stick my hand up your rectum?" Rollie glanced at Tim for his reaction. Tim merely smiled. So did Amy.

Monaghan pulled on a long rubber glove that looked more like an oversized prophylactic with five tumors and asked Amy to pull up her legs. The glove disappeared and so did I. Out to get a drink of water. When I came back, the glove was off.

"Okay, Amy, everything's going along just fine. You're dilated about three fingers, or six centimeters. Shouldn't be long." He looked over at Tim. "You two taken any classes in Lamaze?"

"Yeah. At the "Y." The whole bit."

"Great."

Tim took a small notebook out of his pocket with his free hand and scribbled down some quick notes. Then he asked Miss Waite to bring him a damp cloth and some water which he used to wipe off Amy's sweating brow and to moisten her parched lips, which seemed to dry quite rapidly from the heavy panting. He timed each contraction, from the point Amy would start panting until she stopped, and recorded the durations in his notebook. At the peak of the heavier contractions, when Amy's face was strained and grimaced, he would mumble a few soft words of encouragement to her, but was always very careful, I noticed, never to disturb her concentration with even the slightest aggravation or annoyance.

Amy would pant in a rapid crescendo, always breathing the hardest at the peak of each contraction (or "pain" as the nurses called them). At one point she rolled over on her side and asked Tim to rub her lower back during the entire contraction. Both of them obviously knew what they were doing and were in a far calmer state of mind than imposter Doctor David Dezengremel.

Suddenly Amy changed the rhythm of her breathing. Instead of taking a deep breath, letting it out, panting in crescendo, and terminating with another deep breath, she now began to pant continuously but with sporadic forced blowing.

Tim's face lit up, his eyes danced with excitement. "Transition! We're there! Hang on baby, you're about to drop a watermelon." He flashed me a quick wide-eyed glance, winked, then reached back under his gown and wormed his free hand down the back of his trousers. He bent over, grimaced with growing pain, bent over more deeply, groaned—then suddenly straightened. The grin was spread over his face like fresh blueberry jam—the key, attached to a strip of adhesive, as well as a curly hair or two, was captive between his thumb and forefinger. Two clicks later the handcuffs were on the floor.

Rollie and Miss Waite ran in from Mrs. Henderson's room. A terrible thought flashed into my head. If both women went together, Doctor Dezengremel would be expected to deliver! Gulp. Now was the time to sneak out. But I couldn't. Anymore than I could've put down Agatha Christie before reading the last ten pages. I was hooked.

Rollie pulled the sheet up. I could see that the bedding between Amy's legs was soaked. "Okay, water's broken. Things're on the move. Let's get 'er into delivery."

Suddenly Amy threw her head back and let out the worst groan

I'd ever heard in my life. She blew a few more times, struggling for control, then groaned again. Her face was contorted, grimaced. I couldn't stand it. Why didn't they do something for her! Christ almighty, couldn't they see how much she was suffering? For Christ's sake, Rollie, put her out! I was staring at him, pleading. Reading my face, he came over and put his hand on my shoulder and whispered reassurance.

"Relax, *Doctor*. All she feels is the same urge you feel every morning on the can, only hers is more like passing a load after nine months of constipation. There's really not much pain, if any. In fact, if anything, it feels good. Ever look at your own face in the mirror during an orgasm?"

"No, but it sounds like fun."

"You see, this is when all those medieval doctors we still have kicking around here knock 'em out. But instead of missing out on all the pain, what they're really missing out on is all the fun, the most memorable experience of their lives. Shame. Goddamned shame. Well, come on, Doctor, let's go introduce another soul to life."

There was an expectancy in Amy's face as Miss Waite and Tim wheeled her into the delivery room. And if there had been a mirror close by, I'm sure I could have seen a little in my own, too.

The birth came surprisingly fast. Amy held her breath and with Tim's help raised herself up in the stirrups to push. Tim's face was aglow with delight. Amy fell back, hyperventilated, then raised up once again. The groans were almost obscene. I was certain the entire hospital was listening in bewilderment.

On the next push I could see Amy's vulva swell with the baby's head. Jesus Christ, it was really coming! I mean, it was really happening. Rollie put his fingers around the little head to guide it out. Then he took a knife, and at the height of a contraction, made a small slit to make more room for the baby to pass. Amy apparently felt nothing. But how that head could get through that little hole, even with the episiotomy, was a source of marvel. Tim was craning to watch; his face was flushed with building excitement.

On Amy's next push, the baby's head popped completely out. The room was suddenly filled with an indignant wail, hearty and hale.

Tim was absolutely beside himself with joy. "Oh wow! Outa sight. Oh wow! Outa sight . . ." On the next push the baby was in Rollie's hands, screaming its bloody (literally) head off.

"A girl! It's a girl!" shouted Monaghan.

"A girl!" shouted Tim.

"A girl!" shouted Dezengremel, forgetting his ignorance of the English language.

Tim couldn't contain himself. He kissed Amy, Miss Waite, myself and Monaghan, in that order, then jumped around the delivery room shouting "Outa sight, outa sight, outa sight . . ." and finally stuck his head through the doors to announce to the entire ward that it was a girl. Amy was crying, laughing, glowing.

Rollie clamped off the umbilical cord, cut it, then picked up the flailing, screaming infant and set her right up on Amy's deflated stomach. And despite Amy's superlatives on how beautiful her new daughter was, to me she looked like a shriveled-up, half-drowned, toothless old man—but a miracle nonetheless. Finally exhausted, Tim stood proudly behind his family and beamed down at Amy and the tiny, helpless little soul snuggled in her arms.

And to think I wanted to sleep through the whole thing. Christ, Dezengremel.

The sun was well up by the time Rollie dropped me off at my apartment.

Mrs. Henderson had finally delivered at 6:15, another girl, and after calling her husband in Guam, at Rollie's expense, we dragged ourselves down to Rollie's sunburst-yellow Morgan and started home. On the way, Rollie babbled on and on about "old stone-face Sellman," the head maternity doctor at County General, who intransigently refused to allow fathers in the delivery rooms, despite the many petitionings of mothers, fathers, and fellow doctors, because, as he put it, "why should husbands watch a delivery anymore than an appendectomy; after all, they're all the same thing—major surgery is major surgery; if they get their kicks outa watchin' blood and gore, let 'em all go to the cock fights, or to the stock car races." Rollie got so wound up, in fact, that he ran a four-way stop and nearly wiped out a milk truck and ourselves with it.

"Arrogant prima donnas, all of them. Don't want anybody intruding into their little private domains of pompous importance. Get their jollies out of having women so completely dependent upon them, so completely under their tyrannical powers. Bastards."

A real crusader, this Monaghan.

Under any other circumstances I would have called in sick and slept in for at least the morning—and probably the afternoon, too. But this morning I was flying too high, floating along on that euphoric feeling one gets in a hot shower following a hard-fought, sweaty game of handball. So instead of hitting the sack, I decided to take a leisurely stroll to the office by way of Lincoln Square Park. I sat down on a bench for a while and watched some pigeons coo and scavenge through the dust for some morsel; their iridesence glistened in the early morning sunlight. Some joggers passed me by, some staring privately down at the ground as they puffed by, others greeting me with strained smiles and breathless salutations. One, a man not a day under seventy, passed several other joggers half his age and rubbed it into one by running a full circle around him.

I stopped off at a little lunch counter and had a ham and cheese omelet, my first breakfast in longer than I could remember, then picked up a whole box of "It's a Girl" cigars at a cigar store. I handed one to everyone I met on the street; and at the office I gave two to a dumbfounded Miss Eckert and the last three to an astonishingly perceptive Stanley Walbridge who never noticed the pink lettering on the wrappers until four days later when he handed one to the Lt. Governor after a luncheon in Albany.

I didn't work much that day.

Chapter 16

I was sitting in the office, about a week later, scribbling a caricature of Stanley Walbridge on a legal pad, when the intercom buzzed. My spirits soared as I saw line 1 flashing. Evelyn, the firm showpiece (excuse the pun) centerfold receptionist, would be on the other end to coo something into my ear about an incoming call and would I care to take it. I didn't wait for a second buzz. An incoming call could mean high adventure.

"Dezengremel."

"Mr. Dezengremel, you have a call from a Miss Chesser. She says it's urgent. Can you take it now?"

Urgent? My guts chilled in panic. I've been turned down. Jeff Cummins told Sylly about my falling asleep in church. Christ. Well, shit, it would've been a helluva lot of responsibility, and it would've tied me down, especially on Friday and Saturday nights. I was disappointed but The Singles would still be there, crammed full of eager bodies, as usual, and anyway my pad was all spruced up for another year, toilet bowl and all. The Singles would be restlessly humming this Friday night, I thought, jammed with panicky teachers looking for some action before the end of the summer. All was not lost.

"I'll take it now."

"Okay. Line 5."

"Thanks." Shit, why not ask Evelyn out for Friday night? I mean, how ripe do they have to get? She'd been with the firm nearly two months now, basking around my bachelor turf, and it was about time for harvesting.

I took a deep breath before pushing the lighted button over line 5.

"Judi?" My voice was hoarse.

"Oh, David, I'm terribly sorry. I really am. But I'm afraid I've got bad news for you." Christ, I knew it. Everything had been rolling along much too smoothly. Nothing can go that well. It's obscene. I felt suddenly dizzy and realized I wasn't breathing. "You okay, David?"

"Yeah. Sure. Fine."

"Look, David, I really am sorry about this, but it's out of my hands. There's nothing I can do. You understand?"

I didn't answer. Fuck it. Fuck the world.

"You still there, David?"

"Yeah, sure." I tried to keep my voice in a controlled monotone.

"I mean, if we could do this any earlier, David, we certainly would. As it is we've taken a lot of shortcuts. But I'm afraid the earliest I can take you to meet Charlie is on Friday. And, if you want, you can take him home the next day. That okay?"

"You mean I'm in! Charlie's mine?" I whooped.

"That's the deal, dad. You'll get a letter tomorrow. But I thought I'd call."

"Did you say *Friday*? Christ, Judi, what time Friday?"

Judi was laughing her ass off on the other end.

"Friday evening. I've already made all the arrangements with Mother Mary Noelene. She's the Mother Superior at the convent. It's a convent, too, you know. Penguins waddling around all over the place. I'll meet you at your place about 6:30 and we'll drive over from there. How's that?"

"Great. But what if he doesn't like me? Maybe he doesn't like honkies."

"Charlie knows all about you and can hardly wait to meet you. The only thing he doesn't know about you is how to pronounce your last name. Ever considered changing it?"

"Haven't met the right guy."

"Oh, well, don't panic; you're young yet."

"Do you think I should bring him something? How about one of those new toys we bought him? One of the Tonka trucks maybe?"

"Just bring yourself. Right now that's all he needs. Just you. Okay?"

"Are you sure?"

"I'm sure."

"Are you sure you're sure?"

"I'm sure I'm sure."

"Well, as long as you're sure."

"I am."

I went right out and bought another box of cigars, this time with the wrappers printed in blue, and handed them out to every man, woman and child in the street—even one to a mounted traffic cop. Then I went home and made up Charlie's bed and unpackaged his toys, and just sat in his room. It was happening.

Chapter 17

The Children's Foundling Home of the Sisters of Mercy is located in a part of the city where bankers and brokers once dined in turn-of-the-century elegance, but where cops now gulp down their brown-bag lunches securely locked in their prowl cars. There is a stench of unattended refuse, of neglect and decay.

The Home itself, formerly a finishing school for young Catholic ladies, is a large-dirty-brick building badly in need of general repair. Resting in the shade of towering, but dying elms, it is encompassed by an old wrought-iron fence, sort of a chastity belt in its prime, whose black paint is now badly scaled and in places hanging on by little more than ancient habit. But unlike any of the other properties along the street, it is well-groomed and gayly decorated with numerous beds of pampered summer flowers.

As we entered the gate, rusted open, and approached along a walk leading up to an imposing wooden door, I noticed a number of nuns, draped in black silk, stooped over the flower beds busily weeding and digging. They were humming a hymn, very softly, which I recognized from my early Catholic childhood. A warm flash of nostalgia, of early innocence, flooded through me.

Judi rang the bell and a nun greeted us. She smiled shyly at me, more warmly toward Judi. After Judi introduced us, the nun, Sister Cecilia Ann, led us down a hallway decorated in Modern Institutional: blah yellow walls with heavily-waxed imitation-marble floors. The feeling was of merging into something not quite alive, not quite dead, just sort of hanging there in limbo. There was a residual odor from the supper hour, that heavy odor of starchy spiceless institutional food which I had become thoroughly familiar with during my college days. Stern countenances of invincibility frowned down at us from portraits on the walls, the last of which I recognized as Pope Paul. The others, I assumed, made up the local diocesan hierarchy.

My stomach was aflutter with panic and expectancy over meeting Charlie and I must have shown it. Sister Cecilia kept me distracted from my thoughts with a continuous babble of small talk about Charlie. We climbed a flight of back stairs and walked down another hallway. She kept it all very positive, I noted, saying nothing about his rebellion toward that Great White Bowl of Porcelain. Nice boy. Our pride and joy. Handsome as the Lord Himself. I supposed, all of the usual softening-up bullshit.

We paused outside a door labeled, most imaginatively, PLAY-ROOM 2. Judi turned to me and explained that she would come in to introduce us, but then she would leave us alone for about an hour to get to know each other.

Alone! For an hour! Christ, what'll I do? What'll I say? But before I could do or say anything, we were inside and a little black face was looking up expectantly into mine. I tried to meet the expression but felt suddenly dizzy and weak in the knees. I wasn't breathing. The nun who had been playing with Charlie on the floor, whom Judi introduced as Sister Mary Bernardina, scurried to her feet and sort of bowed and smiled her way out the door. There was a submissive sadness in her eyes, that of a mother whose man-child was being snatched from her bosom by whim of the king. Later Judi explained that it had been Sister Mary Bernardina who had always been the closest to Charlie and the one who had given Charlie his only name. It had been her own father's name.

Charlie ran into Judi's arms and they greeted each other with big hugs. Judi introduced Charlie to me, but I wasn't really listening; I was numb. Then I felt a pat on the shoulder and heard a door close behind me.

Help!

We just stood there, the two of us, silently facing each other across the room, seemingly miles. I was timid, hopelessly awkward and totally out of step with the music of the moment; he was black, foreign, cow-eyed, frizzy-headed and suddenly handing me a Tonka cement truck. He dropped down to his knees and by himself began to play with a little yellow bulldozer. I followed suit with my cement truck. At first I was hesitant and self-conscious, but before I knew it we were a roaring, raucous duet of sputtering, spitting motors. Together we scraped and we bulldozed and we cemented and we graded and we loaded and we hauled and we unloaded. But perhaps more than anything else we built some bridges.

The vibrations from my "motor" were so intense, in fact, that they soon numbed my lips and tickled my nose until it itched. And though the itch was maddening, I decided against scratching it for fear Charlie would think I was picking it. I was going to be the picture of parental exemplitude. Shortly thereafter, however, Charlie paused from his play to stuff an index finger well up his nose and twist it around with searching intent, all without turning off his motor. He then pulled it out, casually wiped it off on his pants and went right back to work. Life's forever one more disillusionment.

I scratched my nose.

After some time Charlie sat up and looked over at me with a face full of host-like deference.

"Wanna play blocks?" he asked.

I smiled. "Sure."

His face lit up and he ran over to an old wicker basket piled high with blocks. It obviously weighed more than he did. But with his face contorted with determination, he dragged the heavy basket over to where I was sitting and dumped the entire contents on the floor. I could see myself picking up blocks and toys until after midnight every night and resolved right then and there to myself that Charlie would be responsible for picking up all his own toys, each and every night. (Yeah, right!)

The hodge-podge assortment of blocks, no more than two or three of any one kind, looked like something scavenged from the coffers of the Salvation Army. But they were blocks. And blocks were blocks.

"Wanna built towers?"

"Sure. What kind of tower?"

"A big way-up-high tower."

Charlie searched around and picked out the largest block from the pile and set in down between us, then sat back on his heels. I took this as my cue and picked out a block and set it on top of his. He picked out another, after considering several, and set it down on top of mine. And so it went. And generally, though not always, each block Charlie picked out was of equal size or smaller than the one before it. Already, to my surprise, he seemed to possess a sense of architectural proportion. And of balance, too. For the higher the tower got, the more cautious and precise he became in placing the next block on top, fully aware, it seemed, that one false move and the whole effort would come crashing down. I was soon fascinated and his willing captive.

We built tower after tower. Each grew taller until it began to lean, and lean, until it had us both holding our breaths. And though I would try to maintain a teetering balance by placing my blocks on off-center, each would finally fall and crash to the floor sending the two of us into wild hysterical laughter. Then, tension relieved, we would start all over again.

I was just in the process of putting that just-one-more block on the most exotic, the most bizarrely constructed, the most precariously balanced tower you could ever hope to imagine, which in height would shatter all previous records, when the door suddenly banged open and sent it crumbling like a rudely interrupted dream. It was Judi.

"Hey, what's the big idea," I snarled, "I thought you said I could have a whole hour?"

"I did." She laughed. "It's been an hour and twenty minutes already. And it's well past Charlie's bedtime."

Incredible. For one whole hour and a third I had lost all sense of time, all consciousness of time. The unhappiest people in the world, I thought, had to be those who knew what time it was.

I stood up to leave, to trudge back to my empty apartment, to return to my empty world of correct briefs, of pompous jargon, of proper images. I felt a desolate emptiness, the same feeling you might experience after three days of diarrhea has sucked your bowels barren. Or perhaps the feeling Bob Cratchit knew every morning as he left the warmth of his home for the cold of Scrooge's office.

Sister Mary Bernardina entered to take charge of Charlie. I said good-bye, hugging him to me, and told him how much I had enjoyed our play together. I was just turning to leave when Charlie broke away from the Sister's grasp and wrapped himself tightly around my leg. "No go! No go!" he screamed. "Play with Charlie. No go."

I knelt down and hugged him close again and felt his wiry snarl of hair against my cheek. A surge of warmth spread through me and I squeezed him even tighter. I explained I had to go home now, but that I would be back to see him again, real soon.

"Where you come?"

Sister Mary interpreted. "He means *when*. When are you coming back?"

I glanced up at Judi for the answer. She was wearing a soft, maternal-like smile but gave me no answers. I turned back to the pleading brown eyes before me.

"Soon, Charlie. Very soon. But you be a good fella, now, and run along with the Sister to bed. I'll be back real soon. Okay?"

"I go too?"

"Not right now, Charlie. But soon. When Miss Chesser says you can. Okay?"

Charlie dropped his eyes and turned up his bottom lip; his eyes began to water. I squeezed him again, to reassure him, then stood up. Sister Mary Bernardina stepped forward and took him by the shoulders. He peered up at me with eyes sad and wounded and I could feel my guts swim over hot coals. All I could think about was a helpless, starving, half-dead baby screaming in the terrible blackness of a stinking garbage can. A lump lodged itself in my throat and I tried to swallow it before anybody could see. Judi blew him a kiss. I winked, then half of me walked out the door with Judi.

Outside I grabbed hold of her.

"When, Judi? When can I take him home? You did say something about tomorrow, didn't you? I mean is tomorrow still okay? What do I have to do?"

Judi grinned. "Sure. It's entirely up to you. I've got the agreement for you to sign right here in my pocketbook. I thought it best to give you two all weekend to get acquainted. If you want, you can sign it now. But, if you'd rather have a little more time to think—"

"Then what about tonight? I mean, right now. Whatdya say?"

"I say sleep on it, David. And let Charlie get some rest, too. You're both going to need it."

"Christ, I couldn't sleep now if my life depended on it. Suppose you're right about Charlie, though. Christ, you're always right."

I turned and ran back into the playroom and scared whatever hell may have been left in Sister Mary right out of her. Charlie ran into my arms and wrapped his around my neck. I grew about a foot and a half taller right on the spot.

"I'll be back tomorrow, Charlie. Tomorrow morning. Early. To take you home with me. And if you want, we can stop by the zoo. Would you like that?" Charlie nodded with obvious delight. "And how about a hamburger at McDonald's. Would you like a big fat hamburger?" Charlie laughed and squirmed around in my arms. "What time do you get up in the morning, Charlie?"

Sister Mary caught her breath long enough to tell me breakfast was promptly at eight and that I could probably come anytime after nine. I said that would be fine. I apologized for frightening her and handed Charlie back. She smiled with the deference a slave might have for her master. I could see Charlie was excited with anticipation and I knew I'd probably blown the whole thing. Now Charlie probably wouldn't sleep a wink either. But at the moment sleep didn't seem very important, not very important at all. Charlie had a daddy; I had a son. That's what it was all about.

I signed the adoption agreement against Judi's back before we got into the car. As we drove off, top down, the world no longer reeked of garbage.

Chapter 20

I was right. For once.

Neither Charlie nor myself slept a wink that night. And by the looks of the sunken-eyed nun who unbolted the door to greet me at the Home, neither had she. When Charlie decided not to sleep, she said, nobody slept. And that was that. Christ.

Judi had refused to come with me, said it was Charlie's and my day to really get to know each other. She said she could only be a hindrance, a fifth wheel. I knew what she meant. Without her we would only have each other to turn to, and that was best. Judi was always right.

On the way home the previous night Judi had explained how Charlie would not become legally mine, of course, until the Family Court Judge made it so, a mere formality at the end of the probationary period. The usual probationary period was only six months, but both Sylly and herself felt Charlie and I should have at least nine, to ensure me every possible opportunity for a graceful exit should I finally decide single parenthood just wasn't my bag. And Charlie an out should he decide I wasn't his.

I knew she added that last bit just to keep my balloon deflated. But I knew she was right, too. As usual. This wasn't only a question of fulfilling my needs, but of satisfying Charlie's too. I couldn't help thinking a similar probationary period might do well for marriage. Judi agreed, but without any real enthusiasm.

Charlie's things were all packed in a single grocery bag and ready to go. It hadn't ocurred to me to bring a suitcase, and I flushed with embarrassment. I myself had a suitcase, so I guess I thought everybody had a suitcase. How easy it was to lose oneself in the teeming world of Have.

The nuns, all seventeen of them, lined up along the front hallway, beneath the sober faces of Paul & Co. Charlie walked down, or was passed down, the line and said good-bye to each sister with a big hug. The last in the line was Sister Mary Bernardina. Despite her efforts to hide them, I noticed the tears in her eyes. Charlie gave her the biggest hug of all. They all said to come back and visit just any old time, that we were always welcome. And I knew we were.

I threw Charlie's bag in the back and him in the front. All seventeen penguins waddled out to wave a final farewell, but Charlie, captivated by the flashy dashboard, completely ignored them. I waved and smiled for both of us. Then, with a throaty roar and a blast of the horn, we were off to the zoo.

Charlie obviously thought riding in my vet was the greatest thing he'd ever experienced in his whole life. The top was down and by kneeling in the seat he could lean over toward the door and catch a blast of wind full in the face. He would then open his mouth, as if to drink in the stream of air, then explode with a laugh so hearty, so infectious, I would find myself laughing right along with him. I liked the way his eyes and teeth stood out against his dark skin as he giggled.

The radio became a particular source of fascination. He approached it with caution at first, making only tentative probes, but soon he was twisting the tuning dial and pushing the ON-OFF dial. I watched with expectation. Charlie clicked the dial on and turned it to full volume, but there was nothing, only a deep, vacuous hum. Then he pushed a button. The radio suddenly blared out at full volume and sent him cowering back against the seat, his eyes bulging with horror. I quickly turned the volume down to a more tolerable level. "Rubber Ducky" was playing, and Charlie's eyes immediately switched from Channel Fear to Channel Delight. He began to bounce up and down in his seat.

"Sesamenay Street! Sesamenay Street! Can I see it? Can I see it?"

I explained as best I could that this was a radio, not a TV, that we could listen to the music but not see any pictures. He frowned with obvious displeasure, and I expected worse to follow. But then to my complete amazement he simply joined right in and began to sing along with the voice on the record, which, he informed me, happened to belong to a little guy named Ernie. Several words got left out here and there, especially during the quick gasps for breath, but he was very often right on key. I tried to follow along with a few melodious mumbles. Singing was not my forte. I was the type who always faked it whenever the National Anthem was sung.

The song finished, but Charlie didn't. He broke right into "Twinkle, Twinkle Little Star," and sang it twenty-three times over, pausing only for short gasps of breath. I sang along with him, mumbled and muted at first, but then, after about the thirteenth time, full out. I noticed people staring at us from along the street. Next, and this one completely floored me, he sang the ABC song, straight through, leaving out only the "u" and the "v." I sang with him again, and when he'd finally had enough, I asked him where he had learned all these songs.

"Sesamenay Street," he said, "on Sesamenay Street." And not long after that he began to point out all the signs and windows and stop lights and license plates telling me which ones were triangles, which ones were squares, which ones were circles and which ones were rectangles, "just like on Sesamenay Street." I felt a little chagrined about all those goddamn hours I had spent watching Buffalo Bob and Howdy Doody. Howdy Doody. Christ.

Though Charlie was fascinated with the novelty of my car, I was equally fascinated with the novelty of him. And while he watched all the many buttons and dials, I watched him. And not the road.

We were just approaching an intersection and I glanced up to check the lights. They were changing, green for us and red for cross-traffic. There was no real need to slow down, so I didn't. But neither did a driver off to our left who was apparently trying to beat the light, which had already changed. Apparently he had committed himself too early and was going too fast to stop. Charlie had his head up in the wind again and was in the middle of a paroxysm of laughter. I had been watching him and was just glancing back for a quick look ahead when I caught a glimpse of a blur of red coming at us from the left. A horn blared and I slammed on my brakes. Tires squealed. There was a heavy thud next to me and a terrible sickening dread chilled my stomach. Charlie was dead! The car veered around us and sped off. Charlie was lying on the floor, not moving. I could feel my heart pound in my throat as I picked him up and cradled him on my lap. He was dazed, but apparently more frightened than hurt. There were no marks. But I was relieved to see the tears flood into his eyes, to hear the lusty screams.

A cop ran up and asked if we were all right. I said that we were, that we were both just a little shaken up.

"Yer damn lucky," he growled, as if the whole thing had been my fault, "but how 'bout next time. How would the kid here look with his head stickin' through that there windshield?" He pointed at the seatbelt lying on Charlie's seat. "Now why in blue blazes do you think they went to all the bother of puttin' that safety belt in there? For the exercise maybe?" I could feel my Celtic face coloring. I had forgotten to bring along a suitcase, now I hadn't thought to buckle Charlie into his seat. Not yet a parent for an hour and already I was a complete failure. The cop turned away to direct traffic. Charlie had stopped crying and was now only sniffling, so I sat him back in his seat, and buckled him in.

Then, for the first time in my life, I buckled myself in.

Chapter 19

Whaleback Park stands atop a hill sculpted, as its name suggests, strikingly like the flawlessly streamlined back of a monstrous, petrified whale. In earlier years, the entire rocky and precipitous area had been rejected by pioneering entrepeneurs as hopelessly unprofitable for economic exploitation. Now, however, as the only convenient haven for picnickers and golfers, its existence was proudly heralded in an endless stream of JCC pamphlets and mayoral proclamations as directly due to the vision of the city's selfless forefathers. Peering down at the rape surrounding it, however, one could better see it for what it really was, a hapless monument to early American innocence, forever gone.

As Charlie and I drove in under the lush canopy of trees and felt the fresh balm of air bathe over us, I immediately felt that sudden gush of euphoria that comes with ultimate escape from something sinister, the same feelings of security I used to experience as a small boy, when I curled up under the bedcovers at night during a raging storm. I was suddenly free, suddenly safe from everything pursuing me.

It occurred to me that I had never been to Whaleback before, had never even made myself one of those halfhearted promises that someday I'd go up there and take a look around. Oh, I had caught a vague glimpse of the green whale through my office window on occasions, often enough to become aware of its existence, but I had never really *seen* it before, had never really brought it to the forefront of consciousness. When one looks up momentarily from the pages of contrived, plastic legalese to stare out of a plastic office into a plastic world, he sees what his eyes know best, only plastic.

At first, Charlie didn't like the idea of being shackled to his seat, not at all. The principle of it would have been quite enough, but unable to sit up on his knees, he also lost view of everything going on around him. This was even worse so he complained and whined for a while, but once we entered the park area he quickly became intrigued with the ancient trees towering over us like bizarre fairyland giants. Whining gave way to quiet awe.

We drove up the winding roads until finally we reached the top of the hill. There we passed a swimming pool so jammed full of splashing, frolicking kids that one couldn't see the water beneath them all. I could, however, see the harried, exasperated looks on the faces of the lifeguards, slumped in their stilted chairs and obviously disillusioned with the legendary glory which is supposed to be the summer lifeguard's reward. Just beyond the pool area, in a more tranquil setting, we passed an extensive, well-kept picnic area where picnic tables, not quite isolated from one another, stood under the cool shade of massive spreading oaks. Even though it was still quite early, every table in sight was in use and some picnickers unable to get tables had even resigned themselves to the ground.

The road wound around the picnic area and back toward the rear of the pool, passed by several stone, slate-roofed pavilions housing more picnic tables, and finally terminated at a small parking lot already crammed full of cars. A sweating, red-faced, bloat-bellied parking attendant signalled for us to park along the curb outside, so we did. By this time Charlie was beside himself with excitement and was struggling impatiently to free himself of the seatbelt. He wiggled and wormed and slipped right out from under it.

The air was pungent with popcorn and ripening animal dung. The latter reminded me of driving through the rural Minnesota countryside in the springtime when the dairy farmers spread a winter's accumulation of manure over their fields from their fragrant "honey wagons." I was strangely attracted to the scent, but felt strong doubts about a similarly scented cologne ever making a smash on the market.

I thought it best to break Charlie of the habit of playing Houdini with his seatbelt, so I grabbed him before he could climb over the side of the car and buckled him back in. As I tightened it against his waist, he made no bones about establishing his position on the matter.

"Gemme outa here! I wanna go see da bears. Gemme outa here."

He was overtired and overexcited, but I knew I had to establish control and respect from the start, whatever the circumstances. I got out of the car and went around to his side and just stood next to his door, arms folded, staring down at him. When he quieted, I explained that he must never take off his belt or crawl out from under it until I said it was okay to do so. I reminded him about what had happened earlier. But to Charlie, earlier was earlier and now was now and now meant bears and that was that.

"Gemme outa here!"

"What do you say first? Judi had told me about Charlie's being a little on the overdemanding side at times and had suggested a simple show of strength and stubborn determination on my part as a possible remedy to his aggressiveness. It was all too easy to give in to him for the sake of peace, she said, as the poor harassed nuns had often had to do. I forced back a smile as Charlie looked up at me with a fierce scowl, but I managed to keep my own frown stubbornly intact. Finally he gave in, at least partially. Apparently the bears were more important.

"Please." Not "please?" with a question mark, but "please" with a period.

I unbuckled him and lifted him out. I was surprised at how light he was in my arms. For some reason I had expected a three-and-a-half-year-old kid to be on the chunky side, I guess, because nowadays most kids were, it seemed. Seated deep in the unconsciousness of American Motherhood was an identity equation between fat and good health, an equation which I had always strongly disagreed with, having been fat and clumsy and left-out as a kid myself. I was glad and proud to find Charlie lean and eager.

No sooner were his feet on the ground than he was grabbing me by the hand, all smiles, and pulling me toward the nearest cage, the refuge, or better, the castle of the laziest, most languidly arrogant raccoons one could imagine, and envy. I bought Charlie a little packet of nuts to feed them, but the raccoons, fat to the point of sin, were just too content to move. One nut Charlie threw landed about a half inch from the nose of one of the coons. He raised his head just high enough to take a couple of sniffs and made a feeble attempt at it with his mouth, but the struggle was too much. He dropped his head back down, sighed, and was fast asleep again.

Watching this, I thought of Stanley Bertrand Walbridge and his probable metaphoric reaction had he been with us. No doubt, I thought, he would have likened the insolent somnolence of these coons with that of those "goddamn lazy, leechin' welfare dregs, bleedin' us workin' people white." Welfare was Stanley's pet preoccupation and the topic of most of his public oratory. If welfare should suddenly cease to exist as a public issue, so would Stanley. It was the adrenalin which kept a heart enfeebled by two major coronaries going.

Charlie's fascination with the inanimate raccoons was about equal in duration to one of his yawns. "Nothin' goin' on here." He grabbed my hand and pulled me over to a cage full of monkeys. There was more action here, and Charlie was soon giggling heartily at their many show-off antics. There was one monkey who could do a variety of especially clever tricks, including a grand finale consisting of several backward somersaults (winter peppers). He ended each performance by suddenly springing against the wire mesh of the cage, rattling it wildly to gain everybody's undivided attention, then staring directly out at anyone holding a bag of nuts. No dummies, these monkeys. At first this final lunge frightened Charlie and sent him fleeing around behind me where he could wrap himself around my leg, but before long he was meeting the monkey on equal terms, jumping and screeching right back at him, to a point, in fact, of causing me to glance around us rather self-consciously for any glares of disapproval. But there were none. In fact, one kid nearby was throwing pebbles at a snorting elk and by the look of wrath on his mother's face was about to catch particular hell. Another kid was scraping up some peacock droppings off the ground with his fingers and was wiping it off on his little sister's crispy pink dress. It was reassuring to find everybody else's kid cutting up too. There was much consolation in numbers.

Next Charlie dragged me off to visit the camels. Which weren't really camels at all, but llamas. But the more I tried to explain, in the most ingratiatingly diplomatic terms possible, that those greasy bodies behind those snobbishly arrogant stares were actually llamas, not camels, the more Charlie absolutely insisted they were camels. So they were camels. I mean, after all, what's in a name. I was beginning to understand why the nuns had finally thrown up their hands in trying to convince Charlie the toilet was a neat place to do business. This kid had a mind of his own. And that was that. And, I have to admit, at the time I couldn't have been more delighted. At the time.

We spent all of three hours visiting every animal in the zoo at least once, several twice, and the bears three times. For some reason Charlie had a special affinity for bears, especially the young ones. Later on I discovered it had a lot to do with a story Sister Mary Bernardina often read to him at bedtime, entitled *The Knobby Boys*, in which a little baby brown bear is left to starve after a band of gypsies snatch away his mother. In the story the mother bear is finally returned to her baby through the enterprising schemes of the Knobby Boys.

It finally took a suggestion of a hamburger and a thick shake at McDonald's hamburger stand to pry Charlie loose. Had we been at the San Diego Zoo, or the Milwaukee Zoo, I'm sure we would've been there for the better part of a month, just to see everything once.

But with the fascination of the zoo and all its many wonders behind him and out of sight, Charlie began to realize just how hungry he really was. And for Charlie, hunger on top of a sleepless night could mean only one thing, irritability; so for me, it meant go faster. At first I didn't see the blue Ford with the PD plates approaching us so rapidly from behind; if I had I might have had time to slow down and act casually innocent. My stomach chilled and knotted to the wail of the siren behind us. I pulled over and glanced back at the blinking red light. Charlie was staring at the red beacon, too, and I could see from his wide eyes and gaping mouth that his hunger had been forgotten, at least temporarily. I considered putting a ten under my license but decided against it. I mean, what kind of example would that be for Charlie. Instead I smiled politely at the officer and thanked God I wasn't wearing long hair and a mustache.

Charlie was captivated with the impressive uniform and the mysterious sunglasses and the Smokey-the-Bear hat. The cop took my license and registration and I could see him feel the undersides for the tell-tale texture of a Federal Reserve Note.

"What's yer hurry?"

"Well, Officer, my kid here's hungry and we were in a bit of a rush to get to McDonald's for a hamburger. You see, we've been at the zoo all morning."

The cop raised his head to eyeball Charlie through his one-way-mirror sunglasses. Why, I wondered, did cops always feel the need to come off like stony Marine DIs?

"*Your* kid?"

"Yes sir, *mine*." I knew what he was thinking, and I felt myself retreat into a little pocket of paranoia lying somewhere between my spleen and my gonads.

"Gimme your keys."

"Excuse me?"

"Your keys, lemme have your keys."

"And may I ask why?" I tried to sound affronted.

"No."

Rather than push it, I handed him the goddamn keys and immediately considered getting out the spare from under the front seat and just sticking it in the ignition for the goddamn cop to eyeball when he returned. After considering it for half a second more, I did it.

The cop swaggered back to his car, the leather of his holster and wide belt squeaking impressively, and sat in the front seat with his legs sticking out the door, apparently so he could spring out should Criminal Dezengremel try any funny business. I could see him using his radio in the rear view mirror and knew he was checking to see if one David Dezengremel, D–E–Z–E–N–G–R–E–M–E–L, was wanted for kidnaping or sodomy or some such thing. He was gone a good ten or fifteen minutes during which the novelty of the new situation wore off for Charlie and he began to realize once again how good and hungry he was. And he proceeded to let me know about it. I began to call the goddamn cop everything I could think of in my head and to compose some stinging letters to the editor. Nobody, but nobody, pushes around D. D. Dezengremel.

Finally the cop returned. First he handed my license and registration back, then he sort of grinned and handed me a little yellow slip, a summons for speeding at 45 mph in a 25 mph zone. The bastard. The dirty rotten bastard. Then he handed my keys back, without so much as a word, and all I could think about was peeling off and spraying the bastard with a fusillade of pebbles and dust. But I didn't. Then he left without noticing the spare key sitting in the ignition, which made me all the hotter.

I drove the rest of the way to McDonald's well within posted limits, despite Charlie's impatient whining. And after I had cooled down a little, it occurred to me, to my logical half, that it was all for the best. The wait would do Charlie far more good than harm. He had to learn that his every need could not be catered to, and I had to learn that there was no easy way for him to learn.

But I still hated that goddamn cop with a passion. And not for the ticket either.

Charlie's appetite was equal to that of several of the larger animals we had seen at the zoo. I made the mistake of buying him only one hamburger, myself two, and was soon trudging back to the counter under orders for another. The sign out front claimed over two billion sold, but with Charlie around it certainly wouldn't be long, I thought, before they'd have to update it.

When I got back to the car I found most of Charlie's thick shake spread over his lap and the car seat, with little dark rivulets flowing down onto the floor carpeting. My once-immaculate vet was inundated with a thick, sticky mass of chocolate. Christ.

We were parked adjacent to a station wagon full of kids, on Charlie's right. There were two kids in the front seat, jammed in between Mommy on one side, Grandma on the other, and four more now-sitting, now-jumping in the back seat. From the time plump, frown-faced Mommy arrived back from the stand with a mountainous order, she did little but scream and scold her brood, mostly with her mouth full of food. "Stop that! Yer gitten it all over my new dress . . .Sit down in your seat, what the hell's the matter with you anyways, don' you know nothin' . . .Mona, you're gettin' chocolate all over that clean dress . . .You told me you wanted vanilla and that's what you got, don't be such a snot . . .Just shut your mouth and drink it . . .Look out for Grandma's shake, stupid, or I'll stick you in the back."

Suddenly there was a loud slap–I winced–followed by a wounded shriek. I glanced down at Charlie, who had stopped eating and was staring over at the sobbing boy with a look of sober concern. I flipped on the radio and turned the volume up loud enough to entertain most of the parking lot around us. Mommy got the message and gave me a glower, which I returned with a wink and a wave. She rolled up her window and turned her back.

Charlie was soon once again engrossed in gobbling up his second burger, and I continued to watch him with fascination. I felt I could have watched him eat all day. And had I let him, I'm sure he would have.

Chapter 20

It was well past Charlie's naptime by the time we left McDonald's, and though Charlie was heavy-eyed and yawning, we had no time for such nonsense as naps on this our first day together.

Late Friday evening, after driving Judi home, I had called Hattie Walker. I asked her if I could bring Charlie by, so the two of them might get at least partially acquainted before having to spend the entire day together come Monday, when I would have to go back to my office closet and Sam Douglasson. Such practical matters as naps (and suitcases and seatbelts) never even entered my mind. Hattie had previously agreed to babysit with Charlie during my working hours, in fact with such an effervescence of enthusiasm that I was convinced at the time Judi had been up to her old cheerleading tricks again. She said to drop over anytime Saturday, that she would be in all day, as usual.

Hattie lived in a petite Cape Cod in a blue-collar residential section on the outer outskirts of the city. She and her husband had saved all their lives for their little dream house, and "Beans" had built it entirely by himself, from the ground up. He had been an electrician by trade, a builder at heart. But just ten days after finally moving them out of their Northside apartment, home for some twenty years, Beans suffered a sudden heart attack and two days later he died in the hospital.

Hattie explained that she had nicknamed her husband "Beans" because, when first married, they had tested a pet theory of his which held that, if, during their first year of nuptial bliss together they were to put a bean in a jar each time they "made whoopy," as she put it, they would never in their lifetime be able to empty that same jar if they were to take out a bean each time they "did it" thereafter. The jar had been snatched empty within six months of the second year and Frank had been known only as "Beans," by friend and family alike, ever since. In fact, most people, even most of the foster children they had raised over the years, had never known his real name until the day of his funeral, when the minister referred to him as Francis Beans Walker during the eulogy.

Hattie must have been eagerly awaiting our arrival because the door opened to a rather stout, massively buxom woman well before I could reach for the doorbell. I knew immediately, perhaps from the maternal twinkle in her eye as she beamed down at little sleepy-eyed Charlie, that the three of us were going to get along very well. Very well indeed. She began to chatter with us as if we were close relatives or next door neighbors dropping by for a visit, and I found myself feeling that we were.

She was an easy conversationalist, and talked so much and so fast that she always seemed a little breathless. But even though she talked—and talked and talked—you always knew she was listening, really listening, to whatever you said to her. She always looked you straight in the eye, rather than inward at her own thoughts. For that alone, I loved her.

She offered us a piece of fresh rhubarb pie, right out of her own rhubarb patch, and though I went through all the usual polite "don't bother" and "we just ate" bullshit, Charlie came right out with a straight forward "Oh boy!" So we sat down at the kitchen table for pie and coffee, milk for Charlie.

I was surprised to discover how neat an eater Charlie was at the table. At McDonald's he had dripped, dropped, and slobbered half his hamburgers and most of his shake over the car and himself, and so I felt I had every good reason to expect him to do likewise at Hattie's, to have himself, the table, and the floor newly decorated with impressionistic collages of pie and crumbs by the time he was through. But I was wrong. Apparently the presence of a table made all the difference in the world, as a few crumbs sprinkled around his plate was the full extent of the damage. I felt a surge of pride and though I knew it was pride *of* rather than pride *for*, I enjoyed it anyway. A selfish feeling perhaps, but a natural one, I felt, and one that would tell Charlie that someone cared, that someone was really his.

Hattie apologized for having a piece of pie too, at her weight, because she knew how much it turned most people off to watch a fat person eat. I immediately flushed with embarrassment (or was it guilt), but she laughed at herself, and I laughed with her, then she set about eating her piece of pie, to the last crumb. She told me about the time, when Beans was still alive that she decided to join up with a Weight Watchers group, with every good intention. However, she was soon asked to *retire* gracefully from membership, with her money back, because she was spending most of her time, and everybody else's, at the weekly reinforcement meeting, discussing her favorite recipes for cheesecake and pecan pie, thereby throwing a monkey wrench into the whole deal. And though she still felt compelled to try out every gimmicky diet that came out in the latest issue of the magazines, she always had to reward herself after a couple of weeks with a delicious devil's food cake (appropriately) or a scrumptious Waldorf Astoria Red Velvet Layer Cake, or both. And that, of course, would be the end of the diet. At least until the next issue of *Family Circle, Woman's Day* or *Ladies' Home Journal.*

Hattie especially enjoyed her reminiscences of Beans and the many adventures they had shared together over the years. Her eyes sparkled when she told about them. But, she had to admit, those times together had not always been good ones. In fact after about four or five years of marriage things weren't going very well for them at all. They weren't on the verge of divorce or anything as dramatic as that, she said. Instead, and worse, they woke up one morning and found themselves sinking slowly but ever deeper into a sort of marital numbness. She was sinking into her rut, he into his. No longer could either of them see any freshness, any romance, any excitement, or any rejuvenation in their lives together. They felt old before time. They rarely went out together anymore, and talked less to each other, watched more television, and went to bed early. They always felt exhausted and beaten down, and they made love more mechanically and with much less frequency. Beans, it appeared, had been right about his bean theory after all. But perhaps worst of all, they didn't fight anymore. This to Hattie had been the worst signal of all. To her it meant each was becoming less involved with the other emotionally, that they were actually growing apart. Instead of man and wife, they were becoming brother and sister.

One day Beans suddenly disappeared. Hattie came home from grocery shopping one Saturday and found him gone, vanished, bag and baggage. A note on the refrigerator read, "We can't go on like this, Honey, will call later." After about a week, it was on a Friday, she remembered, he called and asked her out on a date. After toying around with him for a while, she accepted. Beans arrived that night with flowers and candy in hand and took her to a drive-in movie where he promptly tried to put the make on her. She slapped him and said she never went down for anybody on the first date. So they watched the movie, *Godzilla's Revenge*. The next day, a Saturday, they went on another date together, to the beach, where Beans maneuvered to get her drunk and put the make on her again. So she slapped him again and told him she didn't go down for anybody on the second date either. Beans settled for a cold swim in Lake Ontario instead.

After about a month of this curious courtship poor Beans was an absolute wreck. Each night they went out, which was practically every night, Hattie would tease and egg him on until she had him panting like a mad dog, then would always cut him off and send him "pole vaulting home," as she put it. Usually a model of discretion and caution at work, poor Beans received four accidental bolts of electricity during one week alone.

Then one clear, starry night, they parked in a secluded spot up on Whaleback Park. Beans asked her to marry him, again, and presented her with a diamond engagement ring. Her first, since they had always been too poor to afford one earlier, and still were. It was somewhere around three o'clock in the morning when they routed their minister out of bed and called some friends—they had to be good friends—to stand up as witnesses. They all met at the church sometime around four, their children and the parish organist too, and there in the middle of the night they renewed their marriage vows, and their marriage. After a brief second honeymoon, a day in a motel about three blocks down from the church, Beans moved back in. Their marriage had never gone stale since.

All the time Hattie talked and told stories she laughed. And the more she laughed, the more I laughed. And the more we both laughed, the more Charlie laughed, though he had no more reason to laugh than the fact that we were laughing. It struck me then how much a person's attitude is influenced by those around him. And I hoped I would always laugh as much, for Charlie's sake.

A mongrel dog who loved his dogfood with a shot of whiskey poured over it, Hattie said, along with three or four cats joined us in the kitchen. They sniffed Charlie and me over, the dog taking particular note of my crotch, and apparently accepted us as friendly. Probably because Hattie did. The kitchen also housed two tankfuls of tropical fish and a spacious cage where two parakeets chirped and chattered in obvious contentment. Hattie explained that she once had only one parakeet but that it looked so lonely and forlorn to her that she had found herself lying awake nights feeling sorry for it. Finally she had gotten a companion for it. And watching Hattie's face as she told me all this, I could sense the depth of her own loneliness, how completely alone she was after a husband and 187 children. Then I knew that there had been nothing forced or amplified about her enthusiasm to sit days with Charlie, that she had been genuinely eager without any coaching from Judi.

We stayed with Hattie the rest of the afternoon. And not once during the whole time was I even remotely concerned with what time it was. I just sort of sat back, completely relaxed, and watched Hattie play with Charlie and marveled at the ease with which she could relate to him. She tuned right in on him despite the wide age-gap. Many older people, I had often noticed, even those who had once had children of their own, often came on too strong with a child, almost insulting in their awkward gushy condescension. Not Hattie. As she played with Charlie, she played effortlessly as an equal. And she enjoyed it, really enjoyed it. And by the size of the hug Charlie gave her when we finally left, between teary protests over leaving at all, I knew Hattie was to become far more to us both than just a babysitter.

Chapter 21

Hattie had invited us to stay for supper, had insited upon it, but I declined with thanks. This was Charlie's and my first day together, and this of course included our first supper. And I wanted to cook it. I had a hell of a lot to learn, especially in the kitchen, and I was anxious to get with it. I felt it was the only way.

Hattie was disappointed.

Though I was anxious to serve Charlie his first meal in his new home, I was sober-minded enough not to try anything too impressive. I had been diligently watching the *Galloping Gourmet* on TV, whenever I could catch it, and had accumulated a notebook full of exotic recipes. But when it came down to practicalities, when confronted with naked reality, I wisely settled for cheeseburgers, potato salad from the deli down the block, and a few crumbly slices of Rollie's pumpkin bread. And I served everything on paper plates. No dishpan hands for Dezengremel.

Charlie climbed up into the high-chair and I slid it up tightly against the table so he couldn't jump out. He took one look at the burnt-up hamburger and the mushy salad and the crumbled bread and pushed the plate as far toward the center of the table as he could reach.

"I wanna peena budder sanbitch."

"Peanut butter! Whatdaya mean you want a peanut butter sandwich. I just cooked you a nice big fat hamburger, even better'n the ones you had at McDonald's."

"I don't wanna that to have. I wanna peena budder."

Charlie was rubbing his inflamed eyes and I knew he was just too damned tired to respond positively to any sort of stern discipline. So I whipped out the crunchy "peena budder" and the jar of jam that had been in the refrigerator for at least a year and slopped both over a couple of slices of Rollie's pumpkin bread. Charlie took one bite, screwed up his face, threw the sandwich on the floor, and wailed like a wounded wombat. Christ!

I picked up the dirt-covered sandwich and plopped it back down on Charlie's plate. Then I asked him in a voice strained for patience just what in hell was wrong with the goddamn sandwich. Between sobs he mumbled something about the "dirty stones" in the peanut butter.

Charlie no like crunchy peanut butter.

Charlie like only smooth peanut butter.

So I spread another big gob of peanut butter onto a slice of Rollie's bread and spread it over my fingers as the bread tore and crumbled apart. I pasted it back together with the gluey peanut butter, then, with a fork, picked every lump out. Then I took the jam-covered slice off the first sandwich, slapped the two together, gently, and presented the final draft to Charlie for his approval. He took another bite. I scrutinized his face for his reaction. My stomach was churning with expectancy.

This time there was no grimace. Instead he pulled the slices of the sandwich apart, very carefully examined each, as if for some trace of arsenic, then contemptuously dropped each slice on the floor. The jam side of one slice hit face down and stuck fast. Christ!

I was too exhausted to give him hell. I just wanted to get him packed away in bed, to have a few moments to myself, to regroup my wits. So I wiped the mess up off the floor, then once again asked Charlie what in hell he wanted, if anything. He wailed. I had spoken too harshly, and I realized it, but I found that right at the moment I didn't give a shit. I threw up my hands, thought a cathartic "fuck it," and tossed one of the charred hamburgers on Charlie's plate. It looked sort of pathetic sitting there on his paper plate, all dried up, so I drowned it with half a bottle of ketchup. And while I drank the first glass of milk I'd had in more years than

I could remember, Charlie ate that goddamn hamburger to the last morsel. Which was a hell of a lot more than I could do with mine. Charred sawdust. Christ!

After filing the paper plates away in the trash, I decided to spend some time with Charlie just messing around the apartment, so he could get used to his new surroundings before going to bed. He was tired, very tired, but I thought it would be a good idea to give him some quiet time to make him feel more at home. I wanted him to sleep. *Soundly*.

So I got out one of the new pads of drawing paper and the crayons, and the two of us sat down in the middle of the living room floor to draw. And what I had often pictured in sentimental daydreams during those lethargic, tedious afternoons as father and son reposed contentedly on the floor, bathed in the twilight of the setting sun, sharing curious designs soon turned into father struggling to draw whatever Napoleonic little son requested him to draw.

"Wanna draw bears."

"Well, Charlie, tell you what. I will if you will. Okay?"

It wasn't.

"*You* draw 'em." Lower lip out. Face fallen.

"Why don't you draw some bears too, Charlie?"

"*No*. You draw baby brown bear."

"If you will, I will."

Screams and woeful wails. "No! You!"

Christ!

Finally I decided the solution to the whole deal was a brand-new day after a long night's sleep. So I suggested a fun frolic in the bathtub. "Hey Charlie! How 'bout goin' for a swim in the tub with your new bath-toys?" Under the circumstances I thought a suggestion would accomplish a hell of a lot more than any authoritarian dictums.

Wrong.

"Don't wanna bath to have. Wanna draw potamusses."

I shook my head. The suggestion had become an order.

"Tell you what, Charlie ol 'man, we can draw a hippopotamus

together tomorrow. How's that?"

"Wanna draw potamus *now*."

"Look Charlie, we can't draw a hippopotamus now because all the hippopotamusses (or is it hippopotami? Christ, who gives a shit), because all the hippos are in bed fast asleep, just like all good little hippos should be. And it's time for all good little boys to be in bed too."

Before he could think long about the fallacy of that particular bit of reasoning, I picked him up and started to take off his clothes. He slapped me with his hands and when that failed he stiffened up and began to thrash around in my arms like a captured wild animal. I was astounded at his strength and wondered how those poor nuns at the Home had been able to handle him at all, or even if they had. I began to suspect that my adoption of Charlie had been the triumphant climax to an insidious conspiracy to depose a little king from his throne.

His training pants, which I had neglected to change all day, were soaked through to a point of complete saturation and reeked of ammonia. Christ. But at least there was nothing else lumping in there.

I finally wrestled him into the bathroom, nearly dropping him at one point—his sleek little body was like butter—and held him at bay long enough to fill the tub. With a lot more water than I should have. He wasn't in the tub three minutes before half the water was spread over the floor, that nice clean floor.

He was beside himself with rage, out of control it seemed, so finally I took his little head in my hands and very softly asked him what his problem was. He stopped crying.

He looked up at me with that wounded little face, smeared with tears, and with those two big brown pleading eyes. "You come in with me," he said.

Christ. No matter how much you prepare yourself, no matter how many contingency plans you map out, you can't think of everything. Surprise!

I knew I could refuse quite easily, that is, without too much of a further stink, because I knew damn well none of those nuns had ever accompanied him into the tub. So it certainly wasn't any established ritual. But I also realized Charlie was frightened and upset in his new environment with me, and needed all the security and reassurances he could get. And I knew my harsh words and impatient attitude earlier hadn't helped matters any. So I stripped down and climbed in. And no sooner was I sitting there than Charlie was pointing at that floating mass of funny-looking gear (it floats, you know) between my legs.

"What that is, ya know?"

Here I was, not yet a parent for a day and I was already confronted with all the traumatic dilemmas of sex education. Christ!

What should I tell him? Perhaps I should play it safe, I thought, and hand him one of those circumspect euphemisms? "Why, that's my little *thing*, Charlie. We all have these things. But don't look at it too long or you know what'll happen, you'll go blind." Then I thought it would be best to hand it to him straight, man-to-man. "Well, Charlie, that's my ol 'ramrod, fella. Weird shape, eh?" Christ. What I really wanted to do was simply tuck the damn thing between my legs and squeeze it down out of sight and forget the whole deal.

"That's my penis, Charlie. See, you have one too."

Charlie looked down at himself, then back at me. Then he looked worried.

"Daddy's penis is bigger than yours, Charlie, simply because Daddy's a bigger guy than you are. But someday, a long time from now, when you're all grown up too, you'll have one just as big as Daddy's (and probably a hell of a lot bigger; I'm not exactly a candidate for a pickle jar at the Smithsonian). And you'll have hair like that, too. You see, only big Daddies like me have hair around their penises (or is it penii?). And here, under their arms." I held up an arm so he could inspect my armpit. "Little guys like you don't."

"But someday I will, wasn't I?"

"That's right. Someday."

He was absolutely enthralled. Which surprised me a little until it occurred to me that this was probably Charlie's first encounter with a mature male. After three and a half years of nothing but nuns and other little boys, the sight he was now beholding couldn't help but deliver quite a shock. Like, holy shit, man! Like wow!

Then I did something unforgivable. It made me uneasy to have Charlie just sit there and stare at me. Voices in the back of my head kept screaming at me: "Bad! Vulgar! Indecent! Shameful! Immodest! Wrong! . . ." I was on edge. Then Charlie suddenly reached out to touch that curious source of wonder. It was a natural enough thing for him to do, certainly, but I reacted out of long conditioned reflexes. Not with reason, but with viciousness. Instead of calmly restraining his probe, I lashed out and slapped his hand away. Hard! He looked at me in stunned horror. Then his eyes flooded with tears. His sobs came hard, with pain. Not from the slap, but from a deeper hurt way down inside. And at that moment I was the biggest, most ignorant asshole on the face of the earth. I hated every thoughtless self-reverent bastard who shaded everything sexual in my life with filth and shame. I hated my parents. I hated the nuns at Father McMertry High School. I hated the confessional. I hated myself.

I comforted Charlie with an outpouring of apologies. When he was reassured I offered him a quiet explanation about how badly it could hurt grown-up men to poke them between the legs too hard (Christ, was this really David Dezengremel talking, the same one I had grown up with). I started to discuss the invasion of privacy angle but caught myself just in time. I was going to be invading his privacy quite often, wiping off all that shit and soaping off the stench, so how would I explain the hypocrisy? He would certainly see enough of that without any early contributions from his adoptive father.

After I toweled him off, getting at best the biggest drops, I chased him around the house, finally caught him, and despite a storm of protest, got him dressed for the night. I was so cautious about sticking him with the pins that I put the double-diaper on much too loosely, and when I finally freed him, he stood up only to have his diapers and rubber pants fall straight down over his ankles. He tripped and crashed to the floor, which made him all the madder. So I started all over again, this time bobbing around two arms and two legs flailing in my face, and managed to stick him once and myself twice.

I wanted Charlie to fall right into a ritual of always brushing his teeth at bedtime, right from the start. My own teeth were now more quicksilver than enamel, and I didn't want Charlie's to end up the same way. Every parent, I thought, owed his children healthy, well-kept teeth until they reached an age where they could fully appreciate their value and care for them themselves. But tonight was definitely not the night to press any new issues, so I didn't. Instead I wrestled him into his bedroom and sat him down on my lap in the rocking chair, and read him a special story, *Katie and the Big Show*, which had been my childhood all-time favorite. It had always filled me with warm feelings of security, like those you feel when sitting in front of a crackling fireplace on a stormy winter's day. So, even though the story line wasn't exactly appropriate for a muggy July 31st, I thought it might do for Charlie what it had once done for me. At the very least I thought the setting would be cooling, at least for me. When I had finished it, Charlie, of course, wanted another. Just one more, I said, just this once, then to bed. Yeah, right. How many times had I heard that one myself. So I read him *The Seven Diving Ducks*. Then he wanted *The Knobby Boys*, but I didn't have a copy, and even if I did, I told him, he had had enough stories for one night and now it was time for some sleep.

"Sing to me."

Christ!

The nuns must have lulled him into unconsciousness by humming a few bars of those hymns with those dreamy voices of theirs. The voice of D. D. Dezengremel, however, was certainly not lulling, much less dreamy.

At this point all I could think about was that beautiful bottle of bourbon sitting up on the shelf over the refrigerator (I had moved it up there out of Charlie's reach; one thing I *had* thought to do) and how good it was going to feel as it spread its euphoric warmth through my exhausted body. It was a wonder, I thought, that more mothers didn't become alcoholics.

I hummed a few bars of "Edelweiss," the only tune I found I knew, and was eternally grateful no one was listening except Charlie. Then I said good night, kissed him on the forehead, and started to tiptoe out. My mind was ahead of me, already out the door, reaching up into that cupboard, pouring that velvety amber essence over a tall glassful of crushed ice.

"I wanna cereal some to have."

Christ!

"But you've already had your supper, Charlie. And now it's time for some sleep."

Wails, tears, screams, thrashes.

Well, I couldn't very well send him to bed hungry. I mean, he *was* a big eater and all. And certainly if he were hungry, he wasn't about to go to sleep. And sleep, at the moment, was leading all other cars on the track, by four laps.

So the two of us went back into the kitchen where I fixed Charlie a big bowl of cereal. I sat at the table with him, chin in hand, as he munched away on the crispy flakes. To pass the time I read the ceral box, again, and stole several wistful glances up at that shelf over the refrigerator. I could about taste it. Finally, after Charlie's second bowl, I took him by the hand and led him back to his room, and to bed. I tucked him in, kissed him again, and once more started to tiptoe stealthfully toward the door.

"Whadid we do today, ya know?"

Oh Christ! Now he wanted to regurgitate his day. I trudged back and sat down on the side of his bed.

"You tell *me*, Charlie, tell Daddy about all the things you did today."

Charlie started to tell me about his day, about the things that had impressed him the most. The bears, the big man with the noisy belt and funny eyes, the big lady who played blocks with him, McDonald's hamburgers. And as he babbled on, I noticed he dwelled on only the good things he had experienced, only the positive things. A damn good way for a kid to end his day, I thought, recalling all the happy experiences, forgetting the bad. It occurred to me that encouraging such a positive attitude was perhaps one of the more important things a father could do for his son. Certainly it was of greater value than instilling in him any sordid hang-ups over his genitals.

After Charlie had relived his day for the second and third times, I tucked him in again, kissed him again, and finally made it out to the kitchen. I quickly filled a glass with crushed ice and was just about to reach up for that bottle of ambrosia when I heard a heavy thump, followed by the squeak of a door, followed by the patter of little bare feet, followed by a pair of squinted eyes staring up at me.

And that was only the beginning. I tossed him back in bed, issued a few orders, then tiptoed out the door and waited outside for a moment, sifting the silence with my ears. Then I stole back into the kitchen and once again reached up for that goddamn bottle.

Thump. Squeak. Patter.

Christ!

Back in bed. Stern warnings of imminent pain.

Thump.

Back in bed. Light slap to tiny well-padded buttocks.

Thump.

Had I not been so completely exhausted, so completely at wit's end, the situation might have been appreciated for its humor. But I was in no mood for fun and games. I wanted peace and quiet. I wanted a drink. I wanted to pass out on my bed.

Desperate, half-mad, I finally decided I just had to lock him in his room. It wasn't an easy thing to do, because I didn't want the little guy to feel any rejections, especially on his very first night in his new home, but something just had to be done. He had to sleep. He pounded on the door, rattled it, kicked it, screamed his heart out. I collapsed on my bed and felt my stomach knot up with guilt, burn as if I'd swallowed a smoldering ember.

I pulled a pillow over my head and pressed it tightly against my ears. I thought I'd wait for him to cry himself to sleep, then finally get that drink, or drinks. But as I lay there I began to worry. Perhaps I was frightening the little guy too much. I asked myself, how would you like to be locked in a strange dark room at three-and-a-half, Dezengremel? I answered: but, Christ, man, I had to do something. Neither of us had slept a wink the night before and another sleepless night could only spell disaster.

I laid there for some time and stewed uneasily in my own guilt and lack of confidence. Finally I pulled the pillow off to listen. It was dead quiet. Too quiet. Christ, maybe there was something wrong! The accident! The bump on his head! That's what he's been trying to tell me. That he's hurt. Bleeding inside. Bleeding to death!

I leaped out of bed and flew into Charlie's room. The bed was empty. Oh God! Then I saw a lifeless bulk lying on the floor at my feet. I dropped down, panic chilling my guts with icy horror, and started to pick him up. But when I touched him he sighed with that deep contentment of a slumbering child. Relief swept over me. The poor guy had simply, finally, passed out from exhaustion right on the floor. I felt worse than terrible for having locked the door. I wanted to wake him up and tell him I was sorry, to ask his forgiveness. But, Christ, what else could I have done, I wondered, trying to reassure myself? I mean what would happen if I let him walk all over me.

I tucked him back in bed and stared down at his slumbering face a few moments, then went back into my own room. I undressed and crawled into bed, and immediately began to worry about what sort of grievous harm I had done to Charlie for having locked him in his room like some dumb animal at the zoo, like the bears. Then, recalling the point Judi had made concerning that subtle, insidious kind of prejudice that seems to pervade even the most liberal, the most accepting, I began to worry about whether I would have locked the door had Charlie been white. Then I began to think about getting to sleep. I wondered about the peculiar nature of sleep, about its death-like coma, about the lack of control I had over it, about the exact moment I would fall asleep.

Then I began to worry about falling asleep at all. And the more I thought and wondered and worried, the more wide awake I became. I was suddenly aware of how noisy it was out in the street, even through these supposedly sound-proofed walls. The buzz of the clock, the distant slamming of a door, the rush of the air-conditioning vents, the thump of pipes, the occasional drip from the bathtub faucet. My left arm and side began to ache. Then the luminescence on the face of the clock was too bright. It read 2:20 when I finally turned it against the wall.

Then Charlie was screaming and pounding at his door. The room was strangely brighter. I turned the clock around. 5:34. Charlie was up for the day. Christ!

My brain would accept the presence of but one soothing thought, how goddamned nice it would be to be single again.

Chapter 22

I tried not to think, to keep my brain completely numb. Otherwise I knew it would direct me to phone Judi's number, scream "I QUIT!," slam it down, direct me to the window and instruct me to leap.

I drank four quick cups of coffee, the last one strong enough to kill a bull elephant. Then I got our breakfast. Two broken yokes and two slices of burnt bacon for me, one perfect egg and three perfect slices of bacon for Charlie (all parents are martyrs, you know; it helps us rationalize away all that guilt we feel over the way we abuse our kids).

The blood of America is sixty-eight percent coffee, thirty-two percent room for more. Without it, Joe America would surely hop on his desk and piss on it. Within minutes of the fourth cup I felt almost human again. In other words I could think beyond murder and suicide, could appreciate the more positive aspects of fatherhood. So I decided to take Charlie on a shopping trip. I knew of a supermarket over on Onondaga which was always open on Sundays. (Though I had never been there before on a Sunday morning, of course) and thought it would be fun for both of us. I thought I'd pick up a few ingredients for something more attractive than burnt hamburgers. I was quite certain there wouldn't be many shoppers out on a Sunday morning, so I thought it a most opportune time to introduce Charlie to marketing.

The dazzle and wonder of the supermarket were all new to Charlie and he was agape and goggle-eyed from the minute we walked in. Which was fine with me. I figured the more awed and overwhelmed he was, the less likely he was to get into everything.

I thought him too old for the baby seat on the cart, so I allowed him to follow along behind. At first, he was so totally absorbed, so completely entranced by the novelty of everything around him that whenever I would stop to pick up an item or two he would be unaware of it and bump right into the back of my legs.

There were more people in the store than I had expected. Apparently a lot of shoppers were out to pick up last-minute picnic and cook-out items. In fact we hadn't gone more than half-way down the first aisle when we met up with another cart coming from the opposite direction. A young mother was pushing it. She was very substantial in the chest and I was staring at that particular aspect of her femininity when I looked up and noticed she was looking at *me*. I smiled and felt a little warm in the cheeks. A little girl of about Charlie's age, perhaps a little older, was riding up in the seat. The mother stopped to select a box of detergent from the display.

The little girl stared at Charlie with an expression of deep disapproval.

"Look, Mommy, look at the little boy with the dirty face. He needs a bath, doesn't he, Mommy?" The girl was very articulate for her age, but apparently not from viewing Sesame Street.

Mommy kept her head turned toward the racks. The little girl looked a little puzzled over being completely ignored by her mother, then began to restate her question. This time the volume was more of an announcement. The mother quickly threw a box of detergent into her cart, directly on top of a carton of eggs, and pushed the cart on down the aisle. I wondered what, if anything, she would tell her daughter when they were safely out of sound and sight.

I watched Charlie for his reaction to all this. He watched the little girl disappear around the corner. And she watched him. Both seemed equally fascinated, though for entirely different reasons. Charlie had known, played with, fought with, supped with, and slept with white kids all his life. His fascination, then, seemed to come from the fact that the girl was fascinated. I knelt down and held Charlie by the shoulders and reassured him that he couldn't possibly have a dirty face because he and I had just had a bath together the night before. Then we moved on.

As expected, Charlie's fascination did not long remain passive. I began to glance around behind me only to find Charlie proudly toting along a can of tuna fish or bag of potato chips or jar of jam of some sort. At first he accepted the simple but firm explanation that those particular things were not ours and belonged to the store people. He would have to put them back. But it didn't take him long to see through that one. Down the very next aisle he started grabbing things off the shelves and tossing them up into the basket. Just like Daddy. Christ!

So I had to switch tactics. "We don't really need that today, Charlie, but maybe we'll need it tomorrow. Thanks anyway for all your help." I knew that one would make tomorrow a disaster, whenever it came, but at least it would get me through today. Which at the time, was all that really mattered.

I was approaching one of those displays of bargain beer, one of those ninety-nine-cents-a-six-pak come-on's, when we met up with a little boy trailing along behind his mother. The mother was wearing her Sunday-best hot pants.

The little boy, a tow-head with big blue eyes and unusually long eyelashes, stopped to stare at Charlie. Charlie smiled at the boy, then boldly introduced himself.

"Hiya. My name Charwee. What your name, ya know?"

The boy said nothing, only stared at Charlie with growing perplexion. There was no mistaking Charlie's overt friendliness with those teeth and eyeballs glowing against that face, and it occurred to me, from the contrast of reactions, that the little boy was looking at a strange brown face while Charlie was looking at just another little boy, a potential playmate.

The boy's mother was preoccupied with loading several bargain six-paks into her cart. From the large bag of charcoal, and the beer, I surmised she was shopping for a patio cook-out. People from this neighborhood would never be seen picnicking up on Whaleback with all those sweaty blue-collar bumpkins.

Charlie walked up to the boy. Suddenly the boy's eyes ballooned into two bottomless blue marbles.

"Look Mommy! A chocolate boy." With that he grabbed hold of Charlie's left arm and took a healthy chomp. But what he got was hardly the mouthful of sweet chocolate he expected. What he got was an ear-bursting yeowl that must have curdled every pint of cream in the dairy cooler.

Bewildered, but tearless, Charlie stared down at the teeth marks on his arms, then up, with growing ferocity, into the guilty party's horrified face. Then, before Hot Pants could snatch her son off to safety, Charlie dropped his head and lunged at him like a charging bull. He caught the boy full on the chest and sent him flying into the precipitous display of beer bottles. I buried my eyes in my hands, gasped, cursed fate for bottles instead of cans.

It was over quickly. When I peeked out from under my hands the floor was inundated with foam and broken glass, and Hot Pants was picking her wailing son out of the heap. Charlie came flying into my arms, eyes big as saucers, like a bear cub fleeing a swarm of buzzing horror. He wrapped his arms around my neck and held on like he was never going to let go.

Incredulous clerks and stockboys arrived from all directions. I apologized to the most officious of them, as did Hot Pants, then Hot Pants and I apologized to each other. Then each of us insisted upon paying for the damage much to the officious clerk's delight, and finally, at his suggestion, we compromised and split it. Six-fity apiece. Plus tax. I asked him why we had to pay tax when we were merely compensating for damaged property, but he insisted we had to pay it. Until I told him I was a lawyer. I offered to help clean up the mess, but Plus Tax said they would handle it themselves. I knew that didn't include himself. We left.

After we turned the corner I stopped to give Charlie a big squeeze. He wasn't crying or anything. I just felt like doing it. I noticed he was rubbing his marked arm so I kissed it to make it better. Surprisingly enough it did. Then I put him back down on the floor. I was amazed to find I was absolutely bursting with pride (and not nearly the pacifist I had portrayed to the St. Paul draft board). This was one little chocolate man who wasn't about to be devoured by anybody. And he was mine.

Chocolate Charlie. It fit.

Chapter 23

No nap for Chocolate Charlie again.

The phone rang soon after we got back from the market. It was Hattie. She absolutely insisted Charlie and I join Judi and herself for Sunday dinner. Undoubtedly they both thought we were starving to death. But I accepted anyway, without a moment's hesitation. Among other things I thought it would give Charlie and Hattie more time to get acquainted before being thrown together for the entire day starting Monday morning.

Hattie, the perfect hostess, kept my glass filled with gin and a trace of bitter lemon, and before I knew it I was babbling in lavish detail with just the slightest amounts of exaggeration here and there, for dramatic effect, about the cataclysmic encounters of a stuffed shirt bachelor lawyer and a recalcitrant, kinky-haired three year old boy. They laughed hysterically, especially Hattie, who banged the table with her fists, stomped the floor with her feet, and whose deep booming voice, I was sure, caused the neighbors a great deal of unfulfilled curiosity. It occurred to me afterward, between throbs of a splitting headache, that Hattie had kept my glass filled just to get me talking.

We stayed all afternoon. Charlie gorged himself on all the attention while I gorged myself well beyond the point of discretion on Hattie's fantastic cooking. Perhaps a further part of her devious design that day was to display her culinary talents to us, but whatever the reason, it was great. I couldn't recall the last time I had eaten a homecooked meal, a *real* homecooked meal. There was truth, I thought, in that very old and tired cliche that the way to a man's heart (or anyone else's) is through his stomach.

But certainly Hattie didn't have to know how to cook to win anybody over. She was simply one of those rare persons who was mother, friend and confidante to you the moment you met her.

Charlie fell asleep in the car on the way home, as nearly did I. One moment he was chewing a piece of gum, a bribe—he didn't want to leave—the next minute he was out. And little wonder with the amount of sleep either of us had had over the past couple of days. My eyes burned and smarted all the way to the apartment, and all I could think about from stoplight to stoplight was putting Charlie right to bed, taking a nice long hot shower, then collapsing on that king-sized cloud of mine.

But that's not the way Charlie thought it.

While I was entertaining dreamy fantasies of carrying my innocently slumbering son up to his room and tucking him gently into bed, my innocently slumbering son had other ideas. No sooner had we parked in the apartment lot than Charlie was wide awake and ready to go—that is, anywhere except to bed. I could feel the stares burning through my back as I carried a flailing, screaming, kicking, biting little brillo-headed chocolate man into the dripping elegance of the lobby of my lily-white apartment complex. At the moment, if I had had a spare hand, I would have flashed them all a big fat bird.

I was amazed and startled at how fast and how well I got to know myself, the real me, once placed in an environment of relentless stress, like having to cope with an infuriatingly intransigent child when I was much too overtired to do so. As the body ached, and the head throbbed, and the eyes burned, and the nerves bristled, I could feel my instincts turn inward, toward my own needs. The slightest aggravation seemed to become a challenge to my own survival, something to be lashed out at, driven off. It occurred to me how tenuous love really was and how dependent it was on such superficial things as a night's sleep, or in other cases, a full stomach, or even a strong sense of self-respect. Disillusioning, I thought, especially after viewing for so many years all those family comedies on television.

Charlie's antics were far worse than the previous night's. Soon I found myself not yelling but screaming at him, handling him with deliberate cruelty. I reminded myself of a bony-fingered hawk-faced nun I had once hated in grade school; the thought absolutely sickened me inside but only seemed to aggravate my behavior outside. Charlie's defiance was complete and so was my impatience. Every point of contention became a battle, a contest which I, the aggrieved authority figure, had to win.

Finally, after much screaming and squeezing I got Charlie into his bedroom. He wanted a story. I was too tired. He insisted. I was *too tired.* He wailed, flailed around on the floor, rigid. I relented–"Okay, just *one* story"–and hated myself for giving in, and him for making me.

Usually I sat in the rocker with him sitting snugly in my lap. But tonight I sat by myself on the edge of his bed and read him *Number Nine, the Little Fire Engine* with all the verve and enthusiasm of reciting *Foster vs Jones.* Then, while he screamed for still another story, I stuffed him between the sheets and stormed out. Locking his door outright, I went directly to the kitchen and threw down a couple of burning shots of bourbon. They only deepened the gloom of depression. All I could dwell on as I got ready for bed was having to return to that goddamn office in the morning, having to kiss asses and play the fawning role for some spoiled brat like Sam Douglasson. Christ!

I crawled into bed and lay there like a frozen corpse. Then finally, gradually, as the bourbon began to do its thing, my muscles began to relent. The numbness felt good, very good. In fact, at the time, nothing could have felt any better. But then as the euphoria swept through me, releasing my mind from its instinctual preoccupation with self, I began to think about Charlie, about how cruel and unloving I had been to him. I hadn't even said good night. Haunted with guilt, I knew I would have to go back. There would be no sleep until I did.

I couldn't face any lights, so I didn't turn any on. Glaring lights, like bright mirrors, always make the real appear too real. When I opened my door, I was startled to see a bar of yellowish light on the floor beneath Charlie's door.

Christ! He was still up!

I tiptoed up to the door and listened. Silence. I carefully unhooked the lock, turned the knob, then gently edged the door open.

The odor hit me first, then, with the door fully open, the horror. Shit. The room, and everything in it, was finger painted in shit. The walls, the floor, the bedspread, the curtains, the furniture—and of course, though harder to distinguish, Charlie himself. There were even a few gobs stuck fast to the ceiling. Charlie had completely redecorated his room—in his own shit. Not the sweetly redolent feces of the herbivore, but that fetid, nauseating, putrified shit of the carnivore. I gagged, wretched.

It was the last straw, the ultimate aggravation. Something snapped. I went berserk.

Charlie was naked and asleep on the top of his bed when I grabbed hold and thrashed him awake. His eyes bulged with terror. I screamed at him; squeezed his little body in hands that were vices. I mauled him over onto his stomach and began to beat him. Not spank—but beat. He cried out, wailed in fright, in agony as he struggled to wrest himself from my blows. He was strong and managed to free himself, repeatedly, which gave me all the more license to beat him harder.

Suddenly he began to cough, to gag. I stopped. He was choking. The gum! Jesus Christ, he still had that gum in his mouth! His eyes rolled up at me, pleading. He was choking to death!

I grabbed his arms and held them up over his head, slapped him between the shoulder blades with several sharp blows. He gasped, swallowed, then wailed all the harder. His little body trembled in my arms. Filled with remorse, I held his head against my chest and squeezed him. Then I noticed several marks, ugly marks, down his lower back. I looked closer.

Welts! Big ugly black and blue welts!

A profound sense of inner ugliness swept over me, through me. I was repulsed by myself. I was no father, I was a childbeater. A monster, a hateful beast. A loveless lonely asshole bachelor who should have stayed that way, with no one to abuse but himself.

This was all wrong, wrong for Charlie. He would have been better off with the nuns. I couldn't handle it.

I glanced down at Charlie. He was sobbing, haltingly, and was still trembling. He looked helpless, hurt. I needed help.

Charlie buried his head against my shoulder and wrapped his arms tightly around my neck. I dialed the phone. Hattie answered on the first ring.

"Hello." I could hear her television in the background.

"Hattie. This is David. David Dezengremel."

"Yes, David."

"Can you come over here right away?" My voice began to falter; I swallowed for control. "I've hurt Charlie."

Her voice took on an edge of alarm. "What happened?"

"I spanked him, Hattie, hard. Very hard."

She exhaled heavily into the phone, relieved. "I see. Well, I certainly wouldn't worry too much about that, David. It happens. Happens to us all. Hasn't your own father had occasion to whoop the tar out of you a few times, and harder than you deserved at that?"

"I *beat* him, Hattie." Tears came. "Just come. Please."

"On my way."

She must have made the cab driver run every light in the city. No sooner had I hung up, it seemed, than she was at the door. I was sitting on the couch in the living room holding Charlie in my arms. The room reeked of Charlie's artistry and I could tell Hattie caught the odor as she came in. She was carrying an overnight bag; she saw me glance at it.

"Brought along a few things, just in case."

If she was the least bit alarmed, she hid it well. Her manner was offhand as if she had dropped by for a casual social visit with pie. Coffee and a good gab on the agenda.

"Now what seems to be the problem here?"

I pointed to the welts on Charlie's back.

"I did that. I beat him." I avoided her eyes. I was scum.

Hattie bent down to examine Charlie's back. She probed, gently, with seasoned old fingers that looked more like cracked leather gloves. A smile began to spread over her face, hesitantly, like a tulip opening on a chilly spring morning.

"Haven't you noticed these marks before, David?"

"Before? Of course not. He didn't have them before—I just put them there."

She straightened up stiffly, pressing her hands against her lower back. Her smile gave way to a grin.

"Well, David, I'm sorry to have to tell you this but those little marks have been there on Charlie's back since the day he was born. They're birthmarks."

"Birthmarks!"

Hattie was making a valiant attempt to restrain her amusement. "They're somethin' like the strawberry marks we Caucasians get, like the one I've got here on my . . .well, I've got one. They call Charlie's here Mongolian spots; probably 'cause they're as common to Orientals as they are to Negroes. Saw lots of 'em on my foster kids, 'specially bi-racials. More visible on them. They'll probably be gone by the time he goes to school. They often outgrow 'em."

Hattie was sparkling with amusement over the whole thing. I couldn't help but feel somewhat relieved. Yet inside, there was panic; I was still the childbeater, the monster.

"But I beat him, Hattie, marks or no marks. I mean I really wanted to hurt him. I could feel it. It was terrible. I lost control like some primitive."

Hattie dismissed my lament with a casual flip of her hand as she plopped down on the couch.

"David, it might surprise you to learn that most parents beat their kids at one time or another, some quite regularly, in fact. And I'm not talkin' about just spanking either. I'm talkin' about what you're talkin' about—real beating. You'll find that when we do that we're not really beatin' our kids so much as we're takin' out on 'em what we'd damn well like to take out on somebody else. But for one reason or another we can't. And don't think for one little minute you ain't no animal either—college graduate, big-shot lawyer or not—'cause you are. And sometimes with this little guy in your hair hour after hour, day after day you're gonna act just like you belong in a zoo somewheres. We all do. Sometimes we lose sight of that. Too many fairytales, I guess. Anyways, by the smell of it in here Charlie maybe deserved a couple of slaps to the flab basket. But the important thing to remember, David, is just what you're doin' right now, holdin' 'im. As long as he knows you still love him, he'll be just fine."

"You think so, Hattie?" My eyes met hers.

She nodded. "He'll forgive you anythin', just like the Good Lord will. Too often we parents carry grudges against our own kids which is what really hurts 'em, deep down. Hit 'n' hug, Beans always used to say–'hit the b'Jesus outa 'em, then hug the Devil outa 'em.' That's just what he did. And that's just what you're doin' right now."

Good ol' Hattie. So much wisdom from so unpretentious a sage. I felt suddenly exhausted.

I laid Charlie down on the couch and Hattie and I began cleaning and scrubbing up his room and spraying the air with scented disinfectant. Then I cleaned Charlie up and tucked him back in bed, between clean but unironed sheets, for which Hattie gave me the evil eye. I sat down on the edge of the bed. He looked up at me through big brown eyes.

"Charlie sorry."

"Okay, Charlie." I hugged him. "But please don't ever do that again. You tell me when you want to be changed, okay? Better yet, tell me when you've got to go, so you can go in the potty, where it belongs. Okay?"

He hugged me back. "Charlie tell when the BM's pushin' on 'im."

"Good boy. And if you do that, and go in the potty where it belongs, Daddy'll take you out and buy you a big fat hamburger at McDonald's. And a shake, a big fat chocolate shake. How's that?"

Charlie's eyelids fell down over his eyes, retreated back slowly. He didn't answer. I got up and turned off the light.

"Good night, Charlie."

No answer. Just heavy, peaceful breathing.

Hattie insisted on staying the night, she already had the couch made up. In the morning I awoke to the gleeful shouts of someone bouncing at the foot of my bed, and to the sweet aroma of pan-fried bacon.

Chapter 24

Can you imagine a rookie tackle (you know, the guys up front who do all the dirty work) having to set up an appointment to see his own quarterback?

The following Friday morning the first thing I did upon arriving at the office (five minutes late as usual) was to stop by Sally's desk to make an appointment to see Stanley. Nobody got into Stanley's office without a long-standing appointment. Nobody. Unless, of course, you happened to be another quarterback. Then you could just walk in and slap him on the back and ask him how the fuck he was.

Sally looked up at me with that empty fireplace look of hers. The air-conditioning suddenly felt a little on the chilly side.

"Is this important, Mr. Dezengremel? Mr. Walbridge has a very busy schedule today."

"*Very* important."

"Does it concern the Douglasson matter?"

Nosy, aren't yah?

"No, as a matter of fact it doesn't. It's a personal matter."

"I see."

She knitted her brow with official gravity and drew her manicured finger down her engagement calendar (not "appointment"–but "engagement"). All the way down. I was sure now that her makeup was so well-lacquered to her face that it had not even been smeared during the rape.

"Mr. Dezengremel, Mr. Walbridge is tied up all morning and is leaving this afternoon at three o'clock for the Adirondack camp for a weekend fishing trip. She looked at me coldly. Perhaps you can catch him for a few minutes just before he leaves. He has an appointment at two o'clock with Mrs. Ouderkirk. If she leaves a little early I'll give you a buzz."

Don't call us, we'll call you.

"Thanks." I turned to leave.

"Oh, Mr. Dezengremel; you did say this was a personal matter, didn't you?"

"I did. Personal."

"I see. It's just that . . .Well, Mr. Walbridge always insists upon knowing the exact nature of his appointments. His time is very valuable you know. I'm sure you understand. So perhaps you could give me a better idea of the exact nature of what you want to see him about."

I walked back up to Sally's desk, glanced around surreptitiously, then crouched down close to her ear. I spoke in a restrained voice, not quite a whisper.

"I'm a father. Happened over the weekend."

In a momentary lapse of composure Sally's eyes bulged, her thin-lined lips parted. I left.

The necessity for my urgent appointment with Stanley had come about the previous evening. Hattie and I were sitting around the table after supper, having a cup of coffee together, when Charlie, busily engrossed beneath the table with his blocks, suddenly began to recite a rhyme about the letter "E." Hattie, seeing my astonishment, told me it was a rhyme from Sesame Street and that Charlie had just recited the whole thing verbatim—well, almost. Then, stealing a look under the table, I discovered Charlie had formed a large letter "E" with his blocks. I was impressed. Not a little impressed, *very* impressed.

But, at the same time, I also felt a little left out. Charlie was singing all these songs and reciting all these rhymes, and here I was, just another funky spectator sitting on the sidelines sucking on his paper cup of warm beer. But for me spectating wasn't enough, especially when it came to Charlie. I wanted in—to where the action was.

I decided I would see Stanley first thing in the morning. If I could get past Miss Eckert.

I hadn't been in my little closet a half hour yet, but I was already engrossed in a brain storming session trying to think up a new way of enticing Charlie to sit on the pot—and had just come up with the idea of suspending a McDonald's hamburger on a string over the Great White Bowl—when the intercom buzzed. It was line three. Apparently Stanley wasn't so busy after all.

Sally's voice sounded a little unsteady, almost vulnerable.

"Mr. Dezengremel?"

I'm very sorry but Mr. Dee is in conference right now and simply cannot be disturbed. And I'm afraid he has a full schedule for the rest of his productive career, so would you consider an interview by seance on, say, the 28th of August, in the year 2053, at, say, twelve midnight sharp?

"Yes?"

"Mr. Walbridge has cancelled his nine o'clock appointment with Mr. Rand and wants to see you in his office as soon as possible."

Cancelled an appointment! To see me? You've got to be kidding. I mean why should ol' Stan do that? Rand's an asset, I'm still a liability. "Someday you're going to be a real asset to this team, Dezengremel, just keep up the good work."

"I'll be right there."

Stanley was not, as was his usual wont, affixed behind his desk as if a part of it when I slipped into his office. Instead, he was standing over at his bar and was just pouring a second glass of bourbon into a highball glass. He looked up at me with an expression almost paternal. It was paternal. He handed me one of the glasses.

Though Stanley was an unabashed heavy drinker, I had never known him to be into the sauce at 9:30 in the morning.

He asked me to sit down in one of his plush red leather chairs, the ones usually reserved for the other quarterbacks. They exuded virility. He sat down facing me and crossed his legs. His shoes needed shining—it was Friday. He took a healthy belt from his glass, without a grimace.

"David, your father and I were the closest of friends for many years." He held his head back with an air of total confidence. "In a way, though neither of us ever admitted it out loud, we looked upon each other more as brothers, right from the time we fought together in The War, The Big One, as Marines. And it was your father, as you may or may not know, who eventually talked me into going to law school with him. I was bent on going home to take over my father's insurance agency. So you can see I owe your dad a great deal. The very least I owe his memory is helping his only son out in any way I can. Especially with any of those little problems we males sometimes get ourselves into from time to time. So, David, I want you to know that if you feel obligated to make this girl and her child as comfortable as possible, I stand prepared to extend you a significant loan on a *strictly* personal–"

"Uh, excuse me for interrupting, Mr. Walbridge, sir, but I'm afraid I'm not quite sure if I'm following you here. Is this girl you're talking about a client of ours, or is she somebody I'm supposed to know personally?"

Stanley frowned, lowered his voice. There was an edge of impatience.

"I'm talking about that girl who had your kid over the weekend. Miss Eckert just told me about it. We're all really quite–"

I grinned, tried desperately to contain it–then snorted. Stanley pinked, undoubtedly suddenly seeing himself the fool. The more he colored, however, the harder it was for me to compose myself.

Finally, with the help of my handkerchief I managed to wipe the grin off my face enough to apologize for my outburst and to attempt an explanation. Stanley's ruffled feathers were bristling.

"I'm afraid Miss Eckert has misunderstood, sir. She certainly was correct when she told you I became a father over the weekend, but you see it wasn't really my own kid. There wasn't any girl involved. I adopted a little boy, a little three year old boy named Charlie."

Stanley sat inanimate, without as much as blinking. His expression was that of a father whose son has just offered him a joint. Then he downed the rest of his bourbon and set the empty glass down on the mahogany table adjacent to his chair.

"I see. But Miss Eckert seems to have gained the impression somehow that you have a problem of the utmost importance to discuss with me. She seems to think it's of a very personal nature. *Is* there a problem?"

I could see from the abrupt non-paternalness now hewn into Stanley's face that "David Dezengremel, promising young Law Review lawyer" had just been reclassified to *"David Dezengremel, liberal bleeding heart who might fuck up the Douglasson deal."*

"No sir; that is, nothing of the sort suggested by Miss Eckert. I merely have a request to make and I approached Miss Eckert earlier this morning to set up a time when I might discuss it with you. I certainly apologize for any misunderstanding."

"Then it *is* important."

"Well, it is to me."

"I see. Well, what is it? Come to the point."

I felt a little embarrassed now about coming onstage after so sensational a build-up. The let-down was certain to be disappointingly anti-climactical. I was tempted to make something up.

"Sir, I merely wanted to ask you if it would be all right with you if I traded my lunch hour for the last hour of the day."

Stanley flinched. Christ, I knew I should have made something up. He probably would have laughed the whole thing off, if only I had tickled his toes with some little gem like, "Well, you see, Stan, I've got this terminal case of drip-trigger and I'm allergic to penicillin and sulfa, so I've just made out my will and would be highly honored to have you witness it for me and to serve as executor—and would you like to hear how I got burned?"

He was incredulous. Worse, indignant.

"Dezengremel, what makes you think you have to come in here and ask me about some petty little thing like that? You know damn well all you ever have to do when you're going to be out is leave word with one of the girls and—"

"Uh, excuse me again, sir, but I meant, uh, well, I meant everyday. Well, maybe not everyday, just two or three days. Three days a week. Except, of course, when you need me here during that hour. Then maybe two days."

He was waiting.

You see, sir, I'm having this sneaky affair with Judge Askew's wife—a real pig, you understand, but a sensational lay—and four in the afternoon, while the Judge is getting his massage at the Club, is the only time we can meet. We have a hideaway in this sleazy hotel over on the Northside. Daughter's not bad either. Wink. Wink.

"You see, sir, if it were on over the weekend, I'd be able to watch it, but unfortunately, it's only on weekdays, during office hours. And Charlie's getting so much out of it that I feel I should catch it, at least once in a while, so I'll be better able to reinforce what is presented, and participate more actively in the sort of things he's learning to do. And I guess it would be helpful, too, for me to observe the interactions of other black kids with whites." Stanley's eyebrows rocketed off their pads. "That way I figure our relationship can grow a lot closer, and faster, too, especially during these first trial months together."

"Dezengremel, are you running a fever or something? What the hell's this all about anyway?"

"Sesame Street, sir. It's on at four o'clock every afternoon, on UIIF."

For a moment Stanley looked as if he hadn't gotten the punchline and was deciding whether he should laugh now or wait till later. Then his face assumed a very serious air, one of intense scholarship.

"Dezengremel, what do you think would happen to this firm if we all suddenly decided to go home at four o'clock in the afternoon to watch the kiddies' cartoons on television? This firm has a national reputation of professional excellence to uphold. With seventy-six of the country's finest legal minds here, we are simply not going to casually knock off every afternoon at four with the bricklayers to go home and watch Porky Pig."

I was desperate now. I mean I *really* wanted to see Sesame Street.

"But, sir, it's just a switch in time, a trade. And it's just for me, not everyone else in the firm."

He shook his head, eyes closed, looking inward.

"It sets a precedent, Dezengremel, and precedents are dangerous. Look at what those damn labor unions have done to our free market system with a few precedents. Emasculated it, cut the gonads right off it. Look at England. See what happened to them. It starts with a few innocent little concessions, Dezengremel, then every brainless, beer-drinking rabble rouser on the assembly line is making more money than the man with seven years of higher education. Once the door's cracked they don't stop 'til they got it all the way open. Look at this four-day work week bunk? And, just like that proverbial forest fire, it all starts with one careless match. Why, just the other day I got a bill from this hairbrain plumber my wife called over to fix a leaky sink in the kitchen—no, it was the bathroom—well, you wouldn't 've believed it. Forty-six dollars and thirty-three cents! Little wonder the guy's got a swimming pool bigger than my whole house and a stomach to . . ."

When he held out his hand to dismiss me back to my cell, I wasn't sure whether I was supposed to shake it or genuflect down to kiss his signet ring.

Sally looked up at me as I walked by. Though her face was well masked with the usual somnolent indifference, I knew there was a torment of curiosity raging beneath it all. And I knew, too, that if I had bothered to stop to set her mind at ease, that she would have gone through the rest of the day without having to use another strip of that correction tape she had out beside her typewriter.

Never once had I seen it on her desk before.

Chapter 25

It was a dreary day, one of those that makes you feel half dead. The rain was spraying like hail against the office window and the wind, out of the north, seemed to be blowing right through it. The weather in upper New York State could be unpleasantly fickle, hot and humid one minute, cold and miserable the next. And I couldn't help thinking, at least on this particular morning, that it took an equally unpleasant personality to put up with it all.

On the previous night I had taken Charlie to a semipro baseball game at McDougall Stadium to watch the much-touted Syracuse Chiefs, a Yankee farm team, play our own resurging Metros. The teams were locked in a dead heat for first place, and because it was certain to be an all-out, hard-fought contest, I thought it would be a good time to introduce Charlie to the masculine pursuit of serious athletics.

Afterwards I hewed Dezengremel's First Commandment into the slate of granite that was my head: Thou shalt not take a child of three years to a baseball game of three hours. Dummy.

The score was locked up two-two in the third inning, with the bases loaded and our best hitter coming to bat, when Charlie suddenly grabbed my beer and poured it over the baldheaded man sitting in front of us. I was so busy apologizing and feeling my face burn up that both myself and the drowned victim missed the climactic double down the third base line. Shortly thereafter Charlie wet his pants and asked the lady sitting next to him if she had a penis "as big as his," pointing, of course, directly at my scarlet face.

Then it began to rain—to pour.

The intercom buzzed. It was line one, Evelyn's line. I blew my stuffed-up nose, then answered.

"Dezengremel."

"David, there's a young lady here to see you. Her name is Faye Watkins and she wishes to see you about taking on a case. Can you see her now?"

"What did you say her name was?"

"Faye Watkins. Say, you sound like you have a pretty bad cold there."

"I do. Got caught in the rain last night. Watching the submarine races out at the Lake."

Evelyn purred with a whispery little laugh; I pictured her lying on my bed in her bra and panties.

"You can send Miss Watkins right in."

"Will do. Hope you feel better."

"Thanks. I feel better already."

And I did. By the time Faye Watkins walked through the door I had completely forgotten about how miserable it was outside and how miserable I felt inside. Whatever the nature of her case, I was ready to jump right in.

Faye, black, lean, and strikingly beautiful in a yellow-plaid pants suit that clung to a well-proportioned physique like fly paper, introduced herself as a caseworker for the County Department of Social Services, and close friend of Judi Chesser. The latter fact put me on the immediate defensive. She sat right down before I could offer her a chair. Her brow was deeply furrowed with businesslike intent. I got the feeling she had come in waving a white flag to discuss *my* surrender. To break the ice, and to find out what in hell Judi was up to now, I asked Faye how long she and Judi had known each other.

"Since college. Judi and I were sorority sisters together at Syracuse. Chi Omega. We met when I was only a freshman, she a junior. And after we'd become good friends she asked me to come to one of her sorority's rushing parties. I was pretty excited, but at the time Chi Omega had one of those little clauses—a blue bird is a blue bird and a black bird is a black bird—so her sisterhood blackballed me straight off. So Peg Leg got together a team of third-year law students to bring suit against her own sorority, then tipped the press about it. I was voted in at the next meeting. She more or less got me my job at Social Services, too."

"And she's the one who recommended me, right?"

"Right. She said you were good. In fact she said you were damned good."

I dropped my eyes and mumbled something tritely self-demeaning. When I looked back up at Faye, she was staring me square in the eye.

"We want you to take on the DeLong case."

"The DeLong case?" I was apologetic. Consternation swept over Faye's face.

"You mean you haven't heard about the DeLong case?"

My cheeks were warming.

"Well, I'm afraid I've been rather busy lately, and I haven't read a newspaper or watched the six o'clock news in months, maybe years. So I guess I'm a little out of it. I read Peanuts, though."

Faye smiled, then settled back in her chair to explain.

Alice DeLong, the 21-year-old mother of four, three now, was currently being held in County Jail on a charge of murdering her seven-months-old daughter. She had been there for some months now, rotting away, waiting to come to trial. The trial had finally been scheduled to begin on the 13th of September. Alice and Richard, her husband, were county wards, and had been during all six years of their marriage, since the day Richard, whose world revolved around his prick, as Faye put it, knocked up Alice, who was only fifteen at the time. They had been on Faye's caseload for the past two years. Richard had beaten up the last caseworker, a male, for allegedly sleeping with Alice.

They lived in an old rusted-out tin can of a trailer near a redolent old land-fill dump outside the city limits. Besides Richard and Alice, four children and Alice's mother-in-law—who was now so grossly rotund she could no longer get out the front door, much less the bedroom door—all shared two bedrooms. Three of the four children were still in diapers. The mother-in-law used a bed pan.

Last spring, the baby, who was teething, began to scream day and night; at the same time two of the other three children came down with severe middle ear infections. And Alice was pregnant again. To escape the nightmare Richard jumped on his trusty chopper and took off to shack up with some broad whose husband was safely over in Vietnam, serving his country as a lifeguard at some officer's club. Richard finally returned one night, drunk out of his mind, and immediately tried to transfer a festering case of drip-trigger onto Alice, who hadn't slept in a week. He wrestled her onto the bed where his mound of flesh mother was eating and watching the tube and tried to put it to her. When she resisted, to the point of kicking him in the balls, Richard slapped her up, as he had done so many other times, and stormed off again on his chopper. With all the commotion, the baby, finally asleep, woke up and began screaming, which of course woke all the other children. In a climactic fit of rage Alice picked the baby up out of the oven pan where she slept and dashed her to the floor. They found Alice hours later sitting on top of a garbage heap at the dump cradling her dead baby in her arms.

Alice had been turned in for child abuse on four other occasions during the past three years. Two of the four times occurred while Richard was in jail on various charges, including a sodomy count involving the same broad who had given him the drip-trigger. Faye had been trying to work with them and had recently arranged for them both to see a child psychologist at the County Consultation Center on a regular basis. Things seemingly had been improving, especially since her success in getting Richard to go to the clinic.

There were no known relatives to either, except for the mother-in-law and a sister to Alice, an identical twin, who now lived in Southern California. A real Cinderella story, the sister had been brought up apart from Alice, in the home of a school principal. She had gone on to college as a music major and married a successful real estate developer who had large holdings in California. They had contacted her about Alice, but Alice had refused even to talk with her.

The court had appointed counsel, a young lawyer just out of Albany Law School. He and the DA were now about to make a deal to plead Alice guilty to a count of first degree manslaughter, which would carry a minimum sentence of fifteen years. The lawyer, in apparent anticipation of such a deal, had made no effort to prepare any kind of defense; he had not even so much as interviewed Alice beyond their first encounter. At the Grand Jury arraignment he had entered a plea of not guilty to the murder count only to placate Faye who had threatened him with grievous bodily harm if he didn't. In the past two months he had not returned a single one of Faye's calls. Finally exasperated, she had gone to see him, but his "balloon-chested secretary," who was also his wife, had refused to let her in.

"The dirty bastard's just going through the motions to collect his goddamned fee from the County. He couldn't care less about Alice, about her rotting in some stinkin' filthy jail somewheres. To him, and the DA and all the rest of them bastards, she's just so much garbage, better off on the heap where they found her that day."

I opened the lower drawer of my desk and pulled out a copy of the firm's personnel handbook. I leafed through several pages, settled back in my chair with my feet braced up against the top edge of my desk, cleared my throat, and began reading:

"Section IX. Indigent Clients. It is to be the policy of this law firm, without exception, that no one associated with the firm or employed by it shall in any way represent an indigent client or clients or in any way participate in a litigation or other legal matter involving an indigent person or persons, or volunteer his name and services for court appointment to a litigation or any other legal matter involving an indigent person or persons."

Faye sprang to her feet.

"Hey, baby, you forgot a line. Try this: 'Them trash ain't got no money so let's not waste our precious time on 'em. Fuck 'em.'" She snatched a ball point pen up off my desk and threw it at me; the point stuck in the lapel of my suitcoat. "There, baby, write it in. Then stick it up your ass." She wheeled and started out.

"Go ahead. Run away from another one. That's what you've been doing for the past two hundred years, isn't it—*baby*?"

She wheeled back around and stabbed me with two flashing deep brown daggers.

"You dirty white—"

"Oh, for Christ's sake, Faye, sit your little black ass back down in that chair and cool off. I just read you company policy, not mine. Goddamned uptight, aren't you?"

"You bet your sweet pink little ass I am. And just lookin' at you sittin' here in all this lily-white success reading me all about equal justice in America makes me wanna puke. You bastards. And let me tell yeh, if I hadn't promised Judi I'd come here I wouldn't 've. It's trite, baby, but it's true. Man, is it ever true. Justice in America is for those who can pay for it. Period."

"And who the hell are you to talk about justice? Christ Almighty, you had your mind all made up about me long before you even got in here. Didn't you? And you were just bursting to get the chance to show it, weren't you. Guilt by association. Dezengremel's a white prick because he's surrounded by white pricks." I threw her my letter opener; she caught it. "Here, finish the job, then go pout somewhere else."

She glanced down at the silvery metal blade.

"I would, 'cept I could never afford a lawyer to buy myself the right verdict." She smiled, then sat back down.

"I can see why you and Judi are such good friends. Two of a kind. Two of the hottest hotheads I've ever met."

"Yeah. And now that you've got me cooled down let's you and I discuss this 'run away from another one' bit of yours. I'm anxious to—"

"Let's you and I postpone that one for the bar sometime. Right now I think we should discuss Alice DeLong. Before committing myself on this I'd like to see her. When can we go? And I say *we* because I'd like to have you there with me."

"Why?"

"Well, to introduce me."

"Can't you do that yourself?"

"No."

"What're yeh doin' right now?"

"Sitting on my ass listening to my arteries harden."

"Good. Then let's go right now. My car's parked right outside."

I pulled out my ink-stained lapel and gave it a deliberate examination.

"What do you say we take a cab over there instead and pick your car up later. I'd hate to have you suffer any further aggravations today."

"I'd rather drive." She stood up and put my letter opener in her purse. "So we can discuss this 'run away from another one' bit of yours, in private."

Christ!

Chapter 26

The lawyer-client conference room at County Jail is one with the visitors' room and is reminiscent of a mass production confessional line for facilitating Easter-duty penitents.

A heavy, nearly opaque screen built atop an orangy varnished table and separating parallel wooden benches of the same orangy color extends for nearly the entire length of the room. The room itself is preserved in institutional pea green and inorganic yellow. The brass light switch plates are all so highly polished one trembles at the thought of touching them, for fear perhaps of getting put on some Big Brother's report.

It all reminded me of the military school my parents once took me to, for my personal inspection, in fond hopes I would plead to enroll. Instead I threatened suicide.

Prisoners were systematically regurgitated from the inner bowels of incarceration into our annex. Always there were the rude rumblings and crashings of heavy doors. In their brief flirtations with freedom the prisoners were allowed to embrace their visitors before going to opposite sides of the confessional. I was struck by a complete absence of any self-consciousness displayed during these fleeting embraces, especially between spouses. I wondered what it was like to be starved of something only then to be allowed to touch it, taste of it for one fleeting moment.

Directly across from the guard's desk was a special table, preserved in that same orangy varnish, popular about a million years ago, where lawyers and the clergy could confer with their clients—and in the least amount of privacy possible. There were only four chairs around the table, two of which were presently occupied by a young man dressed in prisoner's garb and a priest. The latter was short, pink and balding. They were engaged in an animated discussion during which the word "pig" frequently boomed out over all others. The guard, seemingly on the verge of his pension, appeared to take no notice.

The priest looked very familiar, and as Faye and I sat there on a bench, waiting—and waiting and waiting—I racked my brain to match the face with a name. Then it hit me. It was none other than Father Cummins, the Episcopal priest from St. Andrews. I wondered, then, from all that Judi had said about him, just exactly who was visiting whom. He looked quite different, smaller in stature perhaps, without all those robes on.

A young black couple sauntered in and sat down on the bench directly across from us. Although I was certain they were something more to each other than brother and sister, in the biological sense, had I come in after them I could easily have taken them for complete strangers. The young man, his hair in a natural afro, looked around in one direction, chewing and cracking his gum with something bordering on muscle spasms, while the girl, her hair also afro, looked around in the other. Never once did they so much as sneak a glance at each other, physically touch each other, or even whisper a word to each other. Nor did they look at us, or anybody else in the room. They looked at things, because they had to, but not at people. Not even at Faye. Then a tall lanky black man, considerably older, was paraded in from the mysterious inner chambers. The couple suddenly leaped off their bench. They slapped hands, hugged, kissed, and babbled in that soul lingo only they themselves seem to understand.

Finally, the remotely controlled steel door opened to regurgitate two women. One, dark and stern, looked remarkably akin to Elma, Monaghan's office nurse. The other, however, a slumped, dumpy form, looked more like some pathetic pauper out of Dickens.

Faye and I stood up as the matron led Alice over to us. There was an odor like freshly cut cheese. Fr. Cummins and the prisoner, or vice versa, were still absorbed in their discussion so the guard offered us his desk. I pulled a couple of chairs around and we all sat down. The matron left.

Faye introduced me to Alice. She looked up at me with eyes vague and liquid and smiled deferentially just long enough to expose a mouthful of severely rotted teeth. The light from the overhead globes glistened off the mucus running out of her nose, down over her upper lip. After sniffling several times in succession, she wiped it off on her sleeve.

I felt uncomfortably out of place in this girl's presence, as if I were intruding into a world completely foreign to me, one in which I shared nothing in common with the primitive natives, but where I was looked upon with all the deferential reverence deserving a superior–a god, king, or conqueror. I was at a loss for something to say. I looked to Faye for help.

"Mr. Dezengremel is here to help you, Alice. He wants to ask you a few questions. Mr. Dezengremel is a lawyer, a very good lawyer."

Alice, nervously using one finger nail to probe the dirt out from beneath the others, glanced up at Faye, then fleetingly over at me. Her face, puffy and much older than twenty-one, was expressionless. Without saying a word she dropped her eyes back down, apparently to concentrate more intently on her nails. She wiped her nose once again on her sleeve.

"Will you let Mr. Dezengremel help you, Alice?" There was an urgency in Faye's voice, as if she was afraid I was being turned off.

Alice pulled her fingers up closer to her liquid, red-rimmed eyes and furrowed her brow with intense concentration. Her nails snapped as she dug at them.

What does a man, suddenly alienated from his own safe little ivory tower, where Motherhood is spelled with a capital "M," say to a girl with dirty finger nails who lives in a garbage dump, one who has taken the life of her helpless little infant daughter? What does she say to you? I felt awkward and distant to the point of breaking out in a seeping sweat.

"Alice, if you feel up to it I'd like to talk to you for just a bit about the reason why you're in here. You see, Faye and I would very much like to help you, to help get you out of this terrible place." It struck me then that "this terrible place" was probably a palace compared to where she had come from; I continued to grope. "So you can go home to your family, where you belong. To your children. But it would help us to help you, Alice, if you'd just answer a few questions for me. Would you do that?" I hated myself for my condescension, for my distance.

At first there was no response, only a continuation of the nail picking. Then she stopped. Her head sank down further, as if to hide. A tear rolled down her cheek, over a scaly patch of eczema, then dropped onto the table. She buried her face in her hands and began to wail. Her whole body trembled as she mourned. I was startled, unresponsive. Faye reached across the table, but before she could do anything to comfort her, Alice was up out of her chair, staggering.

"My baby! My baby! I've killed my baby! My poor little baby. Oh no, no, no, no . . . ."

She turned and suddenly threw herself into the iron bars behind her, headlong. She slumped to the floor, limp. When I got to her side Father Cummins was holding his hand over a gaping wound in her head. Blood was streaming down over her forehead. She was dazed but conscious. She looked up through heavy eyes and saw Father Cummins' collar. Her voice was frail, broken.

"Tell God I want my baby back. Tell Him I'll promise to be good this time . . . "

On the way back to the office Faye drove in silence. She was waiting.

"Faye, I'm sure you're fully aware of the fact that the legal profession, and especially the New York State Bar, somewhat frowns upon the practice of one of its barristers soliciting away another's business. You see, in order to distract public attention away from all the legal hands wandering under the table, we lawyers display only the finest of etiquette above the table."

"I'll go along with that."

"Thought you would. Tell you what, if you can get Alice or her husband to dismiss their present counsel and then to approach me about taking over, I'd be glad to help out, if I can."

I glanced over at Faye. She was grinning.

"That won't be necessary, David."

"Why?"

"It's already been done. We had Richard give this Rogers fella the ax yesterday, after Judi assured us you'd be only too happy to take over. For nothing."

She handed me back my letter opener.

Christ!

Chapter 27

How do you celebrate your son's first BM in the potty?

If he's only two or so you probably don't. The expected is never particularly fussed over. But, if he's going on four, you go right out of your mind. You declare it National BM Day, you hang the flag out, invite the neighbors in to marvel at the unflushed trophy, and apply for a parade permit at City Hall.

By the time Hattie arrived I had already gotten as far as taping a large bow of toilet paper to the outside door, titled beneath, in Charlie's water colors, "REJOICE! HE'S JOINED THE MOVEMENT."

I was, therefore, in a particularly good mood when I arrived at the office later that morning. I even considered announcing the good news to Miss Eckert, or "Ms." Eckert as she preferred it now, but she wasn't at her desk when I arrived. I was early. Imagine me being early for work. I'd catch her later, I thought.

I went right to work on the Alice DeLong case. Sam Douglasson would have to wait. Fuck Sam. For the first time in my law career I found myself eagerly involved, reluctant even to stop nights. Mornings and afternoons had become wedded into a single whole, went by sometimes without so much as a glance at the clock. I was totally absorbed, totally committed to something I truly liked. I hadn't known the feeling since the days after that Christmas, years ago, when Santa Claus gave me my first erector set. Sometimes, like today, I'd even work right through the lunch hour. And if my stomach complained too loudly, I would appease it with a quick sandwich from the Chuck Wagon, a snack cart which came around at ten o'clock in the morning and again at noon.

I had done a lot of legwork and a lot of thinking since meeting Alice that morning. Most of it at the library. Not the law library, but the public library.

Before meeting Alice face to face I probably would have jumped, gratefully, at any kind of deal the DA might have offered to make. With a well documented record of previous child abuse incidents and a better than average looking DA, with even an amateur's flare for painting a gruesome spectre of a helpless seven-months-old infant lying bloodied and broken at its mother's feet, Alice was as good as tried and convicted of murder. The press, always in search of the sensational, had, of course, jumped on this case and had managed to play up the sordid to the public sufficiently to rouse it from its stupor of over-saturation and create what might be termed a stir. And where there is a stir, a general concensus of opinions–those of the friends, families, peers, bosses, neighbors, or heroes of the jurors. There couldn't help but be a biased jury, no matter how subtle or unconscious that bias might be. When the human animal sits in judgment of his fellow, one of his eyes may indeed be on the accused, but the other is invariably on the faces of his nodding, frowning peers. It is they, after all, who will judge him.

So when Faye told me how the court-appointed lawyer was just going through the motions while selling Alice out to a DA deal, I could fully sympathize with him. What the hell else could he do? And previous to that morning when I myself confronted Alice, face to face, I probably would have done the same thing. But thank the Lord I hadn't told Faye that.

After meeting Alice–no, more than that–after seeing, feeling, hearing, smelling Alice, after experiencing Alice, things were different, very different. I found myself feeling strangely fragmented, as if my carefully trained, socratic mind had suddenly crumbled into a million pieces. The next several days were spent groping within a new darkness, trying to put it all together again. But oddly, none of the old pieces seemed to fit anymore.

Finally, that following Saturday, I packed up Charlie and a picnic lunch and drove out into the country to do a little quiet healing, to take my mind out of the arena. We drove at whim and ended up touring along a somnolent little lake nested between verdant, sloping breasts draped with vineyards. We were in wine country. We drove slowly, suffering only an occasional honk of impatience from behind, and breathed in the pastoral beauty, the tranquility, the lack of complexity. It was more than attractive, it was magnetic. And the deeper we drove into its grip, the more difficult I knew it would be to turn back again, to return to our cages.

But we did. Because we had to. On the way back, after eating a leisurely lunch on a bluff overlooking the lake, I decided to explore a little, to delay our return as long as possible and to make it a little more adventurous. I took an old single lane road, away from the lake, but generally heading in the direction of the leaden film hanging low on the horizon, which meant home. The road followed along a precipitous ravine, at the bottom of which trickled a little trout stream, nearly dried up now from the usual summer's drought. We drove slowly, almost at a crawl, taking in the cheery singing of the birds as well as the raucous burps of the frogs. Charlie was even more enthralled than myself. To him this was a whole new world, a different planet even.

When we had driven down the road perhaps ten or twelve miles, I decided to pick up the pace a bit so we could take better advantage of the waning daylight to find our way back home. The road weaved and rolled like a roller coaster and with a little speed at the right places was as much fun. Sometimes I would speed up abruptly while approaching the crest of a sharp grade, then step off the accelerator just at the top so Charlie could giggle with delight at the sudden thrill of weightlessness.

Then it happened. We dipped down into a little depression, where a little spring dribbled into the main stream, through a culvert, and climbed up the other side. I wasn't going fast, by freeway standards, but it was too fast. At the top of the steep incline the road broke abruptly to the right and dropped down again, sharply. Perhaps there had been a warning sign, if so I hadn't seen it. Just a fraction of a second away from us, half lost in the dipping sun, was a small boy stopped in the middle of the road straddling his bicycle. There was a wall of rocks to the left, the precipitous ravine to the right. The boy was between. I hit the brake and jammed the wheel to the left. A solid wall of rock reached out at us. I jammed the wheel back right. We skidded past the boy, missing him by no more than a layer of paint. But I had wheeled too far back to the right. We were going over the ravine! By instinct alone I jammed the wheel sharply left, using every ounce of strength. The car swung heavily, out of control, and spun in circles back across the road and slammed heavily off the massive wall of rock, then stopped.

Charlie's eyes were popping right out of his head, as I'm sure were mine. I fell back against my seat and breathed out a sigh of relief. We both had our belts on. But I knew had we plummeted off that cliff the belts would only have served in helping the troopers find our bodies in the wreckage.

The boy rode up on his bicycle. He was whistling. He was a lad of perhaps nine but had on the badly tattered clothes of a much older boy. He spoke in half sentences with a heavy ruralish twang and bared teeth half-dissolved with decay whenever he smiled, which was often. The near tragedy hadn't fazed him in the least. In fact he thought the whole thing had been great fun and asked me if I wanted to do it again. He was dirty but not dirty like the all-American kid just down the street. He was dirty with filth worn so long it had become a part of him.

The boy mumbled something about our tires so I got out to investigate the damage. All four wheels were severely bent over, almost flush to the ground, from the sidelong skidding. The frame beneath was bent and twisted. The whole left side of the front end was smashed in against the steaming motor, which reeked of hot oil. The old powder blue asswagon was gone.

The boy, whose name was Lonnie Sixberry, said the nearest telephone would be at his house, just a "li'l way" down the road. His mother and grandmother weren't home, he explained, and he didn't have a father, but he thought his brother, whose turn it was to be in charge today, would let us use it anyway.

Charlie enjoyed the novelty of running carefree down the deserted country lane–for perhaps a mile. If that. Then he wanted to ride on Lonnie's bicycle. But there wasn't any place for him to ride, not so much as a rusty fender, and the handle bars were out of the question, so I had to say no. Which, of course, left but one alternative. Me. So for the next three hundred miles, now reining on my hair, now my nose, Chocolate Charlie, dastardly desperado, led a charge down the road atop his trusty, relentless steed. After all, Daddies can do anything. Heigh ho, Daddy!

"Git ap!"

"I can't, Charlie, I'm too tired."

"Why not?"

"I just told you. I'm TOO TIRED."

"Why you tired, yeh know?"

"From carrying you."

Silence.

"Do horses have a penis?"

Christ!

The road followed along the very top of the ridge looking down over the stream below. This exposed us to the full force of the wind, which, though not particularly strong, was relentless and directly against us. Finally too pooped to plod I had to stop for a rest. Charlie dismounted and ran off to lasso a chipmunk with Lonnie while I collapsed down under a big old tree. Above me the wind moaned a melancholy lament through the branches. I looked up. The canopy was bleakly sparse, the leaves tattered and ill-formed. The branches themselves, knobby and grotesquely gnarled, appeared to have suffered a lifelong bout with arthritis. I glanced around at the other trees along the ridge. They were the same. Down below, however, following along the stream bank, the trees stood straight and tall and sported symmetrically shaped plummages of lush green. Just a few feet from hell, it seemed, was paradise.

The rest of the way Charlie didn't feel quite so heavy. Some of the pieces had fallen back together.

Lonnie's house was little more than a cancerous shack. There were burlap covered mattresses on the floor, an old stuffed chair or two, a formica-topped table, and a bleeding heart crucifix tacked up against one crumbling wall. The air was musty, like the inside of a laundromat. Lonnie's brother was watching a fuzzy cowboy movie on a little circular screen surrounded by a big hulk of a box. When he turned toward us, I was startled to find myself staring eyeball to eyeball into a dirty-faced mirror image of Lonnie—an identical twin. He ran up and boldly introduced himself as Lennie Sixberry, man of the house on Tuesdays, Thursdays and Saturdays, then shook my hand with an eagerness I had associated only with lonely grandmothers.

Encouraged by the cowboy movie on the tube Charlie and Lonnie began to have an all-out shootout. Lennie showed me the phone, which was buried beneath a stack of food-encrusted dishes, then joined in with the other two, on Charlie's side. I called four garages before finding one with a tow truck, then sat down in the old stuffed chair, the one with some stuffing still in it, to watch the kids play. Lonnie wanted me to join in on his side, but I yawned and begged off.

Outside the crickets were singing their evening praises to the Great Green Cricket God. I was in no hurry to get home now, for finally my mind was completely at ease. Thanks to Lennie and Lonnie and a big old tree, all the pieces were now back in place, forming a new whole. I had my defense. Alice DeLong was not guilty. Not innocent, but not guilty either.

I was absorbed in a high school biology book, soaking up the chapter on heredity, when the intercom buzzed. I glanced up at the wall clock and was surprised to find it already well after noon. Again I had gone through the lunch hour without a single hunger pang. That is, 'til now. Once I realized what time it was, I was immediately ravenous. Conditioned animals, all of us. And how very much so we rarely, if ever, give full conscious thought to.

I finished the paragraph I was on, then pushed the flashing button without really noticing which one it was. I was disappointed to hear Miss Eckert's steel and rivets voice on the other end.

"Mr. Walbridge would like to see you in his office, *immediately*." There was obvious delight in her emphasis of the word "immediately." She reminded me of the presidential press secretary types, the ones who sniff at the groin of power as it passes through their hands.

Something big was up and Sally knew it. She was gloating with anticipation. And I had a very good idea of what it was.

"Tell Mr. Walbridge I'll be there in a few moments. I'm just finishing some important research here and I've got to scribble down a few notes while things are still fresh in my mind."

"Mr. Walbridge was quite adamant about seeing you immediately, Mr. Dezengremel. He said to send you in even if you were busy with a client."

"Well then, tell the ol' boy I'm tied up with forty-six of 'em."

"Sir?"

"Forty-six chromosomes. Did you know, Miss Eckert, that each cell in that exquisitely manufactured body of yours contains the same forty-six chromosomes that every other cell has, and that if you had an identical twin sister, heaven forbid, she too would have exactly the same chromosomes, down to the—"

Click!

"—minutest little detail."

And did you know, Miss Eckert, that my son Charlie shit in the pot for the first time today and that it stunk just like yours.

Sally was not at her desk when I entered the waiting room. A man, slick and nervous, like a weasel, was just coming out of Stanley's office. He left the door open, as if by previous design. When he spotted me he grinned as a kid brother might do, who was about to witness his elder get the strap. I recognized him immediately. Scoop Curtiss was all too well-known—revered by some, feared by most—as one of the best muckrakers in the business. Best because, although his exposes were always ruthlessly vindictive, they were always just cleverly factual enough to stand the challenges of litigation. He obviously gloated in his work, and I couldn't help but think him a little sick somewhere, sick like the fragile little putdown kid who now had the muscle for vengeance, for dragging down into the dirt whomever happened to be on top, by whatever means necessary.

Stanley's face was a ghoulish white. His lips were drawn tight and his eyes were beady and fulminating.

I started to close the door behind me.

"Don't bother. We won't be that long."

He picked up a little booklet smartly jacketed in clear plastic. I recognized it immediately. It was an executive copy of the firm's handbook, most of the contents of which Stanley had originally authored himself. He considered himself, on these merits, a published author.

He read: "It is to be the policy of this law firm, without exception, that no one associated with the firm or employed by it shall in any way represent an indigent client or clients or in any way participate in a–"

"I know the section, sir. Section IX."

He slammed the handbook down on his desk, an outraged schoolmaster. I could feel the ears pressed against the walls on either side of us, the gapes out in the lounge.

"Then I presume you were fully aware of this policy when you agreed to represent this child-killer, what's-her-name?"

"Alice DeLong, sir–innocent 'til proven guilty. Fifth amendment to Section IX."

"Dezengremel, do you have any idea at all what something like this will do to the prestige of this firm?"

I shrugged.

"Well, let me tell you this much. We have no room around here for any insolent hemophiliac publicity mongers who would have our entire system of justice dedicated to saving the goddamned garbage of this country! I have just informed Mr. Curtiss, who, by the way, was the first to inform me that *my* firm was representing this DeLong broad, that you are no longer associated with this firm. You're fired!"

The veins in Stanley's neck and temples were engorged with blood. He was trembling with rage. I thought of his previous heart attacks and decided against saying anything that would upset him any further. Instead I smiled. Then, before he could react in his own defense, I grabbed hold of his shoulders and quickly kissed him on both cheeks. He was stunned.

"Merry Christmas, Uncle Stanley. Sweet dreams tonight."

I winked, and walked out.

I was giddy with relief as I threw my personal books and belongings into an attache case. I was free. Free at last. Christ, I mean for the first time in my life I was really free.

When I came back into the waiting lounge, Sally was back at her desk pecking busily at her IBM, without correction tape, as if nothing out of the ordinary had happened. I started out toward the reception desk, to savor Evelyn's coquettish purr one last time, but then turned back and walked straight up to Sally's desk. She didn't look up. I leaned over to her ear, and bellowed.

"Go fuck yourself!"

The bow of toilet paper was still on the door when I arrived home.

Chapter 28

Charlie and I were in the middle of breakfast the next morning when the phone rang. It was Rollie.

"Congratulations!"

"For what?"

"For getting yourself fired. Well done."

"Now how the hell did you hear about that? I haven't told a soul, 'cept Hattie."

"Can't begin my day without reading Curtiss's column in the *Herald*. You and Stanley were in the lead paragraph this morning. He's got you both quoted blow by blow."

"Scoop Curtiss?!"

"That's the one. Ol' garbage mouth. He's the broad who writes that daily gossip column, "Heather's World," under the name of Heather Worthington. Didn't know about that one, eh?"

"Why that dirty rotten sonofabitchin' . . .He set it up! He set the whole goddamn thing up!"

Rollie chuckled with distant amusement.

"Could be. He's been known to stick a few pins in just the right places to liven up an otherwise dull day. He's a real pro, that guy."

"He's a real bastard, that's what he is. How come nobody ever assassinates assholes like him? Christ."

"Probably because he's too popular with the rest of us assholes. Makes our whole day. So how do you feel about it anyway?"

"About what?"

"About getting fired, losing your job. How do you really feel about it?"

"I feel like I just got out of jail."

"Thought so. Then Curtiss actually did you a favor, didn't he? I mean when it comes right down to it he sort of shortened your sentence for you."

"Hey, Monaghan! Are you trying to defend that weasel bastard or what? Christ Almighty—oh, now I get it. Turn the other cheek and all that shit. You're Christ The Reincarnated, in disguise, aren't yeh? Well, forget it, fella, 'cause this time you're just never gonna make it around here. We're all very civilized and Christianized now and we just don't go 'round crucifying you radic-libs anymore. The very best we can do now is buy your phone, perhaps start a dossier. So if I were you, I'd get my ass back up there while the seat's still warm and sit it right back down on the right-hand side of Big Bubba and keep my big mouth shut."

Rollie started to laugh, then gagged. When I asked him if he had a cold or something he said no but that he had a mouthful of his famous Christmas oatmeal-banana-honey bread. He always began his Christmas baking in August, he explained, in order to free himself during the Yuletide for other pursuits.

"Well, Dezengremel, what're your plans now?"

"Haven't even thought about them yet. And won't 'til I win this DeLong case."

"Gonna win that one, eh?"

"You bet."

"Confidence is ninety percent of the battle, I guess. Where you going to set up shop?"

"Here I guess."

"Charlie gonna let you do that?"

"Guess he'll have to."

"Sounds like trouble."

"Got a better idea?"

"Glad you brought that up. Got a proposition for you. Strictly business, you understand—tit for tat."

"I'm a little short on 'tat'; how you fixed for 'tit'?"

Rollie laughed, choked on another mouthful of bread.

"If you'll agree to handle all of my malpractice suits, free of charge, of course, I'll let you use one of my spare rooms over here as your office. Got two here I'm not even using. And Elma tells me she used to be a legal secretary, 'bout a hundred years ago, and says she does nothing but play solitaire around here all day anyway and could use a little more action. Says we can share her services, whatever that means. How about it?"

"Throw in all the oatmeal-banana-honey bread I can eat and an occasional nip from your medicinal spirits and you've got yourself a deal."

"Done."

Rollie hadn't been kidding when he said he started baking his Christmas goodies in August. The room he gave me for my office, the one he said he wasn't using, included three purring chest-type freezers already crammed to the brim with frozen breads. Also included, as a bonus, was a life-size human skeleton which (or who) stood propped up in one corner in such a way that it was the first thing you saw when entering the room. And from the dart board on the wall, the one with the jacket from Lyndon Johnson's *Vantage Point* pasted over it, I assumed the room, which wasn't being used, of course, also served as Rollie's personal therapy room. The walls were appropriately papered in one of those gaudy floral prints one associates with the local funeral parlor—apparently Rollie had ambitions of becoming a conglomerate. The three large windows all looked out at a solid wall of greasy bricks.

I spent the weekend moving in and setting up. Charlie, of course, insisted upon coming along to help. And though I had visions of an all-out war between us, surprisingly enough he spent most of his time just leafing through one of Rollie's old anatomy books and marveling at the skeleton in the corner—and, of course, asking questions.

"What that is, yeh know?"

"That's a skeleton, Charlie."

"What a skelekin is?"

I noticed he had the anatomy book open to a page showing a skeleton and was looking back and forth from the page to the "guy" in the corner.

"A skeleton, eh? Well, a skeleton is . . .Well, it's sort of a bunch of bones, see. And this bunch of bones is hidden way down deep under your skin, see, where it helps to hold you up, so you can walk. You've got one and I've got one. Everybody has one."

"Does a skelekin have a penis?"

Christ.

When I arrived Monday morning there were two new lines painted on the door directly beneath "Roland M. Monaghan, MD"—

David D. Dezengremel
Attorney at Law

Each letter was painted in a different color, from purple to bright orange, then back again. The paint was still tacky.

Elma greeted me with a smile and a clutch of the hand that nearly brought tears to my eyes. Rumor had it she moonlighted weekends as a bouncer at some queer bar over on Liberty Street. I noticed fresh paint stains on her hands.

I hadn't been in my new office for more than an hour when Elma burst in to announce that some smooth-talking dude wanted me on the phone, if I wasn't too busy. Said his name was Haskins.

Dick Haskins was County DA. I walked out to Elma's desk, where she had already resumed her game of solitaire, and picked up the phone.

"The lady at your place said I could reach you here. I guess that was your mother, eh?"

"No. My babysitter."

He chuckled. "Oh, I see. You got one of those too, eh?" He chuckled from where he had left off—one of the boys.

"Yeah."

"Look, David, the reason I called is to discuss this DeLong deal with you. I was just talking with Burt Rogers, who was on the case before you, and he told me that you had taken over. He's a little upset, by the way. Says the girl's husband stormed into his office the other day all drunked up and called him everything in the book. Burt thinks somebody put him up to it. Anyway, Burt and I had more or less agreed to settle for manslaughter one on this thing rather than the murder rap. We've got an open and shut case, as I'm sure you know, but there's no sense in dragging this thing into court just to give the papers some juicy headlines. I don't think the judge'll give her anything more than the bare minimum. He's pretty soft."

"Tell me something, Dick, have you ever met Mrs. DeLong, personally I mean?"

"Well, no, not really. I saw her—"

"I'm going for acquittal, Dick. No deals."

"You're outa your mind, Dezengremel." He had fully anticipated my stand. "We can hang her on the murder two rap and you know it. With her record you'll never even get off the ground with a defense of TI."

"I'm not going for temporary insanity."

Silence. This he hadn't anticipated.

"Look, Dezengremel, you're playing around with other people's lives here. I've seen you upstarts go off half-cocked on your little Perry Mason ego trips before. But you're gonna get burnt, buddy, and so's she. God help you both."

"You got any kids, Haskins?"

"No."

"Married?"

"Separated. But what's that got—"

"See you in court."

Chapter 29

Following our first encounter in the bathtub together, Charlie had become exasperatingly preoccupied with the male plummage. So much so, in fact, that whenever Hattie or I took him shopping he would invariably, and always at the worst possible moment, ask some prim and proper little thing, in that unrestrained voice of innocence of his, something like, "Little guys don't have fur on their penis, do they?–just big guys."; or, equally as devastating, "Girls don't have a penis, do they?–they got a bagina."

It was Hattie, fortunately, who had fallen victim to the first bomb blast. It happened at one of the busy checkout counters at the local supermarket. Charlie was sitting in the basket at the time, and had just handed the checkout girl one of the bananas he had torn loose from the bunch. The girl, middle-aged and stiff, was holding it in her hand, awaiting the rest of the bunch, when Charlie suddenly announced to all therein present, "But girls don't have a penis; just daddies do." The woman dropped the banana and turned a brilliant shade of red, what Hattie called Christmas crimson. Hattie nearly swallowed her teeth laughing, she said, and left with tears streaming down her cheeks.

Had it been me that first time, however, I would surely have dropped dead on the spot, charred black from mortification. My face even prickled pink as Hattie told me about it. Which made me all the more thankful for having Hattie around. Under her influence Charlie would come to know personal freedoms I could, at least for now, only envy from a distance.

So it was with no hesitation, and some degree of relief, that I asked Hattie to take Charlie on a little shopping expedition while I got myself properly groomed and manicured for presentation to Alice DeLong's jury. It was a Saturday, and jury selection was scheduled to begin early on Monday afternoon at the county courthouse.

However, in order to economize, now that I had no source of steady income, I decided to drive the three of us over to a section of the city, not too far from the Foundling Home, where I knew I could get a haircut for about half the downtown union price. I wore an old scruffy sweatshirt, a faded pair of grease-stained dungarees, tennis shoes which looked as if they had only recently been dug up, and no socks. When in Rome . . . .

Using what money the insurance company had allowed me in settlement for my vet, I had only a few days before gone out and bought an old clunker of a station wagon which had over 72,000 miles on the odometer, and four bald tires on the wheels. I hassled with the salesman for a good half hour trying to get four new tires thrown into the deal, but the bastard wouldn't budge. Finally, with two of his Elks compatriots well within earshot, I challenged him to an arm wrestling duel with the tires at stake. He had to accept, and did. And won.

The bastard.

I spotted a barber pole and pulled over. On the third attempt I managed to parallel park in the only space available. After the vet, parking an old clunker of a station wagon was more like trying to dock a garbage scow in a harbor full of Chinese junks.

Looking in through the window, I could see that the barber chair was unoccupied so I told Hattie to meet me back at the shop in half an hour. Charlie was already halfway down the block, chasing a mangy old alley cat. Hattie lumbered after him scolding as she went.

The barber, young and scrawny with close-set eyes, peered up over his *Playboy* as I walked in. He smiled a little too eagerly, which caused me to wonder just how many heads of hair he had actually cut in his career, and what mine would look like about twenty minutes from then. Christ, I thought, I had come down here to save a buck but would now end up spending fifty times that for a wig to cover the damage.

"Mornin'," he chimed, setting down his *Playboy*.

"Mornin'," I replied, playing the role.

He made no immediate effort to get up from his chair, so I climbed up into the barber chair and just sort of sat there like a dumb potato soaking in its own sweat waiting to be peeled. When he finally did get up, a little hunched over from the waist, I understood. I fought off a grin.

He wrapped me up in a sheet, already prickly around the neck with someone else's hair–last year's customer, I thought–and was immediately talkative. Talkative, that is, like someone suffering from stage fright. After he had clipped away for a few minutes I noticed his posture had considerably straightened.

"Well, goddamn Yankees lost 'nother one last night. Stayed up 'til after midnight listenin' to the goddamn thing. Jesus, did they ever shit. Christ. Looks like the celler again this year."

I thought about Charlie pouring my cup of beer over that man's head at the ball game and chuckled out loud. The barber assumed I was sneering sympathetically at the Yankees.

"Wouldn't care 'cept I lost 'nother five bucks on 'em."

I was tempted to suggest the obvious, like why not bet on the other team, but I got the feeling somehow that this guy was actually enjoying his losses. Perhaps, I thought, because in losing the money he was actually winning the right to dump all over somebody.

After picking the last morsel of flesh from the Yankees' bones he went on to the weather. Which, of course, was shit too. He was already bound for Florida where, of course, the weather was always perfect. Next came the "fuckin' economy" and how he hadn't been able to get "one lousy stinkin' rotten job" after getting out of the "fuckin' Army," and how he'd had to use his VA benefits for barber school "'cause there wasn't nothin' else to do but go on welfare with all them there fuckin' douche bags."

I found myself only half listening; he kept my back to the mirror and all I could concentrate on were those terribly loud snips of the shears and the gaping holes each was leaving in my hair. Then suddenly I realized he was talking about Alice DeLong, one of "them there fuckin' douche bags."

"Guy in here yesterday was tellin' me all about it. Said while her ol' man was doin' time in the clink she'd lock 'er brats up in a closet where it was about 200 degrees, and take four 'r five guys on just for the 'ell of it. Said she beat one kid up so bad one time the doc thought he was a nigger, he was so black 'n' blued. Jesus, oughta really be some trial, eh? Thinkin' myself 'bout closin' up shop next week so I c'n go see it."

I grunted passive assent.

"But get this. The real topper. This guy says they got some young lawyer dude queer's a three dollar bill to defend 'er. Says he hangs around that doctor feller who got hisself bounced outa priest school 'r whatever yeh call it for blowin' some guy in that confession thing. This guy says he'll probably get the cunt off by blowin' the whole goddamn jury, judge 'n' all."

I was sure, now, that no matter what he did to my hair I was certain to get my money's worth, and more. I egged him on.

"Who's this lawyer fella? From 'round these here parts, is he?"

"Yeah. One of them rich dudes with a coke bottle stuck up his ass; works for that asshole Walbridge. They say he's got a little nigger kid livin' with 'im. Probably breakin' the little bastard in early."

He was scraping my neck with a straight razor and I couldn't help but wonder what would happen about then should an exuberant little black face sudenly burst through the door to claim me as his own.

"Yeh know, before I got drafted inta the goddamn Service, and got sent over to 'Nam, I wasn't prejudice 'gainst them niggers the least bit. Probably 'cause I didn't have all that much to do with 'em, know what I mean?"

I grunted.

"They went to their school, we went to ours. But, Jesus, after havin' to live with them bastards over there in the fuckin' jungle for thirteen months–man, you ain't got no idea in hell what those stupid jungle bunnies 're really like 'til you gotta live with 'em.

Talk about dumb, Jesus Christ Almighty. Act like a bunch o' fuckin' luny retards. And they'd just as soon stick a shiv in yer back as a Charlie's. Could never turn yer back on 'em or you was good as dead. But fixed 'em." He snorted, wiped it off on his sleeve. "Whenever one of them bastards got hisself all hopped up on "H," we'd put the bastard out on point and patrol out into the jungle far enough to make it look good, then POW!—enemy contact." He laughed at the cleverness of it all. "Sent a helluva lot of them 'J' bunnies back to the States that way, all wrapped up in pine boxes labeled KIA. But it weren't no lie though. They was sure enough all killed in action."

He loosened the sheet around my neck and dusted me off with talc, then swung the chair around until I could see myself in the mirror. I nodded shy approval without really looking at what he'd done to me—I always felt self-conscious about looking at myself in the mirror. Just then Hattie and Charlie walked in the door; Charlie was holding a soupy double-dip ice cream cone. Chocolate naturally. He came up and stood possessively beside me, all the time concentrating on the drips flowing down his cone with his tongue.

Shock, in C sharp major, blared out over the barber's face; he looked first at Charlie, then at me. I handed him some money; he took it, mechanically, without really looking at it.

"This is Hattie Walker"—Hattie nodded politely—"and this little guy here, half drowned in ice cream, is Charlie, my son." Charlie offered his cone to the barber, who declined with a stiff shake of his head and a twitch of something that might have been a nervous smile. "His real father died a few years back while on patrol over in Vietnam. Killed in action. Charlie takes the Silver Star to bed with him every night."

I nodded, then the three of us left. Charlie wanted to go get a McDonald's hamburger.

Chapter 30

The only question I asked each of the prospective jurors was, "Have you any children of your own?" If they answered in the affirmative, I accepted them; if not, I challenged. I only had to challenge twice.

Alice sat at the table during the course of the initial proceedings with no more presence than an empty rag bag. Her head hung forward; her tiny hands lay clasped together on her lap. The way she hunched her shoulders and intertwined her legs beneath the table gave the impression of desperately trying to occupy as little space as possible.

I had tried several times since our first encounter to get Alice to talk to me, about anything, but had failed to provoke even so much as another groan of despair. She didn't want to be helped, by me or by anyone else. And this troubled me. I didn't want to deprive her of the punishment she now craved, but at the same time I couldn't just stand by and watch her be punished, alone and vengefully, for an antisocial act, a catastrophic climatic event, for which she as a pawn of circumstance was not at fault. I decided, finally, to let God or Whomever do the punishing.

The first day of the trial was uneventful, undoubtedly of disappointment to the jammed gallery, with little more accomplished than the final selection of the jury—eight women, all mothers, four men, all fathers. I waived any opening statement.

After the matron led Alice out, back to her cage, I took Faye and Judi, who had each scheduled the trial as one of their afternoon field visits, out for a drink at the Brass Rail. None of us, particularly me, was in the mood for much socializing, the first drink seeming only to deepen a latent gloom, so we stayed on only for one drink. I went directly home to eat supper with Charlie and Hattie. Afterwards I asked Hattie to stay on with Charlie so I might go on down to the office to take care of a few last minute details before trial in the morning. She offered to stay overnight, as I knew she would, and I gratefully accepted. I knew it was only a matter of time now before Hattie would become a permanent member of the household, but I wanted to let her do it on her own time, and in her own way. It would not be easy for her to give up The House That Beans Built.

I decided to walk the mile and a half or so to the office in order to do some thinking, to rehearse once again some of the things I intended to say in my closing statement. But instead of thinking, I only watched the faces I passed by; the entire distance went by without seeing one smile. Once at the office I sat in my creaky old chair and stared over at Homer, Rollie's name for my ossified corner partner. I had moved him into the opposite corner from where he had been so my clients would be unable to see him now until on their way out.

I had been there I suppose for an hour when I heard a knock on the outer door. Probably a patient looking for Rollie, I thought, somebody about to drop a baby. And with Rollie out of town for the night that meant Dr. Dezengremel just might have to do his thing again. Christ. The thought stirred up my stomach, already on edge.

It was Judi. And by the look on her face I knew she wasn't about to have any babies. It was a look I had never seen there before, a warring paradox of rage and grief. She limped in sluggishly and fell back into one of the waiting room's chairs. Then burying her face in her hands she broke down.

I laid my hands on her shoulders and knelt down in front of her.

"What's wrong, Judi? What's the matter?"

Collecting herself, she dropped her hands down onto her lap. I handed her my handkerchief. What was there about a girl in tears that was so much like a newborn fawn struggling to stand up on wobbly legs.

"She's dead, David. Alice is dead. She killed herself."

At first I didn't react. I just knelt there, numb, as if suspended in a little bottle of formaldehyde. Then I began to feel strangely heavier, as if Fate's mindless alchemy were transforming my blood into lead.

"How, Judi? How'd she do it?"

"Choked to death. Tore part of her dress off and stuffed it down her throat."

Judi was crying again when I got up and went into Rollie's examining room. I returned with Rollie's bottle of medicinal whiskey and two beakers already filled to the brim. Judi was slouched in her chair, red-eyed and staring blankly through one of Rollie's bird paintings. I handed her one of the beakers; she drained nearly half of it on the first gulp. I sat down in the chair beside her and stared up at a scarlet tanager poised spryly on a blooming apple tree bough. We drank in silence.

Finally after several minutes Judi spoke, her voice tired and phlegmy. She cleared her throat. Her beaker was resting against her mouth in such a way that she could inhale whiskey vapors instead of air.

"Nobody really gives a shit, do they, David?"

I shook my head, still staring at the tanager, and grunted something.

Judi took another slow slurp from the beaker, then turned toward me.

"Do we give a shit, David, you and I?"

I shrugged.

She turned back, sipped. A tear rolled down her cheek, and dropped into her beaker.

Suddenly she gulped down what whiskey was left and threw her beaker against the wall. Glass flew like shrapnel. She struggled to her feet, eyes flashing.

"C'mon, David, get your ass in gear and let's go."

"Where we goin'?"

"To get plastered."

Deke was at Freddie's–all three of him. Or so it seemed. He was the biggest mountain of a man I had ever seen in my life. Little wonder he had carried me home those times with such apparent ease.

He bounded right over to us at the door and greeted us with a smile that revealed several gold teeth, and several vacant spaces. His neck was at least as big around as Judi's waist. Though I didn't exactly remember what he looked like, I knew immediately who it was.

"Well looky whoz here! C'mon in, folks, and join the pardy. We was jest lookin' for a li'l action."

He laughed from the same place an opera star sings, from deep down within. He was dark for a Negro, perhaps partly because of the dusky lighting, but the sweat on his brow made his skin shine like freshly polished boot leather. He put one of his massive arms around each of us and led us over to a table where three other men were sitting. On the way he signalled the bartender to fill six more pitchers of beer, one for each of us.

We sat down.

"Well, 'r' youz gonna gemma the keys to that asswagon o' yours now or doz yeh wanna wait 'til we carry yeh out?" He slapped my back so hard my head nearly hit the tabletop; he roared.

I handed him Judi's keys.

While Judi argued with the other three men about something or the other to do with the county welfare program, I babbled on to Deke, and he to me. We were like old school chums at a reunion.

I told him all about Alice DeLong and losing my job and the suicide. Then I told him about the untimely death of my "asswagon." He sat and listened, his face set hard but sympathetic. Then, when I had finished, he began telling me all about himself, about how he had devoted his whole life to football, to making it big.

He had been too dumb, he said, to get into even the poorest excuse for a college–hadn't even finished eighth grade–so he had had to settle for playing on a semipro all-black team down in Brooklyn. Finally, after a single undefeated season, he had felt himself ready for the big time and had boldly walked into the New York Giants' summer training camp, bag in hand. After a single day there, however, he came to realize that semipro football was far more semi than pro. He was cut, as expected, but the following summer, after another undefeated season with the Brooklyn team, he was right back, same bag in the same hand. But they cut him again. Frustrated and embittered now, he got drunk that same night and got himself into an argument with some white dude over something or other, he couldn't remember, and nearly killed the bastard. That cost him nearly two years in prison.

But for him, at least, prison had been a godsend. By coincidence the warden there had been an all-American for Alabama, and when he heard Deke wanted to play ball, took him right under his wing. Daily, summer and winter, the warden put Deke and a few other losers through a grueling routine of conditioning and practice. Then, the following year, the warden got Deke paroled a little early, and once again he found himself at the Giants' camp, same old bag in the same older hand. But this time he beat out several rookie prospects and a veteran or two for a position on the 40-man roster. It wasn't first string, but it was a uniform with his name on it.

Then, on his first chance to play, as a defensive tackle—it was a game against Cleveland, he recalled vividly—he broke his ankle in three places and was out for the rest of the season. At the end of the season the Giants put him out on waivers but nobody else picked him up. They said he was old, too slow. He had visited several other training camps since, but had not, as yet, met with any success. He had come back from New Orleans only last month.

By the time Deke had finished his autobiography, and me mine, we were all pretty much in the bag. Judi's voice was about two octaves above shrill and despite being outnumbered three to one seemed to be beating her opponents down, by sheer power of her voice if by no other means. Their argument was centered on whether or not welfare recipients should be required to pick up their checks in person at an employment office.

I noticed Judi had bought the last two or three rounds of

pitchers, and not from any altruistic impulses so much as from the fact her pitcher was always empty well before anybody else's.

I struggled to get up from my chair and, achieving success, braced up between the table and my chair, slapped Deke on the shoulder–gently.

"C'mon, Deke, let's go."

"Go? Hey, man, it's too early. Things're jest beginning' ta swing 'round here."

"We're not goin' home. We're goin' someplace else. C'mon."

"Then what's yer gig, man. Where de 'ell we goin?"

"To court."

The others all looked up, as bewildered as Deke.

"Ta court? Like a pig's ass . . .Jesus, man, whadaya wanna go there fer?"

"We're gonna have a little bitty trial."

"A trial!"

Judi began to jump around in her chair like a little girl about to blow the candles out on her cake. Her face was pink with excitement.

"Hey, Dezengremel, sounds like fun. C'mon, Deke baby, let's go have a trial." Judi staggered out of her chair and grabbed Deke by the arm and urged him up–and "urge" was about all you could do to Deke.

"Well, I's donno 'bout this. Last time I was in one o' them there places cost me two goddamn years in the can."

Judi pulled on his arm. "Yeah, but this time you'll have a *real* lawyer on your side."

Deke stood up, wobbling. Judi handed him a full pitcher of beer, me another, then grabbed one for herself. Then taking Deke by the arms we ushered each other outside. Judi and I stuffed Deke into the backseat of her VW; then, with Judi at the wheel, we jerked out into traffic, stalled, jerked forward again, and finally weaved on down the street. We rolled down the windows; and with Deke leading, bellowed forth a medley of bawdy songs all the way to County Courthouse, a large soot-shrouded, unimpressively pillared building surrounded by Urban Renewal nothingness. I was about to prove a point. Alice would have her day in court.

Chapter 31

Once while in Judge Askew's Surrogate office, present at his behest to receive with dutiful subservience a tongue-lashing for presenting him with "illiterate, ill-conceived and ill-designed" briefs—I had dared use comprehensible colloquial prose rather than the classical incomprehensible legalese (such as "herewith therein heretofore to be referred to as the aforementioned party of the second part . . .")—I had noticed that his lone window had a hook lock on it and that it wasn't hooked. I took special notice of it because I had thought of coming back that night with a truckload of pigshit to dump on his elegant deep blue carpet.

Now, standing in the shadows in the alleyway between the courthouse and the mound of rubble that had once been Kroeger's Discount Auto Parts, I mentioned the window to Deke who himself had just voted for a cannon ball body block to the front doors. The window, directly above us, was well out of reach, even for Deke, so Deke suggested that perhaps I would be able to reach it from atop his mighty shoulders. Judi thought that was a perfectly marvelous idea, much more romantic than just crashing through doors, so Deke squatted down and I stepped up onto his shoulders.

But when Deke started to stand up, his hands around my ankles like shackles, my legs suddenly turned to rubber. I clawed the cold limestones for the slightest crevice, but it was no use. I teetered to the right, lurched to the left; Deke danced wildly beneath as he tried desperately to regain my equilibrium. I lost balance and lurched backwards. Deke scrambled back, tripped on an old beer bottle and went down. I crashed behind him—heels, butt, head.

Stars.

Judi howled with delight as Deke helped me painfully to my feet. He handed me my pitcher of beer and we pumped down several quick gulps before regrouping our forces.

The next play was for a touchdown—as expected, the window was unlocked. Deke handed the beer up, then lifted Judi up by the braced leg, all the time looking discreetly toward the ground, and I pulled her in. Then Judi held me while I pulled Deke up, all three of him. The three of us, giggling like five year olds, were electric with excitement.

We grabbed our pitchers and felt our way around the gloomy corridors, half breathing to the desolate echoes of our own footsteps on the marble floors, until we found the doors to the main courtroom. They were locked.

"Christ," said I.

"Shit," said Judi.

"Muddafuck," said Deke.

Deke stepped back a few paces, then suddenly lunged into the doors with his shoulder. The doors flung open and crashed against the walls inside like two cannons going off simultaneously. The explosion resounded eerily throughout the corridors.

The main courtroom was on the streetside of the building and light poured in through the huge cathedral-like windows behind the bench. Judi hobbled in and sat herself down in the jury box.

"Okay, counselor," she slurred, "let's get on with it." She slurped down a chug or two from her pitcher and sighed with the contentment of a spectator awaiting the opening kick-off.

"Okay, Deke, take the stand; you're my first witness. And as a matter of fact, my only witness."

"Who? Me?"

"Yeah, man, you."

Deke shook his head with resignation and muttered to himself as he staggered up to the witness chair and flopped down. The chair creaked under his weight. He took a long drag of beer, spilling half of it down the front of himself.

"Deke, I'm going to ask you a couple of questions here. Just a couple, nothin' too heavy. But when we're done, you and I, together, will have proven that one Alice DeLong, mother of four, was not guilty of murdering her infant daughter, that in fact we were. And by *we* I mean all of us who worship a system that dictates, by its very nature, that many of its subjects be poor so the fortunate few can be rich. Answer honestly, Deke, and please keep in mind that I like you."

Deke's eyes glowed with uneasiness. He sat up stiffly on the edge of his chair, his hands poised on his thighs as if ready to jump with the snap of the ball. His pitcher of beer was resting in the same manner on the railing in front of him.

"Could you tell the jury your name and who you are, please?"

Deke looked over at Judi who waved at him with wild abandon and blew him several kisses. Deke grinned with a boyish shyness.

"Name's Ezekiel Roosevelt Browningham. But ever'body just calls me Deke fer short." He grabbed his pitcher and took several deep swallows from it, then rested it on his thigh.

"And just who are you, Mr. Browningham? Besides a name, that is."

He wormed back into his chair and settled back into it a little more comfortably.

"Whoz I is? Man, youz knows bedder 'n me. Jes' 'nother big muddafuckin' nigger jes' mindin' 'is *own* bizness."

Judi giggled and snorted in the background.

"And how long have you been 'jes' a big muddafuckin' nigger,' Mr. Browningham?"

"'Bout thirty year."

"Are you a ward of the state, Mr. Browningham?"

He looked at me, puzzled, helpless.

"Are you on welfare, Mr. Browningham?"

He nodded.

"And how long have you been on welfare?"

He shrugged, looked uneasy again. "Dunno. Since they dropped me, I guess."

"Since who dropped you?"

"The Giants."

"How about before that, before prison. Were you ever on welfare then?"

"Mama was. I lived with her."

"Your mother? What about your father?"

He shrugged. "Didn't live with us but jes' weekends."

"And how long did you say you were in prison, Mr. Browningham?"

"'Bout two years."

"For what?"

"Beatin' on a dude."

"White or black?"

"White."

"Ever hold a job, Mr. Browningham?"

"Couple, I guess."

"Doing what?"

"Couple things."

"Like what?"

"Washed couple dishes at Toady's."

"That all?"

"'Bout it, guess."

"Did you finish high school, Mr. Browningham?"

Deke took a quick belt from his pitcher, but most of it, in his haste, sloshed down his chin and onto his lap. He shook his head.

"How far did you go then?"

"Six or seven grade. Forget."

"Didn't you tell us earlier, the eighth?"

"Okay, eight. Forget."

"Why didn't you ever finish, Mr. Browningham?"

He shrugged, his smile sadly ingratiating. Behind me Judi was inordinately quiet.

Suddenly I lurched toward Deke and leaned over the railing to stare at him eyeball to eyeball. He quickly dropped his eyes, squirmed.

"Why don't you shape up, big muddafuckin' nigger! Why the hell don't you get your big black ass in gear and make something of yourself? What the fuck's the matter with you, anyway? Don't you realize you and your kind are bleedin' this country dry?"

He made no move to clobber me, only hung his head down, as if weighted.

"Answer me, Mr. Browningham! Why don't you shape up, get with it, become like me? Why don't you work to make yourself better, go back to school, get a decent job, make your own living, get yourself a vasectomy? I can't hear you, Mr. Browningham, speak up!"

I stared at him for seconds that were minutes, listening to the muted roar of traffic in the street below. Then, finally, I wheeled and walked back to the defendant's table where I had set down my pitcher of beer. I gulped down a good half of what was left in one continuous chug.

I looked over at Judi. She was staring over at me, frowning. She said nothing.

Deke was hunched and solemn when I returned to the witness box. I leaned up against the railing, casually.

"Deke, there's a little valley not too many miles from here, a paradise, where the trees grow in what you might call quiet splendor. Their trunks are straight and tall, their branches are symmetrical and faultless, their leaves form lush plummages. They're a credit to their own kind, real pedigrees all of them." I paced to and fro; Deke watched me closely. "But on a windswept hill overlooking that same Garden of Eden the trees are of quite a different sort, Deke. Unsightly mongrels, all of them. Their trunks are hunched and warped, their branches are gnarled and twisted, their foliage is sparse and tattered. The ax would be too good for them."

I strolled back to the table, lingered a moment, then turned and walked back up to Deke.

"Deke, those trees up on that hill are exactly the same kind as those down in that lush valley. Exactly the same, all black oaks. Why then are those trees up on that windswept hill so goddamned unsightly?"

He shrugged. "Dunno. Maybe the wind."

"The wind? Then you don't think that it was something wrong

with the trees themselves?"

He shook his head.

"Deke, if I took two identical seeds, or in other words, the seeds of identical twins and planted one in that valley and the other up on that hill, what would those full-grown trees look like about fifty years from now?"

Deke's face lit up like that of a little boy who knew he knew the answer, and perhaps a little more beyond that.

"Well, man, the one yah planted down there in that valley place, she'll be 'nother li'l angel. But that poor bastard you sticked up there on that muddafuckin' hill, man, she'll be as brok'n as the rest o' 'em up there."

"But why?"

"The wind, man, the muddafuckin' wind."

"Thank you, Deke. The defense rests."

A voice rang out shrilly from behind me. "You mean that's it? That's your whole defense?!" The voice started to laugh. Halting at first, then out of control.

I spun and stared into the jury box. She was sitting there, clutching her sides, laughing. My mother. A sickening cold gripped my stomach. I shuddered. Then I heard jeers erupt from behind me. I wheeled. Stanley was sitting up on the judge's bench, laughing, jeering, chiding. I felt naked, shamed. Another burst of laughter from behind, or was it an echo? I snapped around. Sally was sitting at the stenographer's table, chewing a roll of correction tape as she laughed, pointed. I could feel my head begin to inflate, to pound. I pressed in against it, tried to stop it.

I couldn't.

Suddenly I was climbing up into the jury box, sinking my fingers into warm flesh. There were screams. Footsteps thundered up from behind. I gasped for breath, pulled at my collar. An arm was raised, cocked. A blur of knuckles. A wave of cold fire exploded across my brain, receded.

Chapter 32

My stomach was knotted, my palms clammy, cold. I could smell the stench of my own sweat.

I looked down at the miniature landscape below, blurred now and again as the plane cut through the cotton wisps of a cloud. The drone of the single engine was deafening.

Tracks and plastic landscapes carpeted the entire room, except of course for the area near the door, the area where Mr. Dezengremel kept his control board, his varnished barrel bar, and those two red chairs for his associates to sit in while admiring his H.O. railroad complex. The feeling of just being in the room, alone, was delicious. I savored the forbidden excitement as it fluttered through my stomach.

There was a tiny seafoam green rectangle in each backyard, it seemed. But not many trees. A clump here and there, perhaps hiding a rockpile or a swamp. The miniature cars streamed along the ribbons of concrete like well-trained ants.

"Get away from that, David!"

"Don't *ever* touch that."

I flicked on the main switch. My head felt suddenly lighter, lighter than air. Little glass beads of red and green glowed from beneath the dozens of switches.

The dashboard was a maze of lights and dials of mysterious importance. The miracle of human flight was before me. I felt a compulsion to reach out, to touch that miracle, to be a part of it.

Smoke puffed from the two stubby little black engines as they whirred with ease around the circular mazes of track. Tingles of excitement seemed to gravitate to that little thing that made me a boy. I eased the dual control arms up further on the electrical smelling black box. The little engines flew around their separate tracks, faster and faster. My hands went ice cold as my finger dropped knowingly down to one of the switches. It was painted bright blue. Mr. Dezengremel coded everything.

"Get away from that, David!"

"Don't *ever* touch that."

"Don't *ever* touch that."

"Don't *ever* touch that."

The switch clicked. A length of track responded, slid open. One of the stubby little engines hit the switch and jerked sharply onto the new track.

My heart pounded in my ears. My mouth went suddenly dry.

"Don't *ever* touch that."

One train flew down a steep grade as the other approached from below. The timing had been perfect. Perfect!

"Don't *ever* touch that."

My arms strained the levers for more speed.

"Don't *ever* touch that."

Just yards. I stopped breathing.

"Don't *ever* touch that."

I was throbbing, down there. Inches.

"Don't *ever* touch that."

I jumped to my feet. . . .

My hands closed on the man's collar. The prop blast pushed heavily against the door but the strength in my leg was boundless. With one swift jerk the man flew out, limbs flailing, and plummeted toward the miniature landscape far below.

Shock hit like arctic seawater. The sin was mortal. Final. Unpardonable. Guilt tore at me like a thousand claws. I was ruined, lost, suddenly catapulted into hell.

I couldn't breathe.

"Daddy! Daddy! Daddy!"

Charlie's arms were wrapped tightly around my neck. I couldn't breathe. I sat up, loosened his grip. A shadow appeared in the doorway. The room flooded with light.

"You all right, David?"

Hattie's voice bordered on panic.

"I guess so."

"Bad dream?"

"Yeah."

She sighed. "That's a relief."

Charlie loosened his hold and rested his sleepy head on my shoulder. My voice had apparently reassured him.

"Scairt the hell out of us both, let me tell yeh. Never heard anybody scream like that before in my whole life." There was something strange about Hattie's voice. Then I saw why. Her teeth were missing. "The way Judi and that big black guy brought you in here last night all I could think about was things like hemorrhages and concussions. How's your jaw?"

I hadn't noticed the dull pain throbbing throughout the left side of my face until Hattie suggested it.

"Sore."

"Want a couple o' aspirin?"

"Guess I could use 'em."

"Yeah, I guess you could. And for more than one reason too, eh?"

She chuckled and left. I leaned back against the headboard with Charlie on my shoulder until Hattie reappeared with the aspirin. She set the pills and water down on the nightstand, then left again, switching off the light as she went.

"Good night," she gummed.

"Good night, Hattie. Thanks."

I carried Charlie back into his room and tucked him back under his covers. He was already fast asleep again by the time I got the blankets pulled snugly up around his neck. I sat down on the edge of his bed for a while and just watched his slumbering face. Inside I felt an inner peace, a sense of contentment I had never known before.

For the first time Charlie had called me Daddy.

Chapter 33

It was already late morning when Hattie and Charlie came in to wake me. The scents of homemade pies baking in the oven immediately flushed the room of its bad breath. While Hattie shook my shoulders, I could feel Charlie climbing up onto the mattress.

"Judi's on the phone. She said not to wake you but she sounded a little upset so I thought maybe you'd want to speak with her. She told me about Alice. I'm sorry." Hattie's voice was back to normal.

Charlie, smeared with flour from head to bare feet, was jumping wildly about at the foot of the bed babbling on about the Cat in the Hat as if addressing a convention hall without benefit of amplifiers. Then, without warning, he pounced. Just in the nick of time I cupped a hand over my groin beneath the covers. A few days earlier I hadn't been so lucky.

"Okay, Hattie. Thank you."

"How's your jaw this mornin'?"

"Better. But my head's a little bent out of shape."

"Little wonder." she glanced over at the nightstand. "You didn't take your aspirin!"

I had forgotten. "Guess I didn't need 'em so bad after all."

"Guess not. But I'll fix you some scrambled eggs this morning anyways, so you won't have to chew."

"Fine. Thanks."

I swallowed the aspirin, then picked up the phone. It was dead. Hattie poked her head back in through the door.

"Oh, forgot to tell you, Judi unplugged your phone last night, so you could sleep."

I edged over to the side of the bed, hung down over it and plugged the jack into the little box. My head began to pound with the pressure. Charlie helped out by using my back for a trampoline.

"Hi."

"Oh, David, I'm so sorry. I only laughed because I was so surprised, so delighted with what you did. I thought it was brilliant. But at first I wasn't sure what you were doing, to Deke, I mean. You were leaning on him pretty hard there for awhile. Deke didn't know either. He's here at the office with me, by the way. Been here most of the morning. He feels pretty bad about clobbering you, David. But he had to do it. I mean you do remember–"

"Christ Almighty, Judi; slow down!"

An echo bounced back from behind me, wavering in pitch as its source jumped up and down on my back.

"Kiist alrighty, Yudi! Kiist alrighty, Yudi . . . !"

And to think waking in the morning used to be such a simple act, but a mere extension of the nocturnal numbness.

"Just a minute, Judi." I put my hand over the phone and turned back up toward Charlie.

"Let's try that again, Charlie. The. Rice. Is. Ready. Judi. The. Rice. Is. Ready. Judi. Now you try it."

"The wice is weady, Yudi. The wice is weady, Yudi."

"Good!"

"The wice is weady, Yudi . . . "

I put the phone back up to my ear.

"I remember, at least up until the time Deke clobbered me. I'm really sorry about what happened, Judi. I can't explain it; I don't know what happened to me. Too much beer, I guess. Thank God we had Deke with us though, eh?"

"Yeah. And I think he'd like to hear that too, David. From you."

"Put 'im on."

"The wice is weady, Yudi . . . "

Deke's breath was heavy in the phone.

"How's yer jaw, man?"

"A little on the sore side, Deke–quite a wallop you've got there. Guess I needed it though, eh?"

"Youz was really snapt out, man."

"Yeah. Too much of that draft beer. How about a rematch sometime, Deke, say with both your hands tied behind your back."

He chuckled. "Anytime, man. Anytime at all."

"Okay, you're on. Besides, I'd like you to get a chance to meet my sparring partner sometime soon. Right now he's doing to my back what you did to my jaw last night."

"Yer boy?"

"Yeah. Charlie."

"Luv ta, man. After youz all git back wes'll all hafta git tagether, play a li'l football maybe."

"Get back?"

Judi was suddenly back on the phone. Her voice was cautious, exploratory.

"Has Rollie talked to you yet?"

"Judi, now you know goddamned well Rollie hasn't talked to me yet. You just woke me up, remember?"

Another echo from behind.

"The wice is weady. Godam well. The wice is weady, godam well. The–"

"No, Charlie. Now let's try that again. The Rice. Is. Ready. But. Who's. Got. Sam. Dell. Got that? Now you try it."

"The wice is weady but who's godam Dell. The wice is weady, godam Dell . . . "

"Judi, now what the h . . . What's going on here?"

"Well, Rollie wants you and Charlie to drive up and stay at his little country hideaway for awhile. For a little R & R. He should be on his way over there right now."

"You two bastards set this up this morning, didn't you? While I was sleeping it off."

"The godam wice is weady, you bastards. The–"

"Charlie!"

"Judi, I'm not going anywhere for any R & R. And that's that. For once in your life why the hell don't you mind your own goddamn business."

"I am."

"The wice is weady, godam biz bastards. The wice—"

"Charlie! Go tell Hattie you want a cookie." He didn't want a cookie. "And what's that supposed to mean?"

"You figure it out."

"Well, I'm not going. Period. And that's final."

"Wanna bet?"

"You're on."

"Rollie's got Frank with him."

"The Armenian?"

"That's the one. And Deke thinks you ought to go too. And so do you. Don't you?"

"Christ Almighty."

"Kiist alrighty, godam biz bastards . . . "

It was early evening when we pulled off the narrow country lane onto the dirt driveway. It had been a warm day for September, but now a fresh coolness, heavy with the evening's perfumes, bathed in through the open car windows.

Charlie was still asleep in his car seat in back. Hattie was up front with me and had just awakened. Neither of us made a move to get out.

Rollie's hideaway, a veteran old farmhouse enveloped with enclosed porches, lay peacefully in front of us, nestled in a grove of young evergreens. They were the only firs around, so I assumed Rollie had planted them there, perhaps to attract his birds. There was no lawn, no grounds, only a vestige or two of hardy perennials, long since abandoned to their own devices. Rollie was no hedge-clipper.

A few hundred yards off to the right, at the foot of a gradual slope, a row of trees and shrubs snaked along what appeared to be a small brook. It bulged into a darkly tranquil pond, naked of shrubs on the nearside, then snaked off again into the misty distance. A flock of birds swarmed into the high limbs of a tree near the pond, scolding and chattering as they alighted, over our intrusion perhaps; then, as if on signal, swarmed off again.

Hattie took a deep breath and let it out with a sigh. "It's beautiful. Just beautiful. Just listen to all that quiet."

Hattie had insisted upon coming too. Well, not insisted exactly. She had simply come into the living room, where Rollie and Frank were examining my jaw, three pieces of steaming apple pie in hand, and had announced it would take her at least an hour to get her bags packed. With that she asked me if I could eat the pie with my sore jaw, and when I said no, Rollie asked Hattie if she wanted it, and when she said no, that she was on another fad diet, from *Women's Day* this time, he snatched it out of her hand and grinned his thanks. Frank, tall, dark and quietly menacing, stood up all the time he ate his piece of pie, which I took for a clear act of tacit intimidation.

Rollie scraped off his second plate, to the very last crumb, then threw me the keys to his secret retreat. Along with them was a hastily drawn map, scribbled on prescription paper, which I assumed was for the purpose of showing me how to find the secret treasure house. It looked more like a prescription. Then, as he was leaving, he very surreptitiously slipped me a brown envelope tied in the back with a red string and sealed with wax. It was labeled, "TOP SECRET, Do Not Open Before 1800 Hours." I folded it over and sneaked it into my back pocket.

Remembering the envelope now, I smiled to myself and glanced down at my watch. It was long after 6:00 PM. I leaned forward and slipped the envelope out of my back pocket, and ripping it open, pulled out a fat bundle of dirty green bills, all twenties. Hattie gasped.

Charlie had quietly awakened in the back to his new world.

"That where the three bears live, Daddy?!"

I peered back up at the saggy old farmhouse.

"Yes, I believe it is, Charlie. I do believe it is."

"Oh boy!"

Chapter 34

I was cussing—to myself, I thought—and banging beneath the hood of the old clunker, and Charlie was role-playing by pounding a few more dents into one of the front hubcaps with a wrench, when I heard a car pull into the driveway behind us.

A little man wearing grayish-green coveralls and boots more brown than black got out of a mud-spattered Bronco and greeted us with a drawled-out, nasal, "Hello there, neighbors." He was short to the point of petite, and a balding spot atop an overgrown, matted-down crew cut gave him a facetiously monkish look. I wiped the grease off my hands with a rag and shook his outstretched hand. His grip was powerful, but naturally so, not at all exaggerated. Charlie's face soured to the strange new odor now penetrating the damp morning air.

The man introduced himself as Clarence Hadcock, our "teat-pullin', shit-kickin' neighbor from just down the road apiece," and with a sparkle from eyes wholesomely kind, added that he was also Doc Monaghan's "country cousin drinkin' buddy." He spoke with such casual familiarity I found myself immediately comfortable, at ease. I introduced myself, but before I could introduce the little guy staring up at him, Charlie had handed Clarence a wrench, one smaller than his own, of course, and was introducing himself.

"My name Charlie. Me fixin' the godam car."

Clarence's dark eyes flashed with amusement as he shot me a knowing wink. I could feel a little prickle run across my Celtic cheeks.

Clarence ruffled the top of Charlie's brillo-pad head and thanked him for the wrench. "Fixin' the goshdarn car, eh? Well, just what seems to be the matter with it?"

"Won't go." Charlie spit and sputtered through his thick lips to show Clarence how everything was supposed to work. Clarence wiped off his brow.

"I see. Well, then, let's have a look at 'er."

And look he did. In fact, he took right over. First he climbed into the front seat of the car and tried to start it. And as the motor ground away, without so much as a feeble sputter of encouragement, Clarence shook his head with all the professional gravity of a diagnostic surgeon. Then he climbed out and disappeared behind his Bronco, returning momentarily with a large shiny metal tool box. As he knelt down over it, I noticed a patch on the back of his coveralls which showed a large orange letter "E" standing behind a black and white calf. Printed on it was, "Member, Eastern A.I.C., Inc."

Clarence flipped open the box. I was surprised to find not the wrenches and pliers expected, but a strange assortment of plastic bottles, metal-bound notebooks, and long metal tubes that looked like wispy syringes.

"Shit," he muttered, "wrong box. Every time. Do it *every* time. I got three of these here boxes back there in the Bronc. Keep my first-aid stuff in one–get kicked now and then, yeh know, in this business, 'specially by those blasted Herefords. Gotta watch those Herefords. And I keep my tools in another, and then of course my breedin' stuff here in this here one." A devilish grin crept across his well-tanned but remarkably youthful face. "Reminds me of the day I comes across this here accident. This here girl's alayin' there besides the road, see, half naked, and just bleedin' away like a slit pig. Pretty little thing, she was. Anyways, I runs back to get my first-aid box, see, but as usual I comes back with the wrong one. And just about the time I'm adiscoverin' what I got, the cops pull up, sirens ablarin' and all, and there's ol' man Hadcock akneelin' there besides some half naked, beat-up broad with his breedin' gun in 'is hand."

Clarence laughed as if I'd told the story, then packed up his "breedin' box" and took it back to the Bronco. He returned shortly thereafter with a box identical to the first one; this one, however, was full of tools more appropriate to the present situation. The clunker had already gone through menopause anyway.

"Now, if I could just get myself to put a label 'r somethin' on these here things I wouldn't get myself so messed up all the time. Been gonna do that now for ten, twenty years now. Never seem to get around to it, though. Kitchen sink still leaks too. Mrs. reminds me every blasted mornin'." Clarence raised his voice into a falsetto. " 'Clarence, when 'r' you gonna fix that sink? Clarence! Clarence, are you listenin' to me?' "

He set about taking out one of the spark plugs, with a special tool designed for just that task, and all the time he worked he jabbered on and on as if he were filling me in on all the news since the last time we'd seen each other. His run-on sentences were punctuated only with a clang or two from Charlie's busy repairs to the hubcaps below.

He started to tell me about the time, one night last spring, when he and Rollie had gotten themselves totally wiped out on a bottle of homemade dandelion wine while driving the Bronco through a neighbor's scrubbrush in search of screech owls. Using the four-wheel drive they bulldozed their way over all sorts of brush and stone fences and small trees and thought it was all very funny until they put a small tree through the radiator in trying to run over it. Then, staggering around in the dark, they got themselves totally lost, fell into a swamp, and were just about to be eaten alive by those "little flyin' cannibals" when he pulled a plug out of the engine block and held it up for examination.

"Ah ha! And when's the last time you changed these here plugs, bub? Burnt out worse 'n my old rooster."

I explained defensively that I had never changed them, that I had only recently purchased the car, used.

Clarence shook his head with disgust. "Dealer shoulda put new ones in fer yeh, used or not. Can't trust nobody these here days. Everybody's after that almighty buck; don't give a darn how they get it neither. All think they're amissin' out on somethin' their neighbors got 'n' they don't."

He pulled the other plugs and cleaned them all off with a piece of fine sandpaper from his toolbox. Then he replaced them and climbed back into the front seat. The old clunker started right up on the first try. Charlie cheered with wild exuberance thinking, of course, that he and he alone had been responsible for the successful repairs.

Clarence, obviously pleased with himself for having shown up one more inept city slicker in the fine art of mechanical repair, wiped his greasy hands off on his coveralls and delivered a lecture on the merits of getting a new set of plugs put in as soon as possible. I accepted his triumphant exhortations with several placating nods, then, as he packed up his tools, changed the subject by asking him about the meaning of the patch on the back of his coveralls. He grinned. The look was similar to that worn so very well by my upperclass fraternity brothers just before making us, the innocent pledges, stand up after showing us several deliciously grotesque stag films.

"That? That there's the emblem for the Eastern Artificial Insemination Co-op. Been one o' their technicians now for some twenty-eight years. Longer 'n anybody else in the state." He pulled his sleeve back and held up his watch. "My twenty-five year watch. Comes out to 'bout $1.27 a year."

Charlie scraped a handful of damp manure off Clarence's boots and held it up boldly to his nose. His face screwed up into a gargoyle. "Blaht!" Before I could tell him, he threw the fibrous wad away and wiped his hands off–on his pants, naturally.

I turned back to Clarence who had been highly amused with Charlie's discovery.

"In other words you're a surrogate bull."

"A which?"

"You take the bull's place, do his thing for him."

"That's me."

"Doesn't seem fair somehow. Probably why there's so many ugly bulls around, eh?"

"Hell no. Them champs get more action 'n a buck rabbit under a full moon. Get their jollies ever' time we rob the semen from 'em. See, we trick 'em—they're kind o' stupid, yeh know—we trick 'em into mountin' this here mock-up that looks like a cow's heiny. And it has this here super-duper rubber vagina with temperature controlled water arunnin' through it. Inside it's all nice and warm and soft and flimsy, just like the real thing. So when them stupid bulls mount up, this here guy quickly slips their pricks in and bango!—they never know the difference."

"Fascinating. But what about the poor girls, what do they get?"

"Hadcock!" That devilish sparkle was back in his eyes. "Say, wanna come along and see me 'n action? Bring yer fresh air kid here along too. Good education for 'im. Got a PM Hereford to do over at the Adkins' place. Matter o' fact I could use a little help. Sometimes them blasted Herefords get a little on the onery side, yeh know. Women 'r' women, yeh know—just that some of 'em have hoofs instead o' high heels."

"Sure. Love to. But this guy is certainly no fresh air kid. Charlie's my son."

Clarence looked down and smiled at Charlie, ruffled his wiry hair again.

"Well, fancy that. Sun sure 'as been hot this summer, ain't it."

After the first couple of turns I was completely lost. Obviously, though, Clarence was not. He knew every turn, every curve, every bump, every rut on every back road and cowpath in the area, and drove accordingly. Dust swirled into a cloud behind us as we tore down the dirt roads; our heads bounced off the roof as we flew from bump to bump down those that were paved. There were no seatbelts so I hung onto Charlie with one hand and braced myself against the dash with the other.

Occasionally we padded by a farm where the American Dream had obviously been realized, where the huge clapboard farmhouse was neat and well kept, where the bright red barn was freshly painted, where the fence posts were impressively regimented and the barbed wire shiny new. But those were surprisingly few, and were, for the most part, according to Clarence, owned in abstentia for tax write-off purposes by big businessmen from the big cities who knew as much about dairy farming as he did about the color of Raquel Welch's bedsheets.

Mostly we passed by farms rife with decay and neglect, rundown houses with tarpapered sides and naked cinder-block chimneys, yards cluttered with rusted old derelict vehicles and machinery, broken, abandoned toys, and smoldering heaps of refuse, often seemingly floating atop mires of mud. I was startled. Somehow I had gained the impression that the ghetto could only sink its roots into concrete.

Clarence jabbered on and on the whole time he drove, continuing on from where he had left off at the house, first about him and Rollie, then about his wife–who was so ugly, he said, that he finally had to slaughter the sow to keep himself from raping it–then about his "city-slickin' brother-in-law," for whom he had nothing but the deepest of contempt.

"An insurance 'executive', he calls hisself. Know what an insurance executive is, bub? That's an insurance salesman who's allergic to penicillin, that's what. 'Hey, Clarence ol' buddy,' he says. Gives me that big phony slap on the back, one o' them one-of-the-boys deals. 'I was just alookin' over your policies here,' he says. Sly bastard waited for me to go out to the barn then asked the Mrs. fer 'em. Women. Can't see the bad in nobody. 'Specially in one o' their own kin. 'Lucky fer you I come along,' he says. Said that ever' darn time he come up. Don't come anymore though."

Clarence chuckled to himself, a look of ultimate satisfaction aglow on his face.

"What happened?"

"Well, it weren't nothin' I did, I can assure yeh o' that. Did it all hisself." He snickered. "Yeh see, bub, before we had this here newfangled French straw method of insemination, we had to keep all our semen in our own 'frigerators. Some technicians used to keep it in little beakers 'r test tubes, but often as not I'd keep mine in them there little cream bottles. So I'm asittin' there at the breakfast table, see–same one we use fer lunch 'n' supper–so I'm asittin' there one mornin' after doin' the milkin' and down comes good ol' Roger Dodger. Spoons hisself out a glob or two o' oatmeal, see, and sprinkles a little brown sugar onta it, then goes to the 'frigerator. I'm areadin' somethin' 'n' kinda half lookin' at 'im, see. Never wanted to look at 'im any more 'n that. So what's he do but grab hisself one o' them bottles. 'Oh boy!' he says, 'fresh cream fer my cereal.' Well let me tell yeh, I nearly had to swoller my teeth to stop from breakin' up inta little pieces right then 'n' there. Dumps the whole business right out of a couple o' them little bottles onta his cereal, and digs right in. I wish ta God in heaven above yeh coulda seed the look on that idiot's puss. Lord help us, it was worth every second o' all his bullshit. Puked right there, right in his bowl. Fell right off my chair. Bastard ain't been back since."

Clarence pulled into a driveway and drove up to a weathered old barn with a sagging roof and shingles of green with purple flecks patched here and there with canary yellow. A pack of motley dogs, with balls of dried manure hanging off their fur, ran up to investigate Charlie and myself. A few strategic sniffs at our crotches seemed to satisfy them.

Clarence went right to work as Charlie and I became all eyes. Well, at least I became all eyes. Charlie became partly eyes–but mostly questions.

"What that for, Daddy, yeh know?"

"I don't know, Charlie. Let's watch and find out."

"Can I have that?"

"No, Charlie, it's not ours. It belongs to Mr. Hadcock."

"What's he gonna do with that, yeh know?"

"I don't know, Charlie. I just don't know. Let's wait and find out."

"Why's he doin' that for, yeh know?"

"Charlie, (FOR CHRIST'S SAKE) I *don't* know!"

Clarence pulled the top off a shiny metal tank, which he called an LN tank, and pulled out a rack which had several thin yellowish straws hanging from it. They were coated with frost and fuming heavy vapors. Clarence explained that these were the French straws he had mentioned earlier, which contained the frozen semen. The LN tank itself contained liquid nitrogen at -321°F, he said. There were code numbers on the tank for telling one lucky champ's semen from another's.

Careful not to burn his fingers, Clarence picked one of the straws out of the lot and placed it in a piece of tissue, which he then stuffed into the top breast pocket of his coveralls. Then he grabbed one of the shiny metal boxes, a shiny pail, and a brush not unlike a common toilet bowl brush, and headed for the barn.

"Where we goin' now, Daddy, yeh know?"

Two little girls ran out of the back door of the farmhouse and came down to follow us into the barn. When they saw Charlie they hesitated, stood off.

"Hi! I'm Charlie; who you?"

No answer.

Clarence filled his bucket with water in the milkhouse, which itself sparkled with stainless steel and smelled of antiseptic; then we all paraded on into the barn with Clarence serving as Grand Marshal. Ruminating cows, their necks held in stanchions, lined both sides of the barn. Their heads faced outward, their hind ends inward. The gutters were piled high with a night's worth of butterscotch pudding, a little on the soupy side, but the odor pervading the cool dampness was surprisingly pleasant, more like something, perhaps corn, in the process of fermenting. Innumerable sinfully plump cats were lounging amongst the piles of hay and burlap bags. An old radio mysteriously attached to the ceiling was playing church music—barnyard Muzak.

Clarence set his pail and box down and opened the box only to find it filled with a complete assortment of various gauzes and bandages. He muttered several oaths to himself and went back to get the right box. While he was gone I heard the girls giggling behind me and turned to find Charlie knee deep in one of the gutters making "chocolate pies, like on Sesamenay Street." I nearly wretched as I wiped his hands and clothes off on an old granny sack.

Clarence returned, followed in by a leather-faced woman I assumed to be the girls' mother. She scolded the girls harshly and told them to get "their little asses" back in the house, directly. Before she left she frowned down at Charlie, who was pulling one of the cats' tails, then over at me.

Clarence read my face.

"That was Mrs. Adkins. Does that ever' time. Won't let 'er little virgins witness the dirty deed. Last time I was here they snuck down here and started to watch me through one o' them there broken boards. But she caught 'em and wailed the livin' tar out of 'em." He set down his box. "Last year, just before Christmas it was, she led a little mother's vigilante committee in gettin' a health teacher fired from the local school for teachin' sex education to 'er seventh grader. Nothin' wrong with her my breedin' gun wouldn't fix."

"One would think such things would come a little more naturally on the farm."

Clarence shook his head. "One would think that. And she ain't alone neither. One mother down the road here apiece locks 'er kids in their rooms just as soon as she sees my car comin'."

He opened the box, the correct one this time, and took out one of the thin, tubular breeding guns. Then taking the French straw from his pocket, he inserted it into the syringe-like gun and clipped off the tip of it. He then pulled a long plastic sheath over the whole business and held it in his teeth while he pulled a sleeve-length plastic glove over his arm and washed it with token effort using the brush.

He walked down the concrete aisle between the rows of stanchions to where a yellow tag was attached to a beam up over one of the cows. She was rusty red and white and of much stockier build than the others, the black and white ones. Taking a goggle-eyed Charlie in tow, I followed Clarence down the aisle, noticing as we went the name cards tacked up over each stanchion—Sugar Tail, Glad Ass, Baby Doll, Once Overlightly, Secondhand Rose, Pussy Galore, and, up over the cow Clarence was about to breed, Tight Lips. I wondered what Mr. and Mrs. Adkins were like in bed.

As we stood there, several of the cows around us uninhibitedly squatted and lifted their tails to perform that timeless ritual so well known to us all–but tacitly denied by many. It was a factory. Raw materials in one end, finished product and wastes out the other.

"Why don't cows do *their* BM's in the potty, Daddy?"

I took Charlie a safe distance back and sat him down on a bale of hay, so I could be of assistance to Clarence if needed. I couldn't imagine how I could be.

Clarence positioned himself directly behind the cow, then lifting her tail, suddenly thrust his gloved hand down her pulsating rectum. He scooped out several handsful of feces until his arm was swallowed up to the elbow. Tight Lips squatted in conformity to the apparent act and turned her head back toward us with a goggle-eyed look of indignation.

Suddenly she began to shift back and forth jerking Clarence along with her. Clarence yelled for me to step in beside her, to try to steady her–which, swallowing my apprehension, I did. Then taking the breeding gun from his mouth, Clarence slipped it into the fleshy folds of the poor victim's vulva and slid it home. She jumped; I strained to steady her. Then, just as Clarence's thumb pushed in the syringe to inject the semen, Miss Lips suddenly reared and kicked–one hoof catching Clarence in the stomach, the other square in the groin. Clarence shot backwards across the aisle and splashed into the opposite gutter.

I thought he was dead; he had to be.

Then he groaned. The cow directly above him began to lift her tail. I ran over and dragged him out from under just as she let go. Charlie ran up and wrapped himself around my leg, his eyes bulging right out of his head. Clarence started to struggle to his feet.

"Don't move! I'll call an ambulance."

"What fer, bub? Ain't none near here anyways."

He wobbled to his feet and began to brush off the gobs of butterscotch pudding.

"You mean you're not hurt!"

"Pride's a might ruffled."

"But she caught you square in the . . . Christ, man, aren't you even bleeding a little?!"

Clarence unzipped his coveralls to the waist and pulled them open. A strange looking garment, olive drab, appeared.

"What the hell's that?"

"Flak vest. One o' my boys was a copter pilot over in Vietnam."

Then, grinning, he tapped his crotch with his knuckles.

"Goalie's cup."

Chapter 35

Thump.

The patter of little feet on bare wooden floors nudged my reluctant brain into a twilight of semi-consciousness. I pried open heavy eyes. Inky blackness. The patter stopped at my own doorway.

"Dad–dy? You there, Daddy?"

On any other predawn my reaction most assuredly would have been one of "Christ Almighty (the wice is weady), get your little ass back in that bed." But on this particular morning I actually felt a surge of relief. Charlie had been sick for the past couple of days, following a picnic outing, and I had been on edge dwelling on such things as typhoid, scarlet fever, and the bubonic plague. It wasn't easy, I found, to sit back on your own healthy but helpless ass and watch a little three year old vomit his guts out and burn up with fever. But Hattie, the veteran, had reassured me. She said she had seen these particular symptoms many times before, that Charlie most likely had become overtired on our picnic and had come down with some sort of 24-hour virus that would soon run its course. I was relieved now to find she had been right. Again. Good ol' Hattie.

We had all spent the afternoon together down by the pond, where a few days earlier Charlie and I had explored a little garden paradise atop a small aspen-canopied bluff, whose idyllic peacefulness was marred only by an occasional mosquito or two. It overlooked Rollie's stagnant bird sanctuary, which was probably the reason for the presence of the mosquitoes.

"Charlie hungry, Daddy."

I rolled out of bed and lifted Charlie up into my arms. He put his own arms around my neck. He felt lighter than before.

"Well, I bet you are, ol' man. Feel better now, do you?"

"Charlie *all* better now. No more bomit."

"Good. Then let's you and I go have ourselves some breakfast." I whispered to set the mood. "But let's be very quiet so we don't wake up Hattie. Shhhhh."

We stole down the creaky stairs and felt our way back to the kitchen, located toward the rear of the rambling old farmhouse and away from Hattie's downstairs bedroom. It was chilly there and quite damp; so, heeding Hattie's persistent admonitions on avoiding such unhealthy conditions, I turned up the thermostat. The furnace roared to life with a growl of indignation that rattled the whole house.

I threw some wood into the old Kalamazoo stove, then gave Charlie several pots and pans to play with on the floor, to keep him occupied while I fixed our breakfast. One pot, a large stewing kettle of sorts, was a special favorite of his. He could sit right inside of it and I think he felt especially secure in it, a sort of returning to the womb perhaps.

I peeled several potatoes with a newly acquired expertise, and sliced them paper thin for frying (medium heat) to a crispy brown. Then I laid out several slices of bacon in an old black spider and began to fry them, very slowly, to exactly the point where the fat would begin to turn a golden brown. As the potatoes sizzled I blanketed them with black pepper, turned them, then did the same to the other side.

"Lookit me, Daddy. Charlie Oscar the Grouch." Charlie, crouched in his kettle, had the lid balanced on top of his head. Oscar the Grouch was a character from "Sesamenay" Street, who, by choice, to fit his surly personality, lived in a garbage can.

Up here, though, for lack of a television set, we were no longer able to get Sesame Street. Nor were we able to phone out, or even listen to the radio. Yet none of us seemed to miss any of it.

As the bacon and potatoes simmered and filled the room with their savory aromas, the eastern sky began to grow lighter in a panorama of orange, pink and, closest to the horizon, lavender pastels. Then suddenly the kitchen was filled with an orangy brilliance as the flaming sun peeked just above the silhouetted treeline. There was a promise of another warm autumn day.

I felt a profound sense of peace inside, as glowing it seemed as the sun coming up over the horizon. In the short time we had lived there, in Rollie's little pastoral utopia, I had become hopelessly addicted. So had Hattie. A few days earlier she had come to me and asked if I thought she should sell her house, The House That Beans Built. That afternoon she walked up to Clarence's farm and called a real estate broker back in the city.

I had even begun to think about setting up a little law office in Appledale, a tiny community of only a few thousand apple-growing souls, whose only lawyer, Clarence said, was over seventy now and campaigning this year for Calvin Coolidge.

A flock of honking geese flew over somewhere close by. I peered up from the kitchen door window, but they had already passed by. The annual migrations had begun.

"Say, Charlie, let's you and I take a little walk out into the fields today and see if we can see us some geese."

Charlie looked up from his garbage can.

"What a geese is, yeh know?"

"Geese are birds. Big fat noisy beautiful birds."

"Oscar don't like 'em."

I fried some eggs in the bacon fat, managing to break only one of four yolks, a new record, then sent Oscar in to wake Hattie, a chore I knew only too well Oscar would especially enjoy. She bustled directly into the kitchen with one arm still probing for a sleeve in her robe. Her hair net was down over her eyes and in her apparent haste she had, once again, forgotten her teeth.

"What's wrong!" she gummed, "Charlie says the police 'r' here!"

I laughed.

"I think he meant *geese*, Hattie. A flock of them just flew over."

She sighed with relief, a little more awake now, then surveyed the mess on the sink and counters. Her face melted into one of those lip-sunken, formless grins.

"Suppose you'll leave all them dishes for me though."

"Male privilege."

"Thought so."

Charlie ate as if he hadn't eaten in two months rather than just two days. It was a pleasure to watch him. His plate was nearly bare by the time Hattie got to join us–robe, hair and mouth now intact. She praised Charlie for eating his breakfast, then took several deep savoring whiffs of her own. She was about to pay me due compliment, with a forkful of the well-peppered potatoes under her nose, when suddenly she sneezed. Her teeth blew clean out of her head, eggs and potatoes splattering in all directions as the porcelain choppers landed squarely in her plate. I fell right off my chair.

It was especially pleasant for October. A soft autumn breeze was flowing crisply out of the southwest, carrying with it the balm of over-ripe apples from nearby orchards. Occasionally a dried leaf or two would rustle to the gentle breaths.

Charlie was his old self again, filled with that seemingly boundless energy peculiar to carefree kids at play. He romped lustily through the fields of towering, tangled hay, falling and crashing as he raced from nowhere to nowhere. And though he would voice his annoyance at the frequent spills with unmitigated ferocity, he would always be up and at it once again, more determined it seemed than ever. I ran along with him, falling and crashing, tackling and wrestling, rolling and laughing. It was all too good to be true, yet it was true. It was happening.

When a flock of honking geese would happen by we would lie quietly on our backs and watch the vascillating vees play follow the leader into the distance. Then Charlie would jump to his feet with a lusty squeal of eagerness and be off and at it again. At first enthusiastically, then with increasing reluctance, I would follow along, behind.

Finally sweating and rasping for breath, I suggested we explore back into the stands of trees, where Rollie said he did most of his birdwatching.

"Oh boy!"

The canopies of maple were aflame with red and orange, while most of the oaks, more reluctant to give in to the creep of winter it seemed, still sported proud plummages of leathery green, marred only by occasional splotches of suede brown. Already there was a thick carpet of dried leaves on the ground and Charlie took special delight in kicking through them as he galloped along.

Most of the trees were quite young and seemingly locked in an ultimate struggle for dominance, a struggle often complicated by thick tangles of underbrush growing beneath. Some areas were abruptly sparse, however, especially atop little inclines and knolls where splotches of bare rock showed through lush carpets of green moss.

After some time of mindless meandering we came across an especially interesting tree, one which stood apart in size, shape and appearance from any other tree we had seen. Though obviously old, with a girth truly monstrous, its light gray bark was youthfully smooth and unscarred. Its muscular branches, especially the older, lower ones, projected out horizontally, often along bizarre and fascinating lines. Once Charlie saw it, he of course had to climb it. He ran up and pressed himself against it; hugging its mammoth trunk, he struggled for some kind of foothold. I stood back and laughed at the determined futility of it all.

I took off my leather-soled shoes, grabbed a hold of a low-lying branch and wrestled myself to the top of it. Then, locking my body snugly in a crotch of the tree, I leaned down and pulled Charlie up with me. For a time unmeasured the two of us just sat up there in that old tree and quietly breathed in all the sights and sounds around us–the gossipy chatterings of the many birds, the nasal honkings of geese, the melancholy rustlings of leaves in the branches above us.

Finally, after my leg went to sleep from my cramped position, I lifted Charlie down and we journeyed onward, back in the general direction of the house. When we came to a velvety blanket of moss I flopped down onto my stomach. Charlie followed. The sun, warm like a waning fire in a fireplace, was nearing its high point in the southern sky and already my eyes felt heavy from so early a rising and so active a morning.

As we lay there, savoring the softness beneath us, a caterpillar, all snug in his bristly coat of chestnut and black fur, sauntered boldly past our noses. Charlie, immediately curious, reached out to touch it. When he did, however, it snapped into a little protective ball of fur, reminiscent of covered wagons circling for an Indian attack. I marveled at such an ingenious plan of survival; and the more I thought about it, the more uneasy, embarrassed perhaps, I began to feel about my rejection of God. It occurred to me, then, nose to nose to that little miracle of life, that perhaps in the bustling world of concrete and contracts I had thought too much about the God of the Bible, the God of human invention, and too little about just plain God.

I laid my head down on the spongy moss and reached out to lay my arm on Charlie's back. He was still poking at the little ball of fur. I told him to be careful not to hurt it, then closed my eyes.

Chapter 36

I awoke, seemingly but a moment later, to the bite of a mosquito on the back of my neck. I slapped it. The warmth of the day had apparently brought the pesky little menaces forth from their nocturnal hearths. Soon, though, with the first heavy frost, they would be gone. I could hear a flock of geese honking from the distance. I opened my eyes.

The caterpillar was gone—and so was Charlie!

I jumped to my feet. Panic chilled my stomach as I quickly scanned for a glimpse of that little black face. Nothing. I called. No answer. He had wandered back to the tree. I ran back toward the tree, to the top of a knoll looking down over it. He wasn't there. He had wandered back to the house. I ran, calling as I went. Branches and barbs tore at my face and bare arms. I fell, jammed my wrist. Pain shot through it. I got up, called, listened. No answer. He had to be at the house. He had simply gotten hungry, had gone on back to the house for his lunch. It was, after all, well past noon. I ran on.

I crashed into the kitchen. Hattie gasped from fright, holding her chest.

"Where's Charlie!" I screamed.

Hattie swallowed, shook her head. "Not here. I thought he was with you."

The back shed! He was playing in the shed. He used it often as a substitute for his old refrigerator box. I turned, ran out to the shed. I slammed into the door with my shoulder, called. No answer. I squinted into the darkness. No Charlie.

The pond! Oh God no. . . .

I turned and sprinted past Hattie, down toward the pond. Dread seared my bowels like steel blades. He'd fallen down that bluff; no one had heard his pleas for help. I could see him. Helpless, floundering, gagging, choking. My legs were numb, exhausted. Like rubber. My eyes searched the surface. Nothing. I glanced up at the little bluff, toward our picnic spot. My heart exploded! A tatter of red cloth was hanging limply from a leafless branch. The same color as Charlie's shirt! I approached the pond at full tilt, stumbling with exhaustion. Suddenly one foot dropped down into a hidden burrow. I lunged forward, off balance and plunged, head first, arms flapping, down the slight embankment. My head sank down into the foul mud, my legs suspended themselves in mid-air above. I struggled to pull myself out, gasped desperately for breath.

I cleaned the muck from my eyes and found myself staring at a little but very bewildered boy standing just below the embankment from which I had just swan-dived. He was snuggling a little bundle of fur in his arms.

"Whatcha doin', Daddy? That fun? Can Charlie do that too?"

I sat there in the mud and laughed till I cried. Laughed with relief. Hattie lumbered up, her bosom heaving; she saw Charlie, gasped, then collapsed down onto an old log. I crawled out.

Charlie looked down at his furry friend.

"What this, Daddy, yeh know?"

' Looks like a little rabbit, Charlie."

"A wabbit!"

"Yeah, a rabbit. A bunny rabbit."

The rabbit's fur was stained with blood. And from the dog tracks in the mud along the shore, I surmised Charlie had inadvertently saved it from the jaws of one of the dogs that freely roamed the countryside chasing and killing deer and rabbits just for sport. Rollie, in one of his fits of outrage, had told me about them.

Hattie climbed down to examine the rabbit and suggested we take it to Clarence for repairs. I quickly changed my clothes and the three of us walked down. Clarence got his first-aid box out, the right one this time, and dressed the little bunny's wounds, which were only superficial. Though Clarence was a very congenial veterinarian, when he invited us to stay on a while for lunch, and a "nice cold glass of fresh *milk*," I very politely declined.

It started to rain on the way back, so I put Charlie up on my shoulders to carry him. But when Hattie offered to take the rabbit from him, since it was now sitting on my head, he vehemently refused.

It was *his* wabbit.

Chapter 37

It came on suddenly, explosively.

Charlie was snuggled up in my lap petting his new friend. We were rocking gently back and forth in one of Rollie's old stuffed rockers. A fire was crackling in the fireplace, the room scented with popcorn; outside, in the wild October night, the rain was beating fiercely against the tin roof. Hattie was across from us, her rosy cheeks aglow with the fire's intense heat. She was humming to herself and working on a sweater she was knitting for Charlie for Christmas.

Suddenly Charlie jerked his head up off my chest and vomited, violently. And when everything was out that could come out–all over himself, myself, the chair, and even the rabbit– he continued to gag and wretch until I thought surely he would choke to death. When the paroxysms subsided, finally, he fell back limply into my arms exhausted. But he didn't cry. When sick the days before, he had always cried after vomiting–infuriatedly. But now it was all he could do, it seemed, just to breathe. Hattie rush over and felt his forehead.

"He's burning up again, David."

I looked down into his eyes. They were heavy and swollen, glassy. His head bobbed about when I moved to get up as if it were too heavy for him to hold up.

"I'll get this mess cleaned up, David. But I think you'd better get him right to bed. Use mine. It's warmer down here."

It was all my fault. I should not have taken him outside and allowed him to play so hard so soon after being sick.

No you can't go out, David, it's too cold. . . . No you can't go out, David, it's too damp. . . . No you can't go out, David, you'll catch your death of cold. . . . No you can't . . . you can't . . you can't . . . you can't . . .

His body trembled in my hands as I pulled off his fetid clothes. His eyes were closed, his breathing heavy and raspy. I felt his forehead. It was warmer than before, much warmer. I checked the medicine cabinet for a thermometer, but to no avail. A doctor with no thermometer in his own medicine cabinet! I pulled Charlie's pajamas on and tucked him into Hattie's bed. His lips were parched.

The floor creaked behind me. Hattie tiptoed in. She was holding Charlie's little rabbit by the scruff of the neck.

"I'll go get my aspirin. We'll see if we can knock that fever down."

The old brass bed complained of my weight as I sat down on its edge. Charlie's little form looked lost under the vast whiteness of the blankets. He groaned and began to thrash his head back and forth. Hattie came in with a spoonful of crushed aspirin and water.

"Hold his head, David, and I'll try to get this down him."

I held Charlie's jaw with one hand, his head with the other. Hattie quickly poured the floating powder into his mouth. He swallowed, coughed, gagged—then vomited. I held his head over the side of the bed as he brought up little more than strings of greenish mucus. His eyes remained closed.

I looked up at Hattie's face. Instead of the expected reassurance, that look of maternal confidence from one who has weathered every kind of illness, real or imagined, in or out of Spock, I now saw half-disguised fear.

"I don't like the looks of this high temperature, David. It's probably just a relapse of that flu bug, but just to be on the safe side maybe we ought to give Doc Monaghan a call. Just to ask him if there's anything else we can do."

I glanced back down at Charlie. He thrashed his head from side to side, mumbled.

"Bun–ny . . . bun–ny . . . wan' my bun–ny . . . "

Hattie disappeared, returning momentarily with a little bundle of fur. It smelled like pine trees. She set the rabbit on the bed next to one of Charlie's exposed arms.

I stood up.

"I'll drive down to Clarence's and give Rollie a buzz. Be right back."

Hattie sat down in the old wicker rocker at the foot of the bed, near the rattling window. I could hear it creak in rhythm to Hattie's soft humming as I threw on my raincoat.

The wind was galing out of the northwest; the rain felt like cold needles against my face. A doctor with no thermometer, no phone. Christ.

The domelight on the clunker didn't work of course, so I had to feel around for the ignition keyhole. After several fruitless moments I discovered I had the wrong key. I tried again. Finally jamming it home, I turned it. The motor ground past the usual starting point, then well past. Christ, not now! I paused a moment, took a deep breath, then tried once again. Nothing. My fault again. Clarence had warned me, had told me to get new plugs. But I hadn't. There had been no rush. I climbed out and sprinted toward the only lights visible down the road. Thank God for Clarence. As I ran, I tried to keep my mind at ease, loose–thought about how Clarence would probably run and get his "breedin" gun when I asked him for the phone.

Though I didn't smoke, and never had, I was still disgustingly out of shape, especially for a man under thirty. I ran and ran, yet the light down the road seemed to get no closer; my lungs began to wheeze in the cold dampness. Pains began to burn in my sides. My legs were sore and stiff from the morning's romp in the fields and the wind was gusting directly against me; it felt as if I were doing little more than jogging in place, perhaps even losing ground. I thought about Deke in training camp, what it must be like. I prayed a car would happen by, just one. But none appeared.

Finally I could make out the opaque silhouette of Clarence's white house against the black sky. I ran harder, encouraged by the finish line. I slipped and skidded across the greasy lawn, fell, got up and stumbled up the front porch. It was all I could do to find enough energy to pound a fist against the door.

Clarence appeared in his tattered undershirt, hair bristling from under each armpit.

"What's up, bub? Boogey man chasin' yah? Halloween ain't for a couple more weeks yet, yeh know."

I bent over with my hands on my knees and gasped for breath. There was an odor inside not unlike that of the barnyard. The room was like the inside of an oven.

"Charlie's sick. Want to use your phone. To call Rollie. Ask him what to do."

Clarence's face sobered a little.

"Oh. Sure. Right in the kitchen. Nothin' serious I hope."

"Don't know. Seems pretty sick."

"Get yah anythin'. Snort o' whisky maybe?"

"No thanks."

My hand felt like a lump of wet flour paste as I dialed Rollie's number. Clarence set a tumbler half full of straight whisky on the table beside me, winked. I sipped from it as the phone began ringing on the other end. Something soft and purring rubbed up against my ankle. Sweat began to drip off my chin.

"Monaghan's Moonshine Mecca. Tuffy ain't here."

"You're drunk!"

"Who the hell's this–the AMA?"

"Goddamn you, Rollie."

"Oh, it's only you. What's up? Burn the place down, did yah?

"Rollie, just cool it for a minute. Charlie's sick."

He chuckled with deliberate condescension.

"You hysterical mothers–all alike, 'specially the first time 'round. Well, what is it this time, pernicious anemia or precocious erection?"

"Just shut your goddamned mouth, Rollie, and listen. He's delirious, Rollie. He's lying over there right now burning up and babbling about his bunny. Doesn't even wake up when he pukes."

Rollie's tone changed immediately. I was suddenly talking to a different person. The drunken levity gave way to serious questions, probing questions. And as I answered them his manner grew more and more dispassionate, much too professionally aloof for Rollie—almost as if he were attempting to hide something.

"—by any chance did Charlie manifest any of these same symptoms, say, a day or two ago, in perhaps somewhat milder forms?"

He was onto it now—whatever it was. My heart began to pound in my ears.

"Yes he did. He was sick for a day and a half or so, but this morning he was all better again. Hattie thinks he might have come down with a flu virus or something after getting overtired from a picnic we had."

I was breathing heavily into the phone; I tried to restrain myself. I took another sip of Clarence's whisky.

"This outing, David, was Charlie exposed to any mosquitos that you know of?"

"Sure. We all were." I wanted to add something, something inanely conversational about what a nuisance mosquitos were and why don't you drain your goddamned pond, but I couldn't. It wouldn't work.

There was a long pause. Too long. Clarence swallowed something from behind me. The wind tore at the window. The cat rubbed up against my other ankle.

"David, I want you to listen very carefully. Now, I want you to get Charlie into that car of yours and I want you to get him to St. Jude's Hospital in Syracuse just as fast as you can *reasonably* get there." I stopped breathing; something pressed at my throat. "Get onto 81 and take it south. Get off at the Salina Street exit. Grab the first body you see and ask directions. Tell Hattie to pack Charlie with cold rags or ice, anything to keep that temperature down. Got that?" I mumbled, weakly. "Now, if he should have any trouble breathing before you get there, tell Hattie to give him mouth to mouth, and not to stop—no matter what. Got that?" I couldn't answer. "Everything will be all right, David; just do as

I've told you. Time is the important factor, now, so I'm not going to tell you to drive like any goddamned tourist. But be *reasonable.* An accident won't help anybody. I'm leaving right now, and should be up there before you. Get going."

"What's he got, Rollie?!!"

"Get going!"

Click.

My palms were ice cold.

Oh Christ! The car!

I turned to Clarence. "Can I borrow your Bronco? I've got to get Charlie to the hospital, fast."

Clarence blanched white.

"Jesus, it ain't here. The ol' lady's got it. Out cluckin' with the goddamned hens. What's the matter with yers?"

"Won't start."

"Plugs?"

I nodded.

Clarence jumped up and grabbed a denim coat off a rack by the kitchen door and pulled on a pair of boots. "C'mon. See what we can do. It'd take a goddamed month o' Sundays for any ambulance to get 'ere." He rifled through an open drawer, pulled out a few tools, was out the door.

Clarence ran like a gazelle, boots and all. The wind was now at our backs and we seemed to sail on before it like Clipper ships.

Clarence already had the hood open by the time I caught up with him.

"Got a flashlight, bub?" He wasn't even winded.

"In the house. I'll get it."

I ran in and grabbed a flashlight out of one of the kitchen drawers, the catch-all drawer, then ran in to check on Charlie. Hattie was sitting on the bed pinning Charlie to the bed. He was convulsing, gasping desperately for breath. She looked up, her face ashen, helpless.

"What did he say?"

"The hospital. Take him out to the car." I explained Rollie's instructions, then rushed back out into the raging night.

Clarence was in the front seat grinding the engine. He could have told me what an asshole I was for not getting the plugs, but he didn't.

"Hold the light. I'm going to pull some of these plugs, clean 'em, and heat 'em with my light." He handed me his lighter, then went right to work. He pulled the first plug and held it down low in the engine well, out of the rain, and scraped the points off with the file on a nail clipper. I flipped his lighter open, lit it; Clarence held the end of the plug in the wildly flickering flame.

I heard the door slam from behind. Hattie's silhouette appeared out of the darkness. She was carrying Charlie, all wrapped up in a blanket, and the rabbit, who was dangling by the scruff of the neck from one of her hands. I took the rabbit and threw it in front, then helped Hattie into the back.

Clarence worked fast.

"There. That's half of 'em. Should do it."

He threw his tools at me and jumped into the front seat. The engine turned over, sputtered, then died. He tried again. Nothing. Then again. I wilted, died a little inside. He climbed out. I could hear Hattie's plaintive voice as he opened the door. "Please hurry, Mr. Hadcock. Please."

Panic churned in my stomach. Clarence grabbed the tools out of my hands and went back to work. He fumbled in silence; said nothing, nothing at all. Rain splashed over us as the wind whined and howled desolately through the evergreens behind us. I searched the blackness for headlights. Nothing.

Suddenly Clarence threw the tools back at me. "Goddam thing better work this time 'r I'll kick 'er ass but good." He climbed back in. The motor turned over, roared to life.

I slammed the hood, started to get in the driver's seat. I pushed Clarence rudely on the shoulder.

"Slide over! I'll drive."

"Better let me. I know the roads better 'n you. Besides you're a little–"

"Slide over!"

He slid over, lifted Charlie's bunny off the floor onto his lap.

"Okay. I'll navigate. Where we goin'?"

I climbed in and spun out of the greasy driveway. Charlie was convulsing in Hattie's arms, his little body rigid.

"St. Jude's."

Chapter 38

We raced down a maze of narrow winding roads until reaching route 104, a highway of two lanes but no less a roller coaster. Clarence barked out directions and warnings and from the silent movement of his lips between times apparently prayed I would slow down enough to heed them. The road was wet and slick, the wind gusty, but the old clunker was heavy and stable.

Traffic was surprisingly heavy, despite the severity of the storm, and slow-moving. We passed car after car; but then about halfway to the four-laned Interstate we got behind a car doing about 45 mph. It seemed more like 15 mph. The road alternated between hills and curves and was marked double solid for a hundred miles straight. Approaching traffic was too heavy to take any chances. I blinked my brights on and off, layed on the horn. The car slowed down to 40 mph, going up a hill.

There were four silhouettes, sitting apart, two up front, two in the back. The car was a plain compact—probably headed for a canasta party, in no hurry to get there. I hated them. I hated their stupidity. I hated their preoccupation with themselves, their total lack of external sensitivity. I wanted to run them off the road—and was just about to do it when their left turn signal flashed. Clarence was mumbling oaths. I roared by, off to the right, half in the mud and half on the shoulder. Clarence stabbed the air several times with his middle finger as we skated by.

I could hear Charlie's breathing from the back seat. Heavy, halting, raspy.

"He's trembling all over, David; rigid. Can't seem to get his breath." Hattie's voice was restrained, almost a whisper—but urgent. She couldn't tell me to hurry, outright, that she was scared out of her mind; but I knew her meaning. We were all of the same mind now, all willing to take the ultimate risk. For Charlie.

I floored the accelerator and punched the brights on and off, continuously. As we approached slow-moving cars, and now they were all slow-moving, I turned out into the opposite lane, whether there was oncoming traffic or not. It wasn't fair to make our risk theirs, but I did it anyway. And faced with the necessity of getting the hell off the road, they did.

Rte. 81 was easier. Four lanes straight through Syracuse. I pulled right over into the left lane from the ramp and floored it. With the clunker's weight and age and the sorry state of her spark plugs, we could only do about 95, at best. My leg soon began to ache with the strain of trying to push the accelerator pedal through the floorboard.

Charlie began to gasp for breath, his efforts desperate. Clarence looked back; his face fell. I could hear Hattie begin to give him mouth to mouth resuscitation. Panic seized my stomach, clawed it with cold nails. Tears pressed at my eyes. I pressed harder against the accelerator. Clarence, without a word, eased Charlie's bunny down onto the floor and climbed over the seat to help Hattie.

Festoons of rain streamed down the windows between the rhythmic swipes of the wipers, alternately blurring the nightmare from reality, then cruelly bringing it back again. We passed truck after whining truck, car after car. The night seemed endless. Blasts of wind rocked the car, sometimes nearly out of control. I could hear Clarence begin to blow life into Charlie's lungs.

Traffic began to get heavier, congesting the left lane as well as the right. I flashed the brights, laid on the horn. But the world was both deaf and blind. I screamed out oaths; the trucks screamed back. I had to slow down.

Suddenly the blurred reflection of a flashing red light caught the side mirror. A cop! Jesus Christ, a fucking cop! Some goddamn little frustrated pipsqueak of a boy scout was going to stand me out in the rain and write me out a fucking ticket while Clarence and Hattie sat in the back seat blowing air into Charlie's lungs. The wail of a siren, muted now and then by the wind, filled my ears. I screamed, cursed, damned, jockeyed around a car to the right, pulled back left. My face was on fire with hate.

The light disappeared, then reappeared directly beside us. The domelight inside flickered on. There were two troopers sitting up front, wallowing in that casual arrogance of theirs. The driver suddenly jabbed a finger toward me, then back at himself, then down the road. He repeated. The light went out. Then suddenly, siren wailing, light flashing, the car shot ahead and pulled over into our lane. Cars began to scurry over to the right. I speeded up.

Further up ahead two other red lights appeared, one flashing from the right shoulder, one from the left. We flew by between them, but the lights soon reappeared in the side mirrors. One stayed back a ways; the other shot past us and took up station ahead of the first car. We were being escorted, royally! That drunken bum of a basset hound had called the cops!

Buoyed by a surge of hope I glanced back into the back seat. Clarence was holding Charlie, blowing into his mouth; but Hattie was crumpled up against the door, unconscious. Clarence saw me and stopped long enough to explain. "Passed out cold. Hyperventilated. She'll be all right."

The lights of suburban Syracuse appeared. We were going to make it! Rollie would be there, waiting and ready. The modern miracles of medicine would soon be able to do their thing for Charlie. A warm euphoria crept back into my veins.

The troopers led us off onto the Salina Street exit and on into the city. We sped through the glistening streets, past stopped cars and fleeting glances. We were nearly there.

"I don't think he's gettin' any air, David. Can't seem to get a pulse neither. What should I do?"

"Keep blowing! Keep blowing! Blow harder! Don't stop! Please don't stop!" My vision went blurry.

Hospital. Next Right.

We squealed into a driveway bathed with light and braked sharply in front of two red doors. EMERGENCY ENTRANCE. Rollie and a man in white were suddenly in the back seat. The man in white started to pump on Charlie's chest, hard. Rollie had a blade at Charlie's throat, was cutting. There was blood, a gush of air. Two white uniforms were wheeling Hattie through the doors. A nurse and a trooper were in the front seat, leaning back to assist the doctors. There were shouts, orders, but most of all there was a wheeze of air, the sound of breathing, of life struggling. He was alive!

Bright lights, busy footsteps, aloof faces, groans from open doorways. Corridors, numbers, the rustle of starched cotton.

A small form on the other bed; a tube leading from a bottle of clear liquid. Eyes closed.

Rollie appeared with several orderlies. They wheeled Charlie in, lifted him carefully onto the raised bed. Rollie approached, put his arm around my shoulder, squeezed. His eyes were sunken, exhausted. Words: Charlie has Eastern Equine Encephalitis . . . rare disease with no known cure . . . carried by birds and mosquitos . . . between him and God now . . . you can stay . . . nurses will be with him all night . . .

Clarence appeared. A rich odor of manure washed through the room. Several nurses were scolding him from behind. Rollie barked at them. They left. Clarence pulled Charlie's bunny out from under his shirt, placed it beside Charlie. Winked at me. Left.

The wind roared distantly like a cresting wave, then spent its fury against the large windows. He was still wheezing, breathing. He was still alive. Rain sprayed the window like bursts of tiny bullets. Ghostly shadows floated in and out. Always the sound of water dribbling into basins from sponges. He was still wheezing, breathing. A stir from the other bed. A groan.

The wind pressed my pants against my legs, Judi's skirt between her thighs. Her hair flowed and leaped like billowing flames. It was a struggle to walk. We took each other's arm, pressed on.

Broken windows, deserted shops, sleazy bars, the fetid odor of open garbage cans. A rat scampered out of an alley. Judi screamed. clung to me. The wind gusted harder, threw dust into our faces. Our eyes watered into tears.

An old man stumbled down the opposite sidewalk, fell down.

He got back up, slowly; saw us. He started to cross the street, coming at us. Pocked, unshaven face; rotting teeth. Greasy, torn clothes. Tobacco juice oozing out the sides of his mouth. He dropped to his knees, into the gutter. Filthy water welled around his thighs as it sped toward a drain.

Wheezing, raspy breathing, as if from cancerous lungs. I felt myself repulsed, retreating. He held out a trembling hand, toward me.

"Let me touch you." he wheezed. "Let me touch you. Let me touch you."

I tried to retreat; Judi stood firm.

"Let him touch you," she pleaded. "Let him touch you."

I edged forward. The heavy, raspy breathing deafened my ears, resounded in my head. His stained, gnarled fingers, his broken, torn nails strained toward me, toward my stomach. We touched.

Something hot exploded inside me, shot through my veins. Every cell in my body tingled with joy. I leaped into the air, shouted, danced, sang out. I reached out to touch Judi. The brace suddenly fell off her leg, her deformed arm popped out. She leaped into the air screaming, shouting, crying.

We ran up to others, touched them. Glum faces turned on like long darkened lights. Voices rang out like caroling church bells. Leaden limbs beat the air like fledgling wings.

But the breathing! That raspy, wheezy, rattling sound. It was gone! I looked back, back toward the gutter.

Rollie was peering down at me, one hand gently resting on my shoulder. The window beside me was a pallid glow. Several shadows were rustling around Charlie's bed. There was no other sound. No talking. No dribble of water. No. . . .

I jumped to my feet, pleaded with Rollie's eyes.

He dropped his head, handed me a warm bundle of fur. He turned away.

Daddy! Daddy! Daddy!

Chapter 39

On the night of October 30th, Rollie, Hattie, Faye, and Judi took me to a Halloween party at the Foundling Home. I met a little boy there. He said his name was Bobby—Bad Day Bobby.

His red costume had little horns and a long, pointed tail.

—the end—